Woman Enters Left

By Jessica Brockmole

Woman Enters Left

Woman Enters Left

JESSICA BROCKMOLE

Allison & Busby Limited
12 Fitzroy Mews
London W1T 6DW
allisonandbusby.com

First published in Great Britain by Allison & Busby in 2017.
This paperback edition published by Allison & Busby in 2018.

Published by arrangement with Ballantine Books, an imprint of
Random House, a division of Penguin Random House LLC, New York,
NY, USA. All rights reserved.

A CIP catalogue record for this book is available from
the British Library.

10 9 8 7 6 5 4 3 2 1

ISBN 978-0-7490-2194-8

Typeset by
Allison & Busby Ltd

The paper used for this Allison & Busby publication
has been produced from trees that have been legally sourced
from well-managed and credibly certified forests.

Printed and bound by
CPI Group (UK) Ltd, Croydon, CR0 4YY

For Ellen and Owen,
who have many journeys ahead of them

Chapter One

1952

Movies always begin with a panorama.

A skyline. A beach. A cactus-dotted desert. Paris, Rome, Honolulu, New York City.

This one opens in Los Angeles.

It's 1952, and the city doesn't have much of a skyline. Low buildings squat in front of the Santa Monica Mountains. A few are recognizable. The uninspired bulk of the United Artists Theater. The turquoise-stuccoed Eastern Columbia Building. The highest, the gold-spired City Hall, silhouetted almost alone against the dark mountains.

We zoom in. If not for that opening panorama, it could be any city in mid-December. The cafés, the hotels, the cinemas, the self-important office buildings. The shopwindows decorated with tinsel and artificial snow. It could be New York or Chicago. It could be a studio's back-lot set. Beautiful and busy people hurry down the streets. They hail taxis, they step from streetcars, they push in and out of buildings. They balance shopping bags and gift boxes. They drop pocket change in red Salvation Army kettles. Everyone has a purpose, guided by an inner stage direction. Businessmen with trilby hats and folded newspapers. Young women with lipstick and slim dresses. Older women with handbags dangling from the crooks of their arms. It could almost be stock footage of Christmas in the city.

But then we see palm trees and sunshine between the garlands and strings of lights. We see lighted signs outside the theaters – the Pantages, the Paramount, the distinctive Egyptian and Chinese. We see the Knickerbocker Hotel and the Garden of Allah, the towered Crossroads of the World, the nine giant white letters so stark against the distant hillside and we know: This isn't stock footage. This is Hollywood.

A woman enters left.

Already we know she must be our leading lady. She stands out among the generic businessmen and lipsticked women. She doesn't swing her hips or smile at the passing men. She doesn't check her reflection in shopwindows. She's not pretty, if we're being honest. Striking, maybe. She doesn't have the lushness of a Lana Turner or Rita Hayworth or the fresh-faced prettiness of a Doris Day. But, eyes forward, shoulders back, she walks with a certainty that is infinitely more attractive.

She's dressed neatly, in a crisp white blouse and navy suit. The skirt isn't too short or too long. The jacket is feminine without being fussy. Beneath the turned-up collar of the jacket, she wears a thin scarf the color of daffodils, smoothed down and tied in a square knot. It suggests a man's necktie. She might have intended that.

Perhaps she's a businesswoman, straight from a meeting. Perhaps a saleswoman, fresh from landing a big contract. She carries a soft brown briefcase, creased in the corners with use. Even without knowing what she does, we know she's a woman used to navigating her way through a man's world.

Her stride is deliberate, forceful, confident – that is, until she approaches an intersection. Here she pauses and looks in each of the four directions. She closes her eyes beneath a streetlamp topped with a decorative metal Christmas tree briefly, as if comparing these two crossed streets against a mental map. With a nod of satisfaction, she continues on her journey.

Eventually she turns off the main street. The sidewalks are less crowded here. All white stucco and red tile, it's a residential area. This isn't a neighborhood of mansions, of movie stars and cigar-wielding producers. It's not marked on any "Homes of the Stars" maps. Its streets are lined with quiet apartments and modest hotels.

After a few blocks, she stops in front of a building painted a brilliant blue and tucked away behind a shady green courtyard. It's an apartment building, unofficially called the "Blaue Engel," though Dietrich never lived there. Construction finished the day the movie came out. It's not as fashionable an address as the El Greco or Hollywood Tower, but its apartments never sit empty for long.

Setting her briefcase on the sidewalk in front of the

Blaue Engel, she opens her wide leather handbag and conducts a search. A man with a shopping bag edges around her, as does a woman with a small, furiously yipping dog. The man stares back over his shoulder but, engrossed with the contents of her purse, she doesn't notice. She finally extracts a lace-bordered handkerchief and dabs at her forehead. It's not especially warm out. Perhaps she's dabbing away a headache or a bad day. She refolds the damp handkerchief and glances at a little gold wristwatch. It's a Longines, slim and coppery. The way she turns her wrist and shakes away her sleeve in a practiced movement, it's clear she's a woman with a schedule. Right now she frowns down at the watch. Dropping the handkerchief back into her bag and retrieving the worn briefcase, she heads for the arched courtyard doorway.

The courtyard is leafy and dripping with bougainvillea. It's a bright, wild backdrop for this woman, in her serious suit and neck scarf. A man in a rumpled black jacket looks up from a potted geranium.

"Louise Wilde," she says, before he can ask.

The jacketed man dusts off his hands. He eyes her, but there's no recognition.

She's been in films since '39. Two dozen of them, to be exact, nearly two a year. But surely they aren't his kind of films. This old man, with potting soil under his fingernails, doesn't go in for frothy pictures about showgirls and romance. The Betsey Barnes series, *Tap-Dance to Heaven,* *Red-Blooded Rita,* that new high society picture. All featuring "a small-town girl with big-city dreams," as the studio is fond of saying, all with a grand makeover scene, all with a husband won successfully by the end. He hasn't seen them, she's sure.

The man in the black jacket still waits by his geranium.

"I'm meeting Mr French," she adds.

He taps his head. "The lawyer fellow? He didn't say he was expecting a gal."

She tightens the grip on her black handbag.

"Well, he's upstairs." He pushes open a gate and indicates a set of metal stairs. "Number twelve."

Louise walks up the stairs by herself. The man has already gone back to his geranium. She finds the door marked "12," hung with a scrawny wreath. Of course, the door is blue.

For just a moment, she pauses in front of that blue-painted door. It's been a day and she'd rather be back at home in her bathrobe than here. All morning she'd been at the studio, arguing the new script. Fruitlessly. They'd nodded, smiled, and told her to be on set Monday or else. And then she finds a stack of messages in her dressing room from a lawyer with instructions to meet him at the Blaue Engel. Her fingers twitch for a Manhattan.

Before she can decide whether or not to knock, the door swings open.

Mr French looks exactly like a lawyer, with a three-piece wool suit and unnaturally white teeth. His hair is dyed and Brylcreemed to within an inch of its life. He's probably fifty, sixty years old, despite what the pancake makeup under his eyes wants you to think. He's more Hollywood than she is.

11

"Mrs Wilde?"

Her back straightens. "Miss." Every ounce of that earlier confidence is back. "Miss Wilde."

"You're a hard girl to get a hold of." He peers over her shoulder. "Did your husband come with you?"

"Was he named in the will as well?"

"Ha!" Mr French flashes another toothy smile. "Of course not. But I just thought—"

"I had many reasons for marrying him. His legal expertise was not one of them." She draws her heels together. "Shall we get to our business?"

He stares a moment, as though trying to decide whether he's been insulted or not. "Of course. Yes. Will you come in, please?"

The apartment is small and tidy, with pale yellow walls and a scrubbed tile floor. A tiny Christmas tree, dripping with tinsel, perches on a bookcase in the corner, the only concession to the season. Stepping in, she slips off her gloves. "This is all very surprising. I'm still not quite sure how I merited a mention in Miss Daniels' will. As I said on the phone, I scarcely knew her."

"Are you sure?" Mr French shuts the door behind Louise and goes to the tiny dining table, where he's left a sheaf of papers and a pair of horn-rimmed reading glasses. "I assumed she was a family friend."

Louise had grown up in Newark, New Jersey, with a widowed father and far too many games of checkers. The most she could hope for were visits from Uncle Hank, a balding man with a perpetually spotted tie who owned the butcher shop with her father. He came for dinner most

Sundays, always with a meringue-topped pie. No other visitors. No family friends, and certainly none as exciting as a Hollywood screenwriter.

"I didn't know her before I moved out here." Louise sets her white gloves and handbag on the table. Her briefcase she tucks under the dining chair. "But, really, I didn't know her much even after. I met her a handful of times at parties. Once at the Brown Derby. And half a dozen nods passing in the hallway at MGM. I didn't even know that she lived here at the Blaue Engel until today."

He's brought three paper cups of coffee. Obviously he really had expected Arnie to come. And why wouldn't he? *Movieland* once described her as the "effervescent muse to Arnold Bates's genius" and *Modern Screen* said she brought the "pop and sparkle" into his screenplays. As though she were the pretty and the fun to Arnie's wisdom. As though their careers were intertwined from the moment they exchanged vows. She's never effervesced outside of the klieg lights' glare, but Mr French doesn't know that. After all, if you can't believe the Hollywood rags, what can you believe?

One cup is half-empty, the other two covered with cardboard lids. She wonders how he carried them all from the diner down the street. He opens both until he finds one pale with milk. Clearly that one is for her. He untwists a paper napkin holding two sugar cubes, but she saves him a step and reaches for the other cup.

He raises thick eyebrows. "You drink it black?"

The coffee is tepid and bitter, but she doesn't relent. "Who doesn't?"

She sits and crosses her feet at the ankles. It's the blocking this scene calls for. The leading man, with his important papers and his important news, is the center of this scene. The leading lady – she minimizes, crossing her legs, lowering her shoulders, looking down at her fingers laced around the paper cup. The coffee is awful, but it's something to hold on to.

Mr French plays the part of the scene's hero well. Of course he does, with his artfully arranged hair. "As I mentioned on the phone, I'm Florence Daniels' executor. You've been named in the will."

Louise hadn't seen the obituary at first, but she'd looked it up after Mr French's phone call. It was brief and effective.

DANIELS, Florence, passed away December 13, 1952, at Mount Sinai Hospital. She was born June 12, 1898, in Orange, New Jersey. In lieu of flowers, contributions may be sent to the Screen Writers Guild. Services will be held at Blessed Sacrament.

"May I ask, how did Miss Daniels pass away?"

"Cancer, I think it was." He unfolds his reading glasses. "When she made the appointment to draw up the will, she said it was the second time she had imminent death on the schedule and maybe this time she'd just go ahead and do it."

Louise can't help it – half of a laugh sneaks out. Mr French looks suitably shocked. So much for not effervescing.

"She wrote the will herself. Near the end, she wasn't able to do much, but it's in her own hand." He slips on his glasses. " 'I, Florence Jane Daniels, being of sound mind and reasonably intact body (minus a wholly unnecessary appendix and twelve teeth), do write my last will and testament, the final act to the screenplay of my life.' "

This will is better than most of the scripts Louise is given. "I may not have known her personally, but her sense of humor was famous," she says.

Mr French sets down the paper. "The reason I called you here to Miss Daniels' apartment instead of to my office . . . Well, you aren't just named in the will, Mrs Wilde." He leans back and rests his hands on his knees. "With the exception of a few small bequests, you are Florence Daniels' sole beneficiary."

With a slosh, Louise spills lukewarm coffee down the back of her hand.

He has the good sense to jump up and move the will out of the way, but a trail of coffee runs across the table to her white gloves. He goes in search of a paper towel, continuing to talk to her from the kitchen. "I've started probate proceedings. But there should be no contest. That means—"

"I know what that means."

"Right." He emerges with a handful of paper napkins, which he passes across the table. "Like I said, there should be no contest. She has no living parents or siblings. And, as you can see, no husband or children. Spent too much time at the studio for either, I imagine."

She mops at her hand and the table and her sodden gloves. She's still trying to process his announcement. A woman she'd admired but barely exchanged two dozen words with had just left everything to her.

"Just a few things to distribute, and then the remainder of the property is yours. The apartment here and its contents, her savings, a Schwinn kept down in the gardener's shed." He takes a gulp of coffee, scratches his chin, and picks up the will again. "She left a grand to the Hollywood Studio Club. One hundred dollars each to Blessed Sacrament Church, the Entertainment Industry Foundation, the Los Angeles Public Library, and the proprietor of Chen's Dragon Café. Twenty-six years' worth of *Variety* back issues to one Howard Frink. She also left three dollars and . . ." He squints and straightens his glasses. "Three dollars and an orange sombrero to Miss Anita Loos, 'to thank her for that rhumba.'"

"I was introduced to Miss Loos once. I think it was when she was working on *When Ladies Meet*." She takes another sip of whatever coffee is left in her cup and makes a face.

"Coffee that bad?" he asks.

It is, but she doesn't want to be rude. "It's not that. This is just all so strange."

Mr French takes off the glasses with one hand and rubs the bridge of his nose. "You might not have known her, but she knew you, and must have thought well of you. Howard Frink was her neighbor for seventeen years, and all he got was a stack of old magazines."

As she picks up her coffee again, she sees it has left

a ring on the table. Though technically the table now belongs to her, she feels guilty. When Mr French turns back to his stacks of paper, she rubs out the ring with her thumb.

"I think I read something about your husband recently."

She hopes he isn't talking about the *American Legion Magazine* piece. Something about Hollywood screenwriters and their "red" pens. Mr French looks just like the American Legion type. "It must have been something about Korea." She remembers to smile. "He just came home, you see."

"That must have been it." He talks without glancing up from his reading and initialing. "Well, I bet he's glad to be back. Home cooking sure beats anything army mess serves up. Or was he navy?"

"Neither. He went over as a journalist."

"Is that so? Well, sounds better than trudging through a jungle, that's for sure. The whole time I was in the Philippines, I thought about coming home to my wife's custard pie. Do you make pie?"

"Not often."

He looks up then and gives a wink. "Maybe now would be a good time to start."

She can't think of a response, so just keeps the smile pasted on.

"I have to sort through the things that won't be staying." He glances around the room. "Also, I have to find an orange sombrero."

"I could help you look for it."

Really, she wants an excuse to peek around, to see the life she's inherited.

He nods. He seems relieved.

She takes the coffee cup to the narrow kitchen and empties it into the sink. A lone saucepan sits upside down on a dish towel. Judging by the pantry, Miss Daniels had subsisted on saltine crackers and peanut butter, raisins, and can after can of tomato soup. A whole shelf of the pantry holds nothing but red and white Campbell's cans. The fridge doesn't offer much more: club soda, half a jar of pickled onions, and a paper-wrapped slice of chocolate cake with all of the icing scraped off.

Maybe that's all Miss Daniels really ate. A Hollywood diet, straight from the pages of *Pageant* or *Photoplay*. Louise understands. She's been on one for the past decade and a half. Shaken egg yolks for breakfast. Single scoops of tuna salad for lunch, poised on a curve of a lettuce leaf. Veal for dinner.

Or maybe Miss Daniels was simply an indifferent cook. Louise can't see more than salt and pepper in the cabinets. Nothing to suggest culinary brilliance. All she sees in the way of cookbooks is a single typewritten recipe for chicken croquettes tacked inside the cupboard door.

The main room looks more lived-in than the kitchen. Near to the door is the little dining table with two chairs. The lawyer's papers cover nearly the whole thing. A low sofa strewn with velveteen pillows faces a row of bookshelves and a framed lobby poster for *The Temptress*. Louise wonders if it was a favorite film or if

Miss Daniels had worked on it. She'd made her name in the twenties, after all, working her way up from scenario girl to screenwriter.

Above the sofa is a small, framed painting, done in oranges and aquas and moss greens. In front of a pueblo, two women sit, one combing the other's hair. It's a quiet little watercolor, nothing particularly noteworthy. It's done right on paper with faint hints of pencil lines behind the paint. Somehow, though, it suits this unpretentious apartment.

A small and meaningfully cluttered desk is tucked in the corner, by the window. It's dominated by an Underwood Champion and scattered stacks of white paper. A few framed photos are propped here and there on the papers. There's no television or radio in the apartment, but there's an old crank record player and a modest stack of albums. Mostly old jazz, like Bessie Smith and Ethel Waters.

Louise runs an index finger along the bookshelves. There are few novels, though Miss Daniels seems to have had everything by Elinor Glyn and Radclyffe Hall. Face-out on a shelf is a crisp new copy of *The Price of Salt,* with a bookmark tucked in halfway through.

Most of the shelves are taken up, unsurprisingly, with black-bound screenplays. One by one, Louise pulls the manuscripts from the shelves and flips through them. She recognizes a few. There, Miss Daniels' adaptation of *Miss Ogilvy Finds Herself.* That was the first film that brought her acclaim. And her screenplays for *Wild Winds* and *Such Is Love.* Louise remembers seeing *Wild Winds* one rainy afternoon as a girl and passionately vowing to set off on an adventure of her own one day. Her adventure wasn't to Africa, but Hollywood felt far enough away to an eighteen-year-old girl with thirty dollars and a whole lot more determination.

Others on the shelves are unfamiliar. Florence Daniels was known for her adaptations of women's stories, the sorts of films that Cukor or Goulding directed and women flocked to see. But not all of the manuscripts are her well-known adaptations.

Louise takes down original screenplays, unfamiliar, unpublished, unproduced screenplays. She scans the titles, opens the pages, so white they were likely never read. No rings from coffee mugs or smudged fingerprints. These manuscripts hadn't made the rounds.

They're stories about women. Women strong and successful, leaving their marks on a world determined to forget them. Women not all too different from Louise and Florence Daniels herself. One is about an actress carrying her performance throughout a tentative marriage. Another about a young mother struggling to hold tight to an almost forgotten girlhood passion. One about two friends dying of, yet living despite, radium poisoning. They're the kinds of stories Louise longs to see on the screen. Already, she's casting the screenplays in her head, picturing the blocking, the gestures, the inflections, the sweep of the camera. This one she could see Gene Tierney in. Maybe Constance Bennett. That one, Pier Angeli, with her delicacy and strength. And this one, she decides, could only be Lauren Bacall.

The papers on the desk are scraps of more screenplays, ideas waiting for the rest of their stories. She rifles through the pages, but it's the framed photographs that catch her eye. Miss Daniels at a premiere with Anderson Lawler. At a costume party with Sonya Levien, both dressed imperiously as biblical queens. Sitting poolside in a group at George Cukor's in wide flowered pants and a sun hat. Miss Daniels had been an attractive woman.

But one photo doesn't have other Hollywood notables in it. It doesn't even include Florence Daniels herself. It's a little older than the rest, somewhat fuzzy, as though it had been taken with an old cardboard Brownie. The snapshot is of a young woman posed by a desert rock, squinting at the sun. Dark bobbed hair whips out from beneath the scarf tied around her head. She's pale, either from the sun's shining straight on her face, the film processing, or the weariness of travel, but she's smiling. Whatever rock in whatever desert she leans against, she's happy to be there.

Louise recognizes the woman, though she's not famous. She recognizes her from another photo, a stiff studio portrait that she knows well. And she should. The portrait, of a couple in modest wedding finery, has sat for the past thirty-two years on her father's piano.

A thousand thoughts flood her mind, but the first is a wash of relief. There's the connection. Florence Daniels knew her mother.

Maybe it isn't too surprising. Dad always said that Mom went to California. Drove all the way across the country, only to die somewhere between here and there. Maybe she reached Los Angeles. Maybe, in her last days, she met a young screenwriter.

She knows she's wrong the moment she opens the desk drawer. Inside the desk is a large, heavy envelope, and inside that there are more photos.

She spreads them out, straight over the typewriter and the stacked manuscripts. Her mother, forever young in her memory, is in them, but so is a young Florence Daniels. The two women, with arms around one another, are posed against trees, mountains, lakes, and a battered Model T in snapshots of a long-ago adventure. Even without reading the smudged captions on the backs of the photos, Louise knows they are a record of her mother's final trip.

The last two items to slip out of the envelope confirm this.

One is a lined notebook, like the ones schoolgirls use for compositions. It's filled with penciled script, sometimes neat and flowing, sometimes cramped with emotion. A makeshift travel journal, dated 1926. She flips pages to see how far it goes. Journal entries fill about a third of it and a sketched-out screenplay fills another third. It's titled *When She Was King,* the same as one of the screenplays on the shelf. At the very back of the notebook, past dozens of blank pages, is the single, lonely line, *"Holding your hand, I suddenly wasn't as scared."*

The other volume is a small cardboard-bound book, the kind given out for free as a promotion or advertisement. A little family accounts ledger. This one says "Feldman's Pharmacy – Sellers of Vit-A-Milk" and has preprinted pages to keep track of weekly budgets and expenses for the year. In the columns are indeed household items, printed in rows of tiny letters: groceries, expenses, planned meals. Sometimes, in the corners of the pages, little sketches in ink, of trees and cars, of a little girl's face, of windmills and cacti.

But, as she flips through it, she sees more than lists and plans. There are personal notes, notes that stretch and push beyond the succinctness of a household record. Sometimes only a sentence, sometimes a crisp paragraph, they're little glimpses of the woman behind the housewife.

The lists of groceries, the mundane details about cans of tomatoes and fryer chickens, are written in the same hand as Louise's birth date in the front of the family Bible. Unexpected tears spring to her eyes.

"Is everything fine?" Mr French comes out from the bedroom with an orange-dyed sombrero in his hands.

Louise blinks and starts catching up the scattered photographs. She'd forgotten she wasn't alone in the apartment. An actress is always on camera. "Yes." She shakes her head to clear it. "Are you almost finished?"

"I've found all of those *Variety* issues. I'm going to see if the caretaker has a box or two."

"Fine." She turns the envelope over to slide the photos back inside. She hadn't noticed before, but it's addressed to her, in those same small inked letters. Addressed, but never mailed. *"For AL, who has many journeys ahead of her"* is written across the unsealed flap.

Apart from the wedding photograph and the early

23

death, Louise never knew much about her mother. This envelope, with its photographs and makeshift diary, hidden in a stranger's apartment, holds more of her mother's story than she's ever had before.

While she waits for Mr French to return, she pours a glass of club soda; she doesn't find any gin. With glass in hand, she sits at the table and opens her briefcase. The script inside she extracts with two fingers. *The Princess of Las Vegas Boulevard.* She'd only flipped through it earlier at the meeting. It's so gaudy and girly she's surprised the front cover isn't sequin-studded. She opens to the first page and wishes she hadn't. Stilted dialogue, right from the start.

She abandons both script and drink and wanders back to the bookcase.

What she wouldn't give to star in a script like one of these. Stories about smart, daring, resourceful women, doing more than blushing and sighing up at their leading men. She wants one of these roles so bad she can taste it like sugar at the back of her tongue. Drawn by the title *When She Was King,* Louise takes the screenplay from the shelf. She loves the contradiction and the complete absence of the word "princess" in the title.

Right away, she's impressed.

The writing is crisp, the dialogue playful. The characters are so real she can almost shake their hands. From the snippets she reads, it's about two women rekindling a friendship on a drive across the country. There are campgrounds and card games and a very resilient Model T. There are tears and regrets, and also yearnings held tight to the chest. She wonders if her mother's last trip was like this. She wonders if that's why Florence Daniels started writing it in the back of her travel journal.

She hears Mr French's voice outside and slips the script into her empty briefcase. On impulse she takes another from the bookcase, and then another. She stuffs them in the briefcase until it's full.

Those few pages of *When She Was King* had brought up a surge of defiance so sharp she can almost taste it. Two women driving across the country with the same stubbornness that had brought Louise out to Hollywood all those years ago. Back then she'd had a determination that she'd almost forgotten until this moment. "Just like your mother," Dad had always said. It had taken guts to set off on a journey with nothing but a Model T between you and the unpaved United States.

Mr French comes in with a cardboard box and Louise latches shut the briefcase. Though it's all hers, she's sure she's not allowed to take anything yet; lawyers thrive on red tape and paperwork. She doesn't even know why she's trying to sneak the briefcase full of screenplays out. Maybe because, reading this one, she's been reminded of Mom and her courage. Maybe it's because she wants the same courage, through the dialogue of the script and in real life.

She retrieves her coffee-spotted gloves and handbag and says all the right things to Mr French, hoping he won't notice that her briefcase has grown in size, hoping he won't notice the gaping holes in the bookcase. He doesn't.

It's not until she's back out on the sidewalk that she remembers she left the two diaries sitting in the envelope on the desk.

Chapter Two

1952

It's started raining.

She takes a taxi. With her overstuffed briefcase, she feels almost like she's setting off on a trip. The cabbie even asks if she's headed to Los Angeles International Airport. She sets her purse on the seat, brushes rain from the sleeves of her jacket, and gives him an address on Rodeo Drive.

Lights are starting to go on around the city. Hollywood Boulevard is lined in neon signs and electric lights. Every lamppost holds a metal tree blazing with colored bulbs. Strung across the street are bells, wreaths, and incandescent stars. Louise rests her head against the window.

The crowds of umbrellas hurrying home thin as the taxi turns onto Rodeo Drive. The bright glitter of the theaters is replaced by the yellow glow of porch lights. White felt "snow" and strings of Christmas lights skirt the edges of roofs. She loves Rodeo Drive, with its quiet bungalows and old bridle path running straight down the middle of the road. Framed in squares of lighted windows, aproned women stand at ranges, children bend over schoolbooks, and men pour themselves whiskeys.

"Home late for supper, aren't you?" the cabbie asks, and for a moment she wishes she could give him a different address. That she could point to one of these warmly lit houses and go in to a supper of pork chops or hot pot or whatever was on the stove.

But she doesn't answer him. The whitewashed bungalow they pull up to is dark. No Christmas lights. No tree framed in the window. It used to have evening primrose and bright yellow geraniums planted in front. Even in the dusk, she knows the porch is in need of a coat of paint. The cabbie turns and seems about to make another comment, but she pays him quickly and exits the taxi.

The house is quiet. She sets the briefcase on the rug inside the front door and steps out of her heels. In her stockinged feet, she walks to the kitchen, leaving rainwater like breadcrumbs behind her. She unpins her white hat – the soaked buckram has gone soft – and tosses it along with her purse and navy jacket onto a kitchen chair. Goosebumps fleck her arms. Only then does she switch on the kitchen lights.

It's just as she left it that morning. Curtains flap wetly against the open window; her breakfast bowl, still on the counter, is speckled with rain. A saucepan with congealed Cream of Wheat sits on the stove. She swears under her breath, one of those muttered, self-conscious swears her father always uttered. She scrapes the cereal into the trash can and sets the pan in the sink to soak. As she reaches across the sink to shut the window, her knotted scarf dips into the stream of water from the faucet. She steps back and brushes drops from the front of her blouse, and a red light catches her eye. The percolator is still plugged in. She yanks out the cord and burns her hand on the side of the coffeepot. With a dish towel, she pulls off the lid. The coffee is sludge now. Suddenly she wants to cry.

"Where have you been?"

She doesn't turn around, but dumps the overwarmed coffee into the sink. "I could ask you the same." She swivels the faucet and watches coffee swirl down the drain. "Why are all the lights off?"

"I didn't notice it had gotten dark."

She wishes it were because he'd been writing or typing or even just sitting and reading the newspaper.

"Are you hungry?" she asks, shutting off the water and reaching for the dish towel. "I was just going to . . ."

But she's turned and seen Arnie in the doorway. Six in the evening and he's still in his pajamas.

"You haven't even gotten dressed today?" She throws the dish towel back onto the counter. "You didn't eat the breakfast I left, you didn't shut the window, you didn't even get dressed."

He doesn't answer, just looks away.

She's spent the day arguing with men who called her "sweetheart" and assured her they had a great role for her involving a ukulele and bikini. What had Arnie done? His pajama shirt is spattered with brown. "I see at least you got out of bed long enough to find the coffee."

For an instant, she thinks she sees a flash of hurt in his

eyes. A flash of anger. But just as quickly, it's gone, and his face is blank. When he retreats to the bedroom, she sags against the sink.

She shouldn't have said that. She knows better.

The day before Arnie arrived back home, her neighbor Pauline had brought over a ham loaf. Pauline was married to a B-list actor, a man who gave up Westerns for the army. Louise wasn't the sort for neighborly potlucks and bridge games, but Pauline was young and lonely and determined to be nice.

"When Bert came home from Korea, he was different for a while," she told Louise. They stood on the porch with the towel-covered loaf pan between them. "It wasn't just losing his hearing. He wasn't the same man who left."

Louise could see him over Pauline's shoulder walking to his car. He'd been back a few months now. He didn't look any different. You'd never know he was deaf in one ear if he didn't tell you.

"Oh, everything's fine now," Pauline said, maybe a bit too brightly. "Just fine."

"I'm glad."

"So, be patient with Arnie." She passed over the ham loaf. It was still warm. "You might not know him right away. But he's there, deep inside."

Be patient. Louise repeated it the whole drive to the airport. Repeated it throughout that first awkward dinner, with slices of ham loaf, thin tomato gravy, and boiled potatoes. Repeated it that first night lying side by side in bed, both holding their breaths, both pretending to be asleep. *Be patient.*

She tells it to herself now, leaning against the sink in the cold kitchen. Patience. Even though it's been weeks since he got home. She's lost ten pounds, which the studio loves, and gained circles under her eyes, which they don't. She's been careful around Arnie, so careful about what she says. But all it takes is one long day and she's forgotten Pauline's advice.

She takes a deep breath. Putting her hand against her chest, she counts to ten to the rhythm of her heartbeats, the way her dad taught her when she was young and stubborn and prone to foot-stamping tantrums.

Deep breath. She heads to the squat liquor cabinet in the living room. This is her favorite room, sleek and modern. A low sofa, curved like a wave and the color of the Pacific. Two round orange chairs like upturned buckets. A wide glass-topped coffee table with two carefully arranged white vases and a book of Jackson Pollock paintings. Walls that used to be pale brown now painted something called "Columbia Green." She redecorated the entire room, made it all fresh and smelling of paint for Arnie's arrival home. She even bought him a silver Googie ashtray, shaped like a flying saucer, though she'd always hated when he smoked in the house. And yet, since he's been home, he's hardly spent an hour in the living room.

Though it's less than two weeks until Christmas, she hasn't gotten out any decorations. None of her strings of bubble lights or ropes of plastic holly. No bowl of artful glass ornaments. No mistletoe. She hasn't put on a single holiday record. She's been throwing away Christmas cards unopened. The Ebenezer Scrooge of Rodeo Drive. These days, she doesn't know if she cares.

She turns on the lamp, the one that looks like a flower sprouting straight up from the floor. She finds the whiskey, the sweet vermouth, the bitters, and measures out a Manhattan. On the way back to the kitchen she drinks enough to make room for the two ice cubes she'll twist from the metal tray. The bedroom door is shut, but lamplight shines from underneath.

The Manhattan does its job, and she starts to relax. Warmth spreads out along her shoulders and down her goosebumped arms. She turns on the little green radio in the kitchen and adjusts the dial until she hears Jo Stafford's voice. She takes another sip. From the pantry and the Coldspot, she pulls tins and packages and bottles. Rain rattles against the window. She melts butter, slices onions and dried beef, pours far too much milk. The electric toaster pops. By the time she finishes her drink, she's made two plates of creamed chipped beef on toast. Diet be damned.

She makes another Manhattan and fortifies herself with a healthy swallow before picking up one of the plates and heading for the bedroom. She starts to knock, but changes her mind. It's her bedroom too. "Arnie, I brought you something to eat." She pushes open the door.

He's next to the dresser in his wheelchair, pajama shirt caught halfway over his head. He's swearing in Latin.

"Oh, Arn." She hurries into the room and sets the plate on the dresser. "Here."

She reaches for where the shirt twists across his chest, but he flinches as though she's touched him with an iron.

She bites the inside of her cheek. Careful not to let fingers brush skin, she eases it over his shoulders.

He takes the shirt right from her hands. "I could've done it."

Time was Arnie could run to Roxbury Park and back without breaking a sweat. Now he sits in the wheelchair, hunched over a crumpled pajama shirt, out of breath.

Silhouetted against the gray window, the curve of his ribs is clear against his chest. Since the accident, he's subsisted on little more than black coffee and saltines straight from the tin. Though she isn't much of a cook, she borrows Pauline's cookbooks and makes bowls of farina, pots of custard and of oyster soup, plates piled with liver and onions or fried pork chops. All the things the doctor recommends. As tired as she is after a day on the set, ignoring leers and dodging pinches, she comes home and pretends to be a cook. She plays the role of a regular housewife just taking care of her husband. She wishes she'd been better about doing that all along.

But he ignores whatever she puts on the table. She even bought a TV tray to put in the bedroom, so that he doesn't even have to get out of bed, but he ignores it. Sits in his chair at the bedroom window until she gives in and brings out the cracker tin. He's as skinny as a street mutt.

"Do you want me to . . ." she starts, with a gesture to his waist, but he shakes his head, far too quickly.

"My pants are fine." He tosses the pajama shirt onto the bed.

"You haven't changed them in days."

She knows it's because he can't bear to be touched, at

33

least by her. Those times when he let her help him into the bathtub, when he first came home, he made her dim the bathroom lights. Now he has a bar attached to the tile wall. He does it alone.

"I said they're fine," he snaps. "Why can't you leave me alone?"

If I did, then who else would take care of you? she wants to ask. *Who would want to?* On the back of her tongue, she tastes whiskey and swallowed bitterness.

He turns his head. "Is there more coffee?"

"No, but I have supper for you. Over on the dresser."

"I told you . . ."

"Arn, you have to eat."

"I'm not hungry." He wheels next to the bed. With one hand on the bed and one on the wheelchair, he heaves himself up onto the wrinkled blanket.

"Do you want me to . . ."

Lying down, he turns his face to the wall. "Why can't you leave me alone?" he says again.

She tries. She goes to the studio earlier each day, even before her call. She's waiting in the makeup chair with a glass of tomato juice and the script before the artists get there at six-thirty to lay out their brushes and sponges. She stays late, changing into slacks and a sweater, going over the next day's lines, taking off each and every smear of makeup before the car arrives to take her home. Every day, she lives a little more away from home.

But she can't do that anymore. "They threatened me with suspension."

He freezes at this. His head turns, just a fraction, enough to let her know that he's listening.

She picks up his plate of food, now cold. "Merry Christmas, Louise." And she leaves the room.

By the time he follows, she's seated on the floor of the living room, back against the wall. She's taking off her blue skirt and stockings, and is eating the creamed chipped beef on toast with the plate resting against her bare knees. She should be starting to read *The Princess of Las Vegas Boulevard,* but *When She Was King* is open in front of her. A third Manhattan sits on the book of Pollock paintings.

"The soldiers call that 'SOS,'" he says, and picks up a cardboard book of matches from the ashtray. "'Shit-on-a-shingle.'"

Louise looks up in surprise. Not because of the language, but because this is the first time he's mentioned the war.

She swallows the bite of gravy and toast. "I know."

Now it's his turn to look surprised.

"I read that article of yours," she says. "The one about the food soldiers miss from home."

"Bah." He throws the matchbook back into the ashtray. "I wrote what they told me to write. The kinds of things the folks at home want to hear. The kinds of things a good American would say. You think any of that was real?"

In the past thirteen years, she's played showgirls and coeds and secretaries and debutantes. She's been a princess and the girl-next-door. She understands pretend. But if "real" wasn't the articles he wired home from Korea, if it wasn't the soldiers eating chipped beef and missing their wives, then what was? Arnie's jeep on the road to Taegu, the land mine, the hours he spent pinned under the vehicle waiting for someone to find him. The three coffins that came home on his airplane. She knows that's real.

But he doesn't talk about it. All she knows is what she's read in his articles.

"Do you want to eat yours?" she asks, suddenly ravenous.

He shakes his head no, and she slides his plate toward her.

As she eats, he sits quietly, maybe waiting to talk, maybe waiting for her to. It's odd, this. He doesn't much come out from the bedroom. When he does, it's never to the living room. And it's never this expectant bit of waiting. She bends her head to her plate and keeps her mouth full. She doesn't know how to start the conversation.

When he finally says something, it's "What did you do with Klimt?"

The art book that used to be on their coffee table was all gold-tinted Klimt paintings. Strength and myth. She isn't sure she even likes Jackson Pollock, but the designer had assured her that he was as modern as the room.

"In the attic."

"We bought that in London." He doesn't look at her as he says it. "Remember?"

"It was Ireland."

"London."

She'd been in Europe that summer of '44 with the USO. All the soldiers wanted to see Betsey Barnes, and so she obliged with Betsey's signature giggle and flutter and rendition of "A Polka in my Pocket." Arnie was on assignment for the Associated Press, stuck farther from the front lines than he would've liked to be. Louise didn't care – he was in Plymouth to meet her boat. They called it a belated honeymoon.

That's where he bought her the Longines. The watch was already a few years out of fashion and plain next to the jewel-studded Cartier watches and sleek Omegas popular then. It felt wildly indulgent to shop for a luxury watch in the middle of wartime London, but back at home they lived on hot dogs and cheap beer and far too many kisses. It *was* wildly indulgent. Arnie called it a wedding present, so that she'd always make it to the set on time.

"It could have been either," she says. "Either London or Dublin." And, with the cocktails making her head swirl, it could have been. "We were all over those two months."

"Where did you say it was?"

"The attic." She puts the plate down on the coffee table. "Want me to go get it?"

"No." He shakes his head. "Don't."

She doesn't know why he brought it up just then. But she doesn't have the words to ask him.

It didn't use to be this. Time was they'd stay up all night talking over pots of coffee and candlelight. Not Hollywood gossip or anything like that, but books, politics, philosophy. That was when neither was working much. Enough to pay the rent and keep the pantry stocked with peanut butter and Ritz crackers, the fridge with hot dogs. That was just before the first Betsey Barnes came out. Before both of them had been sucked into the Hollywood vortex.

Even then, they talked. She'd come home as soon as

filming was over for the day. He'd close up the typewriter and flick off the desk lamp the moment he heard her key in the lock. They'd do the crossword puzzle together over dinner. They were young, smart, and mad for each other.

But, somehow, between there and here, all those words had disappeared.

He clears his throat and shifts in his wheelchair. In one hand he shakes something, and she knows it's a pill. Bottles line his nightstand. Some nights, by the light of the hallway, she eyes the row of bottles and wonders if he has something there for her.

She scoots up on her knees to reach for her drink. It's left a wet ring on the picture book and she tries to rub it out with the cuff of her blouse.

Arnie clears his throat again. "Got another of those?"

He hasn't touched a drop since getting back. She'd figured that would be a thing. Returning from war halfway to being a drunk. She wouldn't have blamed him. But not Arn.

"Sure." She jumps to her feet, sways a moment. "Do you want this one?" By the third glass, it was mostly whiskey.

"I can wait," he says.

It's what she feels like she's been doing for weeks.

"Let me get some more ice."

She brings the ice bucket into the kitchen and takes her time. The radio is still on, now playing Rosemary Clooney. She rinses the dinner plates and wipes them down with a towel before pulling out the ice cube tray. There are only four cubes left. Arnie was always the one to remember to refill it before they ran out.

She puts her hand on her chest and counts to ten again, one for each heartbeat. She turns the radio up before leaving the kitchen.

When she gets back, he's just where she left him. She hadn't noticed before, but he'd put on fresh pajamas. White, with a thread of a red stripe running up and down. At the liquor cabinet, she mixes his drink and wonders if he's watching her, standing there in just her white blouse and underwear. But when she turns, he's looking down at his hands.

She hands him the drink. He hesitates, then says quietly, "Thank you." As Rosemary sings, Arnie shakes the pill in his hand into his mouth and chases it with his Manhattan.

She sinks back onto the floor, her back against the Columbia Green wall. She's added fresh ice to her glass, and it sweats against her palms.

"When did you get suspended?" he finally asks. The question he's put on pajamas for. The question he's finally come out of the bedroom for.

"Monday."

"What do you mean, Monday?"

One, two, three, four . . . She breathes. "I went to the studio today to read the latest script." *Five, six, seven* . . . "I'm tired of these scripts. I'm tired of these roles. Charlie came along with me. He's going to insist on script approval with my next contract." She drinks and wipes her mouth indelicately with the back of her hand. "I even wore my lucky scarf."

"The yellow one?"

She nods. "They all but patted me on the head. Said that

they knew what was best for me. That they had the perfect part lined up." She stares at her drink. "A cabbie's daughter who becomes the toast of Las Vegas."

"Of course."

"Of course."

He's already weaving in his chair. "So you said no."

She nods. "I thought I'd show them I *could* say no." She licks her lips. "They just ignored me. Told me the filming starts on Monday in Vegas. Said to get myself to Nevada and be on set or else."

"You're going with the 'or else.' "

"Yes." She sighs. "Yes. No. I don't know." She drains the rest of the Manhattan. "It's just a suspension if I don't show up. Maybe I'll get the contract I want." She looks into her empty glass and snorts. "Maybe."

For a moment, the only sounds are from the radio and the ice in their glasses. "Could be it's not a bad part. Who's writing?"

"Rachmann."

He takes a gulp of his drink. His eyelids are starting to droop. "Could be it's not a bad part," he murmurs again.

She pulls herself to her feet. She sets her glass up on the liquor cabinet, where she's set the bottles and dripping ice bucket. Finding her balance, she stumbles across to where she's left her briefcase by the front door. It's suddenly heavier than it was earlier, but she heaves it over.

"What's that?"

"Not a bad part." She opens it over the coffee table. Bound manuscripts clatter across the table. The ashtray falls to the carpet. Arnie drops his glass with a splash but she's too drunk to care.

He doesn't make a move toward any of the scripts, even though once they'd been his livelihood. Once he would've been unable to leave off sifting through the pages. Today he just stares at them, as though they're snakes raining down in his living room. Maybe he can't reach them there on the table, or maybe he doesn't want to. She's still feeling furious over today's meeting and his casual dismissal of her anger. Furious at these scripts, sitting quietly forgotten on Florence Daniels' bookcase. Furious at Arnie and their dark bedroom, his coffee-stained pajama shirt, the gleaming and unused Googie ashtray.

She picks up one of the manuscripts and thrusts it at him, daring him not to take it. "These are the parts I should be trying for." She picks up another and pushes it at him. "These are the scripts you should be working on." And another. "These are the characters who should be on the screen. I know you'll agree."

Bewildered, he juggles the books in his hand. "Where did you get these from?" He squints down at the white tag on the front of one. "Florence Daniels?"

"She gave them to me." She doesn't feel like explaining, not yet.

"And you brought them all home . . . Why? You don't get to pick your scripts." His voice is getting back that edge of irritation.

"Not yet I don't."

"Then what are you doing with them?"

"I wanted to read them. To be prepared." She picks

up two more and adds them to the stack in his arms. "I wanted *us* to read them." The combination of liquor and anger makes her bold. She looks him straight in the eyes. "Remember when we used to do that, Arn?"

Once the Betsey Barnes series hit it big and he was given an MGM contract, he wrote less and less for the newspapers and magazines. She loved that he was on the lot each day to eat lunch with her. He loved that he could slip in to watch her on set every now and again.

She hadn't been able to argue about what scripts she was given. But she could bring them home and pore over them with Arnie, their empty dinner dishes pushed aside. He'd help her suss out the story, find the lines to hold on to. With Arnie reading by her side, she'd understood the character even before the first day of filming.

For a moment, his eyes soften. Maybe it's the drink, maybe it's the pill, or maybe, just maybe, he remembers too.

"If you read them, you could go talk to the studio. They'll listen to you." *Because he's a man,* she tells herself, *because he's a writer, because he's a broken remnant of a war nobody notices. Because, this time, he got closer to the front lines.* "They're good stories, Arn. The sorts of things we always wanted to work on together. Just read them and see." She piles more in his arms, until they stack up almost to his chin. She scoops up loose manuscript pages and adds them, all in a jumble. "With me acting and you writing, it'll be like the good old days."

He's out of bed. He's drinking a Manhattan. For the first time in weeks, they're actually talking. And, from the kitchen, Eddie Fisher is singing "That's What Christmas

Means to Me." For an instant, it's like everything is back to normal.

But he says, "Stop," and the instant is past. "Louise, you're drunk."

She is, but she doesn't know what that has to do with anything. Most evenings she's drunk. It doesn't mean she's done. It doesn't mean she's ready to stop acting.

She picks up the last manuscript from the floor, the one she was reading over her creamed chipped beef. "But you need a project. If you just—"

"Stop," he says again, and leans forward to put the stack of manuscripts on the coffee table. But with the pill, the whiskey, the towering pile of screenplays, he leans too far forward and loses his balance. With paper raining down around him, he falls from the wheelchair and onto the floor.

She jumps forward, though it's too late to catch him. He's on the carpet, stretched out, looking helpless.

"Arn."

She reaches down to him, but he smacks her hand away. "Leave me alone." That phrase, the one she's heard so many times since he's been back, comes out as a snarl.

She creeps back against the wall. She swallows.

He pushes himself up on his hands, slowly, painfully. By the time he gets himself into a sitting position, leaning against the coffee table, he's panting.

"Arn," she says, and steps forward again, uncertain.

"It's no good." He swipes a hand down his face. "Don't you see I can't?"

She stumbles to the bathroom. She trips over his toilet bench, bumps against the low shelf with his unused shaving supplies, catches herself on the metal bar above the bathtub. All the little reminders that he can't. Hand to her chest, she counts to ten as she turns on the faucet. It's ice cold. The tears wait until she's in the shower. She turns her face up to the water streaming down, and she cries.

Louise wakes on the aqua-blue sofa. She doesn't remember turning off the lamp or falling asleep here.

Resting open across her chest is the script. She remembers coming out of the shower and making another sloppy Manhattan. After the shower, she'd been wide awake. She didn't want to stumble into the dark bedroom and the too-quiet bed. She wanted to get lost in the mountains of Pennsylvania, the flat prairies of the Middle West. She wanted to change a tire and play cards in a tent and take pictures of the sun rising over the desert. And so she propped up her feet and let herself fall asleep reading *When She Was King*.

She's wrapped in only a bathrobe. Outside, it's still dark. The glow from the streetlamps pushes from between the curtains. She checks the clock on the wall, the one that always makes her think of outer space, of planets orbiting around the hour. It's morning. Just barely.

Her tongue feels thick and her head stuffed with yarn. She flexes her calves before getting up. She'd rather be still asleep, but nights are never as long as they ought to be. The kitchen floor is cold. She automatically measures coffee from the blue tin, fills the percolator with water, and plugs it in.

As the percolator bubbles, she washes her face in the

bathroom, wiping away the last streaks of mascara. She runs her wet hands through her hair. It's dried in waves from last night's washing. She rubs in curl cream and combs, twists, and pins her hair until it's all up in loose, pinned curls. It isn't perfect, but it's better than looking like she's slept on the sofa.

While her hair sets, she remakes her face. Not all the way, but enough that she can go out of the house without feeling half-naked. She smooths on some powder, fills in her eyebrows, rubs on some pale pink gloss. She begins the transformation back into "actress."

She steps on Arnie's shaving brush. She vaguely remembers knocking over his little shelf the night before and bends to collect everything that's rolled under the sink. His toothbrush and tube of Pepsodent. His comb. His Old Spice shaving mug, soap, razor, unopened package of Gillette blades, shaving mirror, now cracked in half. She arranges everything back on the shelf, everything except the mirror, which she pushes to the bottom of the Lucite trash can.

She automatically straightens his toilet bench, pats down the bubbles in the rubber bath mat, refolds the towel on his low rack. It's bone-dry.

Once the coffee's made she drinks a whole cup leaning against the kitchen sink. She can't stomach any breakfast. She can barely stomach being awake. The bathroom mirror agrees. Her face is icy white with circles dark-smudged like bruises beneath each eye. She dabs on more powder before unpinning and brushing her curls.

Arnie used to drive her in every morning. One hand on

the wheel, he'd drink his second cup of coffee in the car. He always drove as slow as honey; he never spilled. She could drive herself, if she wanted to. She has a car in the garage, a bullet-nose Studebaker Champion convertible. Deep red and as shiny as a new apple. Arnie bought it for her the day before he left. But she's never driven the Champ by herself, not in all those months he was gone. It makes her nervous, being behind the wheel. Besides, it just isn't the same.

So the studio sends a car. She checks the clock again, this time the one on the kitchen wall, as round and sunny as an over-easy egg. Five minutes. She's still naked under a satin bathrobe.

The bedroom is dark, but she knows her way around it by the glow of the hall light. Underthings in the top drawer, stockings beneath that. A stiff, folded girdle. She opens the narrow closet and feels for the silky touch of rayon, the crispness of linen, the soft caress of jersey. She picks a fir-green dress, with long narrow sleeves and white turned-back cuffs. She'd bought it for a funeral once where she couldn't bear to wear black. She ties the white ribbons at the collar. She slips into alligator pumps and, last, as always, fastens on her gold watch.

It's only when Arnie rolls over and murmurs, "Where are you going?" that she remembers.

There's no car coming. No makeup artist waiting. No one expecting her at MGM.

"Are you going to Las Vegas?" Even half-asleep, he's remembered the night before. She'd drunk enough to forget.

Last night she'd been angry. Her talk about risking

suspension, about thumbing her nose at the studio's threat – it was Manhattan-fueled. She can't really. If she doesn't show up, if she's suspended, if she's *let go,* who buys the cans of coffee? The chipped beef and toast? The Googie ashtrays? It's been too long since Arnie's drawn a paycheck. She has to go to Vegas.

A good actress. It's all she's tried to be for the past year.

"I don't have a choice," she says, and steps backward toward the hallway.

In Arnie's office, she switches on the desk lamp. It's been ages since she's been in here. Arnie too, apparently. The desk is gray with dust. She blows on the typewriter cover and sends up a cloud. It's exactly as he left it when he flew out to Korea. The green blotter. The covered Remington in the center. Three sharpened Ticonderoga pencils and a single red pen in a souvenir mug from the Golden Gate Exposition. His pipe stand and the black telephone. Along the edge of the blotter, she traces "Lou was here" in the dust with a finger, then wipes it out with the side of her hand.

She should have made travel arrangements yesterday, before leaving the studio. But after the meeting and the phone call from that lawyer, she hadn't even thought of it. Now it's Saturday. She's on her own.

The phone book is in the upper-right-hand desk drawer. She doesn't know which airline flies to Las Vegas, but starts with Trans World. It's what she flew on that single transcontinental trip all those years ago, when she stopped to see Dad before heading to Europe with the USO. Eight years is a long time for nothing but phone calls. Maybe after this picture wraps. New Jersey isn't going anywhere, but she misses Dad.

The Trans World agent is far too chirpy for this hour of the morning. They do fly to Vegas, yes. Would madame like to make a reservation?

She takes a pencil from the cup and opens the drawer where Arnie keeps notepaper. The paper's there, but also a folded pink sheet. She sees "House of Representatives" and "Committee on Un-American Activities" and hangs up the phone without replying.

She stalks into the bedroom holding the subpoena between her fingertips. Arnie's still in bed, but she knows he's not sleeping.

"When did this arrive?" she asks. She's simmering. She's steaming.

He doesn't answer.

"I know you're awake. When did this arrive?"

She doesn't specify what "this" is, but he knows. The covers shift. A shrug. "I don't know. A week ago."

"And you were just going to ignore it? Shut it up in a drawer and pretend it never came?"

"Maybe." Another infinitesimal shrug. "Maybe they'll forget about me."

"They haven't in nine months. These aren't the kind of people who forget. Arnie, this is a congressional subpoena."

The light from the hall throws a splash of yellow across the bedspread. Arnie doesn't stir, and he doesn't reply again.

She goes to the kitchen and pours another cup of coffee, but doesn't drink it. She paces from the table to the pantry,

48

from the sink to the refrigerator. When she sets the still-full mug on the counter, it's with decisiveness.

"We'll set up an appointment with Dr Keller," she says, coming back into the bedroom. "You're scheduled to be in DC next month." She unbuttons her cuffs. "I know you haven't been doing your exercises. You aren't in any shape yet to stand in front of the committee."

He rolls over. "Stand?"

She flushes, and is glad it's dark. "You know what I mean."

"Yeah, I do." He pushes himself up on one elbow. "You mean that I need to polish myself up so that I can go in front of the House Un-American Activities Committee and make nice. Just what you didn't want me to do back in March."

Back in March a subpoena would've been an interruption to a writing career going at full tilt. These days there's nothing to interrupt. She throws the subpoena on top of the dresser. "Make nice. Tell them to get lost. Something. *Anything.*"

He lies back down. "Maybe anything is exactly what I don't want to do."

She's tired of the dusty, unused typewriter and the laundry basket full of nothing but pajamas. She's tired of cracker crumbs in the bed. She's tired of him not making an effort, at a single thing. Not at eating, at doing his exercises, at starting to work again. Not even at fighting for the things he believes in. She wonders if he believes in anything anymore.

She's tired too. Exhausted. Deliberately long hours at the studio. Solitary dinners. Quiet nights. But she does them. She does the laundry too.

She wants him to do something. Give in or fight, it doesn't make a difference. Giving in would keep them safe, but fighting, well, that would be a flash of the old Arnie. The one who – yes, don't tell a soul – might have been to a rally or two in his day.

"You always tell me not to back down," she says. "You used to say you'd be right behind me to push me back up."

He's facing away from her. "In case you haven't noticed," he says to the wall, "these days I can't even push myself back up."

She gets down on her knees and reaches under the bed for a suitcase. She has a matching set – white, monogrammed, with gold clasps – that she bought in a splurge before her USO trip, but that's not what she reaches for. The suitcase she pulls out is ancient. She hasn't used it in ages. It's a battered old thing that she brought with her on that bus ride from Jersey fourteen years ago. Faded wicker, lined with purple-pink fabric, something excessively flowered and ugly. It was Mom's. It's hers now, and it's perfect.

She goes to the living room and drops the suitcase on the coffee table, right on top of the scattered manuscripts, then returns to the bedroom. Gray dawn starts to seep in at the edges of the curtains. She throws open the closet, slides open the dresser drawers. "I'm leaving."

Arnie's awake. He pulls himself up to a sit. "What do you mean, leaving?"

"For Vegas." She's yanking clothes out haphazardly. Skirts, blouses, sweaters, shawls. Dresses and pajamas. One pair of twill shorts. Stockings, underpants, girdles, brassieres. A silky slip of a scarf. "It'll take me a day or two to get there." A black stocking slithers from her arms. "I don't want to be late."

She carries the clothes out to the living room and drops them on the sofa. She folds them with suddenly sure hands and packs them into the wicker suitcase, one by one, stacked and wedged. The suitcase is enormous. There's room enough for weeks' worth of clothes. Maybe if she'd planned ahead, laying outfits on the bed, checking items against a list, folding them between sheets of tissue paper, she'd have been able to fit that much. As it is, she hasn't packed half that.

She ducks back into the bedroom and into the shoe closet. Gray heels, shiny black slingbacks, a neat pair of red flats. Her favorite sandals, with straps that twine around her ankles. One pair of pristine white Keds, in case she chances upon anything athletic. They never told her how long they'd be shooting. A girl must always be prepared for tennis.

"How are you getting there?" Arnie is at the edge of the bed.

She thinks of the journals, of the envelope of photos. Of the two women alone with their Model T. "Maybe I'll just drive myself," she says suddenly.

It's not that ridiculous. Though she's never driven the Champ by herself, she knows how. Before he left for Korea, Arnie took her and the car out, introduced them to one another. She drove even slower than he did, but she didn't hit a single thing.

He doesn't reply, doesn't offer to drive her the way he would've once upon a time. He shifts, moves first one leg, then the other, over the side of the bed. Of course he doesn't offer.

"I can do it," she says. Insists.

"But you don't have to. There's probably a train—"

"I said I can do it. Leave me alone," she snaps, unthinkingly throwing his own phrase back at him. "I don't need a train. I don't need your help."

"The studio should—"

"If we're listing the things the studio 'should' do, we can start with 'listen' and 'respect' and 'treat me like an adult.' For the rest of the list, we'd be here all morning."

"Why are you so defensive?" He runs a hand through his hair. He needs a trim and a shave.

"Why don't you think I can take care of myself?" In the studio she holds her head up, despite everything at home. A good actress. "What do you think I've been doing all these months?"

"I didn't say that. I only asked about your drive to Vegas. I'll . . ."

He doesn't finish the sentence. She waits. *Worry. Wait. Miss you.* So many things he could end it with. Even *manage without you* she'd accept, because that would mean getting out of bed and eating more than saltines.

But "I'll leave you alone" is what he says, before adding, "Fine."

It's a pin to her heart. She pulls her shoulders back so she doesn't deflate. "It's what we do best." She spins and leaves the room.

Though driving to Vegas in the red Champion started

as a whim, it's solidified. It's independence, it's escape, it's proof. Of what, she doesn't know. But she needs to do it. She can picture it now, a shot on the screen in Technicolor. The red car, the brown desert, the dark-haired actress running away from it all with her wicker suitcase.

She digs for spare corners in the suitcase where she can tuck the shoes. She adds a satin bag with earrings, a pearl necklace, a silver bracelet studded with turquoise. In the bathroom she gathers her curlers and pins, her Aqua Net, her cold creams, her makeup. She finds her old blue vanity case on the closet shelf, the one she used to carry back and forth to the studio when she was still unimportant enough to do her own makeup, and she packs her toiletries. She adds a bottle of Four Roses. In the bedroom, she fills a cardboard hatbox.

Arnie finds her out in the living room, kneeling in front of the suitcase and vanity case, snapping them shut. He rests his hands on the wheels of his chair.

"You're really leaving now?"

"I don't get to spend all day in bed. I don't get to live on pills and coffee and complaints. I don't get to hide from the HUAC, pretending that everything is okay. Someone has to make decisions. Someone has to go out and work. Someone has to hold the house together."

"But you said the script was crap. That they patted you on the head and didn't listen to a word you said."

"What do you want me to say, Arn?" The clasp on the vanity case is jammed. She smacks it with the heel of her hand. "That I'll put on my lucky scarf and try again?"

"Anything's better than giving up."

It's what she'd wanted him to say last night. It's what she'd wanted him to say when she confronted him with the pink subpoena. Words that sounded like the old Arnie, when it was them against the world. Words that made her feel like it was worth it.

She stands, tall in her alligator pumps, and looks down at him. "It may not be the career I want, but it's something. *One* of us has to have something."

The two glasses from last night's Manhattans are still there, his empty on the floor, hers up on the liquor cabinet, sticky and half-full with melted ice. She takes them to the kitchen. He won't clean them up while she's gone. Before setting them in the sink, she drains her glass. She tastes the ghost of whiskey in the water.

Arnie's still in the hallway, hunched in his chair.

She pins on a curve of a white hat with a pouf of netting. She takes her coat from the closet. Mink, lined in scarlet. Like she's leaving for a premiere, she holds it out to Arnie.

"Lou," he says, and hesitates. "When will you come back?"

Tomorrow, she wants to say. *Never.* She doesn't know what the answer is. "I don't know."

He takes the coat and a deep breath. He unbuttons it and shakes it out. Sitting in his chair, he holds it as high as he can.

She bends backward and slips into the coat.

Turning, she holds it tight against her neck, as though to leave it open would leave her heart open. Arnie stares at her tightly clasped hands. "Last night you said you didn't want to go," he says. "That you wanted the suspension. You wanted the fight."

"Arn," she says, picking up her luggage. "I don't know what's worth fighting for anymore."

Scene: The front seat of an overstuffed Model T. Two women are inside, both wearing raincoats and wet hats. Beryl is turned around, kneeling on her seat and looking out through the back window at the city disappearing behind them. Francie is driving, facing straight ahead.

Beryl removes a handkerchief from her eyes and waves it at the city.

FRANCIE

(smiling)

It's not going to wave back, you know.

BERYL

Don't make fun of me.

(looks at Francie and sticks out tongue)

I'm saying adieu to the city.

FRANCIE

You *will* be back.

BERYL

(turning back around and sitting down)

You're the one who's never coming home. Don't you want to say goodbye?

FRANCIE

Goodbye? No.
(her eyes on the road)
Not with all the hellos ahead of me.

—Excerpt from the unproduced screenplay
When She Was King

Chapter Three

1926

**Mrs Carl Wild: Household accounts,
week of April 4–10, 1926**

Sunday

· ·

Supper: Pot roast and carrots. Popovers filled with prune whip for dessert. Carl ate two helpings.

Beef, round	*gratis*
Salt pork	*gratis*
Tomatoes, can	*12 1/2¢*
Carrots, bunch	*5¢*
Prunes, box	*25¢*

Monday

· ·

Two library books returned, two more checked out for the

week. *Tik-Tok of Oz* for Anna Louisa, *The Young Diana* for me. She said she'd rather the newest Hopalong Cassidy. Carl must be reading that to her.

Supper: Meat croquettes with white sauce.

Parsley	*2¢*

Tuesday
· ·

Rain today.

Supper: Pork chops and buttered peas.

Pork chops, three	*gratis*
Peas, two No. 2 cans	*20¢*

Wednesday
· ·

Rain.

Supper: Ham and boiled onions.

Ham steaks	*gratis*
Pound of pearl onions	*9¢*

Thursday
· ·

Florrie Daniels appeared on my doorstep. Seven years, three weeks, and two days since I saw her last. Offered her coffee (the good stuff), but she said she was just saying goodbye.

She's going to California. Never thought she'd really leave.

Supper: Chicken à la king with ~~mashed potatoes~~ toast.

Fryer chicken	*gratis*
Mushrooms	*6¢*
Pimentos, jar	*10¢*

Friday
. . . .

So much rain it's flooded the backyard. AL built a raft of matchsticks.

Supper: Pork chops (again) and fried potatoes.

Pork chops, three	*gratis*

Saturday
. . . .

Supper: Pork chops. Also, Carl left me.

Pork chop, one	*11 1/2¢*

The Journal of Florrie Daniels

April 10, 1926

I bought this notebook thinking a travel journal would keep me company (of course, only a writer would make friends with A NOTEBOOK). How many lonely nights are strung between New Jersey and California? A tent, a cot, a lamp, and enough ink to last me three thousand miles. I'd observe all through the window of the Model T – every curve of mountain, every ripple of golden field, every last stretch of desert – and then scribble it all down once I made camp for the night. I have a Folding Autographic Brownie to help me capture the trip, once I read the owner's manual, that is. There has to be inspiration in a journey like this. The ad in Variety had said MGM would provide each aspiring scenario writer the contract (three months!) and salary (near to $75 a WEEK), but the ideas, I have to bring with me.

But then, as I was pulling away from the apartment, everything I hadn't sold stuffed in the back of the flivver, I heard my name and suddenly I didn't need the notebook because I had a friend, a real friend. Ethel was running down the sidewalk in the rain with a suitcase. It was like the final frame of a movie, only she splashed her way right into the beginning of this one. Take me with you? she asked. She tried to explain, with tears all over her face, about Carl and her daughter and wanting a ride as far as Nevada, but all I could think was She's here and Yes.

I'd gone to see her earlier in the week. When she saw me on the doorstep, she dropped the bowl of potatoes she'd been holding. Potato and butter and crockery all over my shoes and the daffodils, but I was too nervous to say a word. It had been too long since I'd seen her last and she looked so different but exactly the same. I just stood as butter soaked into my stockings and listened to her babble about her day, her week, the last seven years. She invited me in for coffee, but I'd come to say goodbye, for now, forever, and I knew if I came in I'd never want to leave her again. I still ached over ending our friendship all those years ago.

But I didn't have to. Because, when I was about to drive away from Newark and everything, there was Ethel and her soggy suitcase crawling through the door of the flivver and I didn't have to say goodbye. She'd been crying all night, she said. Carl had left her, she said, and took Anna Louisa too. A few months at his aunt's Nevada ranch to establish residency for a quick "Reno divorce." I said the right things like That's terrible and Of course I'll help but really my heart was pounding.

So I'm not doing it alone after all. Not driving across the country or camping or looking for inspiration across the prairies and deserts. Though I can scarcely believe it, I have Ethel and, at least for a while, I don't have to say goodbye.

Later

Ethel cried herself to sleep. We were still seven miles outside of Wilmington when she dozed off, sliding farther and farther down in the seat until her head rested on my shoulder. When we got to the campground, I sat for half a minute. Her hair smelled like Watkins Cocoanut Oil and, besides, I didn't want to wake her.

I paid our twenty-five cents for the campsite, but I didn't set up the tent, even though yesterday I couldn't wait to try it out. I did shake out the blanket, that red tartan one that the man at Montgomery Ward swore would be warm enough for an arctic night. It was big – I'd planned to wrap it twice around myself – but I tucked it around Eth still lying there across the front seat. I dug out my extra sweaters from the duffel strapped to the running board and made myself a little nest in the backseat.

I'm writing this by the light of my new battery flashlamp. Tomorrow I'll ask her more about Carl. About what reason he could possibly have to walk away from her. I'll ask her what she means to do when she gets to Nevada. I'll ask if it's all worth saving.

Tomorrow I'll ask her all that. Tonight, for now, I'm content to just listen to her breathe.

After all I said about not needing a journal as a friend, look how much I've just confided.

FRANCIE

Do you think I need a pseudonym? A lot of scenario writers have one. Frances Marion does.

BERYL

Well, that's a good one. Use that.

FRANCIE

Do you think I look like a Velma? A Blanche? A Myrtle?

BERYL

Does anyone truly look like a Myrtle?

FRANCIE

I don't have the cheekbones to pull it off.

BERYL

Was it Shakespeare who asked, "What's in a name?"

FRANCIE

I think it was Will Rogers.

BERYL

No! Really?

FRANCIE

Well, anyway, I'd like to hear what he says about the subject.

BERYL

He'd probably say, "Names are like socks. Change them only if they stink."

FRANCIE

He wouldn't say that. That's awful.

BERYL

Fine. I'm saying it. A Francie by any other name wouldn't smell as sweet.

—Excerpt from the unproduced screenplay
When She Was King

Chapter Four

1952

No one has called her "Anna" in decades, not since she legally transformed from Anna Louisa Wild, daughter of a New Jersey butcher, to Louise Wilde, MGM star, Hollywood beauty, and East Coast heiress. The latter is not, technically, incorrect. She does stand to inherit a used upright piano and an excessive collection of Gurley Christmas candles. Her publicists just never specify.

But when she stops at a motor lodge outside Ludlow, it's not "Louise Wilde" that she signs in the ledger. She pulls the curve of her hat lower and signs the book with the name she wore for eighteen years. Without thinking about it, she loops the As and the Ls like a schoolgirl. The desk clerk, a teenage girl with a ponytail and peppermint-pink lipstick, just smiles brightly.

"Did you have a nice drive?" the clerk asks.

After driving the first sixty miles white-knuckle nervous, the next sixty miles lost, and the third bored to bits, she wouldn't say "nice." But the desk clerk looks so hopeful that Louise politely says, "It was fine." There'd been no flat tires, no collisions, no inadvertent roadkills. She supposes that counts for a successful day of travel. "There wasn't much traffic."

"You drove in from . . ." She consults the ledger. "Oh, from Los Angeles! That's a pretty stretch, isn't it?"

The clerk starts waxing on about Cajon Canyon and Mount Pisgah, dry lakes and volcanic craters. Between concentrating on the signs and the dwindling gas gauge, Louise hadn't noticed much. Desert on all sides, with distant peaks shimmering like mirages.

Louise muffles a yawn. "I'm afraid I didn't stop."

"Though you have some of the best of Route 66 ahead." The clerk procures a handful of brightly printed brochures from under the Christmas light-bedecked counter. "Tomorrow morning you'll pass the Bristol Dry Lake. It's not far off the highway, at Amboy." She passes over one showing what looks like a dried-up lake bed. "There are smaller dry lakes and lava hills. The Marble Mountains. The Colorado River. Oatman is worth a stop. Loads of mining history there." She holds up a glossy brochure whose cover shows a delighted-looking child brandishing a gold nugget. "Have you vacationed in this area before?"

As though movie stars flocked to Ludlow, California, to get away from it all. She's just driven through the town center. It's no Palm Springs. "I'm traveling for business," she says.

The girl just blinks. "Business." Her pink smile widens. "But of course you'll want to see the sights on your way there." She unearths more brochures, all featuring shiny cars and smiling families.

Louise is too tired to argue, so she lets the perky desk clerk push one after another across the desk. On each is a car (always a sensible sedan) driven by a man and woman (both stylishly thin and overdressed) and two children (always one boy and one girl, just to be fair) scrubbed, pink-cheeked, and eager for whatever America has to offer. A happy family in search of adventure, as long as that adventure is middle-class and moderately priced.

She cuts off the clerk's cheerful babble. "Do you have anything on Las Vegas?"

"Taking a detour?"

"No, that's where I'm headed." She rubs her eyes. "My business."

"Oh." The girl glances down at Louise's hand, at the thin line of her wedding band. "Oh!"

Louise wants to cross out the name in the book, tell the girl who she really is and why she's going to Vegas. Not for a rendezvous or a divorce or an otherwise scandalous weekend. But she's exhausted and not in the mood to get into it. The girl doesn't mean any harm. "Las Vegas?" Louise prompts.

The girl keeps her eyes on Louise's ring. "You're taking the scenic route to Nevada, ma'am."

"I am?" Louise asks in dismay. She'd watched the signs. She thought she was on the right road. Miles and miles on straight, desert-lined road. She's less than a day into her trip and already tired of sand. "Where am I again?"

"Ludlow, California," the clerk says, a touch too proudly.

"You'll get there all right, but your best bet would've been to take Route 91 from Barstow."

"I guess if I'm heading to Vegas, I should make my best bets better."

The girl draws in her bright pink lips. She doesn't have much of a head for jokes, it seems.

Louise sighs. "How far off course am I?"

Arnie never gets lost. Even the few times they've been out of the city for a party or out-of-town preview, he needs only one glance at the map to know exactly how to get there. It's one of the reasons she doesn't mind that he always drives. He gets her wherever she needs to go.

Got. Past tense. He'll never drive again. Despite her nerves and her awful sense of direction, it's all up to her now. She draws in a breath. "Can you show me a map?"

She half-watches as the desk clerk unfolds a map, marks with a pencil where Louise is supposed to turn onto 95 to go north. "Not much once you get into Nevada. You can fill up in Needles."

"And then how far to Las Vegas?"

"Four hours? Five? More if you stop to see the sights." She taps the map with a pink fingernail. "You'll be very near to the Colorado River. You'll see wildlife all along the Dead Mountains."

As if rivers and canyons and interesting stretches of desert are enough to beat the loneliness that has been squeezing Louise in her very middle.

All she wants is to fall straight into bed, but she asks, "Where's a good place for dinner?"

Though there can't be more than a handful of places, the

desk clerk sticks out her lower lip and thinks for a measure. "That would be the Ludlow Cafe." She nods. "But you should hurry if you want to miss the rush."

She can't imagine there are enough people hiding in Ludlow to warrant a rush, but nods knowingly along with the clerk. "I will. Thank you."

"Your room will be to the left." The clerk passes over a key on an oversized plastic key ring. "You really did pick the best hotel in Ludlow."

The motor lodge had probably been the height of modernity in 1932, but in 1952, it looks worn around the edges. Behind the counter, a small TV set is showing *This Is Your Life.*

"Don't forget your brochures, now. They'll keep you company at dinner."

Louise gathers them up. "Thank you," she says again, and hefts up the wicker suitcase. "At least I won't have to eat alone."

The stack of brochures goes into the bin underneath the ashtray by the elevator.

The worst part about those two hundred miles today was the loneliness. Standing under the fluorescent lights by the elevator, she admits that now. She's used to being surrounded by people, all day. From the moment her driver picks her up in the morning, she's never alone. Makeup artists, hairstylists, men with scripts, women with armfuls of dresses, assistants with coffee and sandwiches and too much cheerfulness.

Even Arnie, withdrawn, ignoring, is at least there. He snores, he aches, he sometimes complains. But she can still feel him. She falls asleep and the space next to her in the bed is warm.

She's used to people. She's not used to the absence.

The Ludlow hotel room is unimpressive, but clean. Green carpeting, bleached-white bedspreads, curtains an orgy of desert flowers. The desk is scratched from decades of suitcases. She nudges aside a square ashtray and drops in a tumble her handbag, her keys, her vanity case. The suitcase she lifts up to the bed. She takes out a dress for tomorrow and shakes it over the desk chair.

She hauls the vanity case to the tiny bathroom and begins unpacking. She needs to organize her temporary space. She needs to arrange her cold cream and toothpaste, so that she can find everything at bedtime. She tells herself that she's unpacking and arranging because she has to, and not because she's trying to avoid a lonely dinner. It's just dinner.

But she had too many of those in the months Arnie was gone. Too many nights eating dinner off a TV tray. Easy, unremarkable things, like tomato soup or buttered rice or pineapple rings straight from the can. She filled the space with the radio, playing anything. Guy Lombardo, Patti Page, Johnnie Ray. *Jack Armstrong, the All-American Boy.* The World Series. Each night, she drank enough to fall into a dreamless sleep. It worked. While Arnie was gone and after he came home, it worked.

From the bottom of the case, past the Aqua Net, the curl cream, the talcum powder, she takes out the bottle of whiskey. There's a pair of tumblers on the desk, upside down beside a plastic ice bucket, and she fills one with an inch of booze. But she doesn't drink it. She wanders over to the window and leans against the glass, whiskey warming in the tumbler.

From her window she can see a far-off stretch of mountains, a break of color against the blue of the sky. Other than that low ripple of mountain, just sagebrush, greasewood, the occasional spit of a cactus or palm. The sun is stretched out across the horizon, a streak of orange against the blue and brown, but it hasn't yet started getting dark. She should go to find dinner, but she doesn't. She leans against that window, by the riotous curtain smelling of cigarettes and old perfume, and watches the sun slip farther and farther away.

Only when the orange has faded and the first fingers of dark edge the window does she toss back the whiskey in one big swallow and feel for her keys on the desk. She leaves the curtains thrown back as she shuts the door.

It is the next morning when Louise runs out of gas.

She left Ludlow late, after a breakfast in the café, where she explained three times that she wanted her eggs poached. "Scrambled?" the waitress asked, as though she couldn't conceive of another way to cook eggs. "Poached," Louise said firmly.

They had no grapefruit, no melon, no fruit whatsoever on the menu. They had tiny glasses of orange juice, which the waitress reasoned was the same thing. Everyone in Los Angeles is on a diet, and Louise has to remember she's no longer in Los Angeles.

She did, finally, agree to a slice of walnut pie, wrapped in cellophane and taken to-go. "The best pie this side of the Pacific," the waitress insisted. Louise wondered if she realized that included a whole hemisphere. She left a too-big tip on the table; she didn't have enough change.

But, when her car rolls to a stop in middle-of-nowhere Nevada, she's glad for the pie. According to the map, she's seven miles from the hopefully named Searchlight, the nearest town with a Shell station. She eats the pie with her fingers, sitting on the hood of the car. There's not much to keep her company here, apart from a weathered green signpost, an ambling tortoise, and the distant Dead Mountains. The signpost is shaped, roughly, like a cactus. The paint is peeling so that the writing is illegible. Maybe it's advertising a prickly pear farm, maybe indicating the spot of a long-forgotten botanical battle, maybe memorializing an untimely death by cactus-spining. She'll never know. Unconcerned, the tortoise ambles on.

It's hot and the road is quiet. In December, not many tourists are driving between Needles and Las Vegas. Every so often, when a car goes past, she thinks about waving it down. She could inch up her skirt and flash a calf, like Claudette Colbert. But that could get a girl anything from a stolen suitcase to a hasty burial in the desert. She licks walnut and sugar from her fingers and wishes she had a drink of water.

The sun is rising higher and her hair sticks to the back of her neck. She dabs at her temples and upper lip with a handkerchief. She shouldn't be so hot. She's wearing a crisp white dress, with a full skirt and turned-up collar. She's topped it off with a wide white mushroom hat, very New Look. It's well after Labor Day, but rules are for middle-class housewives and squares. Sitting on the hood of a car, sticky with pie, she's neither. A housewife never would've let the gas gauge go unnoticed. A square would've walked the seven miles.

Arnie is always fanatical about the gas gauge. He keeps a notebook in his glove box, marking each gallon of gas he adds and how far he drives before the next fill-up. He drives a monstrous Hudson. At least he used to. Sometimes on the weekends, he'd drive them to the beach. They'd sit hip-to-hip, bare toes dug into the sand, reading through scripts and eating through a hamper of chicken sandwiches and tomato salad. Arnie adored that beast of a car. He never would've run out of gas in the desert of southern Nevada.

Not for the first time in the past twenty-four hours, she closes her eyes and summons up his face. She had months of that while he was in Korea. Months of trying to remember the little things – how his eyes dipped down like he was perpetually sleepy, how his bow ties were always slightly crooked, how he'd wink at her before stepping out the door, as though she were in on some great, beautiful secret. Maybe she had been. She wraps her arms around herself. It sure doesn't feel like it anymore.

The sound of tires against gravel reminds her to open her eyes. A sedan, as black and sober as a priest, slows to a stop beside the road, and she balls up the cellophane. Automatically, she arranges her white skirt so that it falls in pleats across the red of the car hood. Against the white is a hint of color from the stones on her turquoise bracelet. She imagines it through the lens of a camera.

All angles and brightness. One of those shots that hurts your eyes with artistry.

A man in a short-sleeved checked shirt leans out of the car window. He's as clean-cut as a marine, but Jack the Ripper likely looked respectable too.

"Are you okay, ma'am?" he asks. His friendly words come with a watchful look, as though he's also trying to decide if she's harmless. Maybe she has a machete tucked underneath her white skirt.

"As well as can be in Nevada," she replies, and slides from the hood of the car.

He's younger than she is, with a spatter of good Midwest freckles across his nose. A spotted beagle wriggles across his lap. "Do you need help?"

She brushes off her dress, but doesn't answer.

He rests a forearm on the open window. An army tattoo peeks from beneath his sleeve. He's young to have already been in and out of the army. She wipes the back of her neck with her handkerchief. The other arm could have a tattoo that tallies the number of actresses buried beneath his garage, but at this point she's thirsty and starting to perspire.

She tosses the cellophane in through her open window and retrieves her purse and white gloves. "I seem to be in need of gas. Are you headed toward Searchlight?"

"Hop in."

His name is Duane. The tattoo on his other arm is a red rose, for his wife. Louise scratches the beagle's ears and listens to Duane talk all about her. She's a model, one of those busty girls Louise sees posing on the beach in sarongs or ruched bikinis. "You've probably seen her," he says. "Magazines, catalogs." He stares at the steering wheel. "A calendar, once."

Louise had done a touch of modeling in her day, something to pay for sandwiches between casting calls. Nothing too risqué – back then she was too provincial to pose in a swimsuit and too skinny for anyone to even ask her to – but there are still a few ads out there for hubcaps and Ivory soap featuring her teenage self.

Those are the kinds of ludicrous things that the House Un-American Activities Committee digs up. *Miss Wilde, did you knowingly pose with that bar of soap in a subversive manner? Did you know it would be marketed to Communists as well as to morally upright citizens?* With Arnie, it was a single rally he'd gone to at Berkeley as a teenager. Youthful enthusiasm breeds regret.

She wouldn't let herself appear on a Red list. These days she avoids parties. She rarely visits bookshops. She doesn't know what's safe to be caught reading anymore. She double-checks her scripts. It wouldn't do to inadvertently deliver a fiery line with too much conviction.

But high heels and tap shoes keep her safe. Songs and dances and empty-headed giggles in front of the camera. A good actress.

Duane doesn't seem to recognize her, but he doesn't exactly seem like a Betsey Barnes-watching guy. She doesn't lie. She says she's driving to Las Vegas for business. He doesn't flinch when she introduces herself as Anna.

Searchlight, Nevada, isn't much of anything. A few

houses, a lot of dust. A handful of bars and scrawny casinos. She wonders if she should've stayed out on the side of 95.

After filling her gas can, Duane treats her to lunch at a hamburger joint. Louise hasn't had a hamburger since she was a teenager. When he asks her if she likes onions on it or chili, she doesn't remember.

Duane eats his with a little bit of everything. Pickles and onions, chili, cheese, and an optimistic slice of tomato. She takes one with a spoonful of chopped onions and a thin slice of orange cheese. The first bite makes her feel ecstatic, the second guilty, but by the third, she's settled back at ecstatic. For a brief, irrational moment, she vows to eat a hamburger every day she's in Nevada.

"I followed Mavis to LA three years ago. She was the biggest thing to come out of Comstock."

"That's good," she says through a mouthful. "Isn't it?"

He seems to want to confide in somebody. Louise, in her white dress, like a vestal virgin, must look trustworthy. Duane tells her about early morning casting calls and screen tests, about tears, about finally meeting that one producer, who turned out to be a louse, and that one photographer, who turned out to be only marginally better. One career took off in the place of the other. Even without having met Mavis, Louise knows her story.

"She was just hitting it big when I was drafted. She'd send me letters telling me about this ad campaign, about that magazine spread. They sounded important, at least." Duane runs a hand over his short hair. "Things were looking up."

"She got that break."

He sighs down into his bottle of cola. "But then I get out a few months ago, I'm back in LA, and she's never at home. Always out on one shoot or another."

Her hamburger is far more interesting than his complaining. She focuses her attention on that. "But she's successful."

"She was in that Frigidaire ad. The one with the champagne bottle? That was Mavis."

"I see that ad all over the place."

"Sure. I open up just about any magazine and there's her face." He drains the bottle. "The rest of the country sees my wife more than I do."

"She's working. Most women aren't."

"Yeah, she's working. And I'm the one sitting at home by the ironing board."

She puts down the hamburger. "What do you expect, with you off in the army? That she was supposed to sit back and wait for your paychecks? She had to find her own."

"That's not what I—"

"Isn't it?" She wipes her mouth and crumples up the napkin. "If you would be so kind, I'd like a ride back to my car now, please. Like your wife, I have a job to do."

They don't talk much on the drive back to where her car waits. Duane had brought the rest of his hamburger, wrapped in a paper napkin, which the dog happily eats in the backseat.

"You know, I thought about getting a divorce," he says quietly.

She just shakes her head.

"I came out here on a fishing trip with my brother. A couple weeks camping on Lake Mead. Fishing. A chance to see the kind of stars you don't find in Los Angeles."

She thinks of last night, of the sun setting silently over the sagebrush and sand. She understands. There's something about that quiet.

"But out there on the lake with nothing but a fishing pole and my thoughts, I wondered. I mean, divorce only takes six weeks in Nevada. Mavis wouldn't even miss me."

"Why are you telling me this?"

Out of the corner of her eye, she sees him shrug. "I don't know. I thought you'd understand."

She doesn't respond. Instead she takes out a compact and reapplies her lipstick in front of the mirror. There's no reason for him to think she'd understand, to confess so much, to expect absolution. She drops the lipstick back in her purse. In the distance, her red Champion gleams.

Duane pulls up to her car, but doesn't shut off his engine right away. He rests his forearms on the steering wheel. "Look, I haven't been out of the army long. Nothing's like I thought it would be."

"Isn't that just life?" she asks, looking at him finally. "Nothing is as we expect."

"I shouldn't have unloaded all of that on you. But I haven't talked to anyone in days, and that's no exaggeration. Mavis and I, we hardly speak."

She closes her purse, but doesn't open the door.

"I suppose I wanted someone to tell me it was silly. The whole idea of divorce." Outside, the wind picks up, swirling sand. "That, if marriage wasn't worth fighting for, nothing was."

"And would you believe me if I told you that?" she asks.

He shrugs.

"You've been through a war. But when you have to choose which battles at home are worth it, you have no idea which way to point your rifle."

He reaches in the backseat and hefts up the metal gas can. "Don't forget this."

She takes the hint and the can. "Thank you for the ride, Duane."

She waits until he drives off before starting to fumble with refilling her tank. Enough to get her into town, at least. And then fifty miles up to Vegas. When she gets there, she'll take a bath. Send her dresses to be pressed. Call to find out where she's to report in the morning. Maybe have a Manhattan or three.

She wipes off her face again with the handkerchief, knowing she'll have to pull over and reapply her makeup before arriving at the Flamingo. An actress never knows who might be watching. The publicity department would collectively faint at a Louise Wilde Sweats headline.

Does she really want to go through with this? If she shows up on set tomorrow, shows up for that bikini and ukulele and insipid script, that'll be it. There will be no negotiating a better contract. No fighting for better roles. She'll be giving in.

But giving in is better than hiding. Better than ignoring her problems, hoping they'll just go away. They won't.

Life requires patience and, these days, she doesn't have much of that.

She slides behind the wheel and pulls on her gloves. Beneath them she can just barely see the line of her wedding band. She turns on the car and looks out onto the road.

But she doesn't get too far, because she's staring at that cactus-shaped sign again. It stands in front of another road, barely a track of dust between the sagebrush. It suddenly comes to her that she knows exactly what that sign says. Though she still can't make out any of the letters, not with the paint peeling in the relentless sun, she suddenly knows she's read it before. Prickly Pear Ranch – An Oasis in the Desert.

Vegas would have to wait.

She turns down the road.

BERYL

Did you hear the one about the artist who ran out of ideas?

FRANCIE

No . . .

BERYL

He was drawing blanks.

FRANCIE

(groaning)
Oh, Beryl. That was terrible.

BERYL

Got you to smile, though. I think that makes it pretty good.

—Excerpt from the unproduced screenplay
When She Was King

Chapter Five

1926

Sunday

. . . .

Rain. Matches my mood. Best not let F see. With these roads, she has enough to worry about.

Supper: Restaurant meal: chowder, coffee, one shared slice of custard pie.

Boonsboro Camp	*50¢*
Gasoline	*$1.96*
Postage stamp	*2¢*

April 11, 1926

Ethel wasn't in the front seat when I woke up.

I found her outside, sitting in front of the fire at the next campsite, her hair wild around her ears, sipping from a borrowed tin mug. I didn't want to wake you, she said, so I made a friend, and offered me the neighbors' coffeepot. So like Eth, introducing herself and flashing her dimple wherever she goes. She was wearing a borrowed cardigan and eating a doughnut. Her benefactors were off at the showers.

She looked brighter this morning. All cried out. Through mouthfuls of boiled-over coffee, she told me about yesterday. She'd returned from the market to an empty house and a folded note from each. Anna Louisa's said that Daddy was taking her on a vacation to see horses and sagebrush and cowboys. Carl's, without explanation, that he wanted a divorce. The house echoed, she said. AL is only six. Ethel misses her like the circus.

It's been just as long since I've seen Carl. When I knew him back in school, I never would've thought him the kind of guy who'd walk out on his wife, the kind of guy who'd take a girl from her mother. He was a good kid, quiet, studious. Fragile, almost. A whiz on the piano. Loved Shakespeare, ice-cream sodas, and jazz music. The three of us were inseparable. We played and sang and acted, with me writing the scripts. We sat in a circle knee-to-knee and swore with crossed pinkies that we'd make it into the flickers someday. But we grew up. Carl went to war, he and Eth got married, and I was left alone to plan my trip to Hollywood. Maybe now too late, but better late than never?

These seven years later, I don't know Ethel and I don't know Carl. I don't know what would cause that kind, timid boy to walk away and leave her alone and crying. I would never leave. At least not again.

Later

It started raining before we left. We made it across Delaware by lunch and to a site outside Frederick, Maryland, before deciding to quit for the night. Lots of hills. Far too much rain. E kept up cheery conversation, mostly about Carl and the movies they've seen (they're both mad for Gareth Hughes) and about Anna Louisa and the books they're reading. (AL reads the Oz books when Ethel's looking, C's dime Westerns when she's not.) As white-knuckled as I drove, I couldn't help but feel a twinge of irritation.

But then she told me to relax, that I was driving just fine. She reached out and squeezed my hand. She said that she trusted me. The rain stopped right then and there and we saw a sliver of blue sky that had her singing "I'm Always Chasing Rainbows." The hills and the puddled roads didn't seem so bad after that.

When we got to the campsite, I stood for a moment in front of the pile of canvas and poles, stood still and nervous until E asked what was wrong. I only have one, I told her. I didn't mean to sound so apologetic. I hadn't known she was coming. One tent and one cot.

She just waved her hand, like it was no matter at all, like it hadn't kept me up for hours the night before just knowing she was there. What do they call it these days, a "pajama party"? she said. We've done it before. Remember the time you slept over? We both fit in my bed.

Did I remember?

I spoke in a rush. I told her it wouldn't work, that we couldn't possibly fit on the cot, that I'd be happy to sleep in the car and leave her the bed, at least until we could buy another. In the end, she took the car. I'm left alone in the tent, with just this notebook and the rain on the canvas above.

Monday

· ·

Rain. Dizziness and I'm out of my tonic. Ankle aching. Wish it would stop raining. Wish I was already in Nev. Wish I understood what was happening to my careful little life.

Supper: Sandwiches (again).

Shipway's Tourist Camp	*50¢*
Gasoline	*73¢*
Parson's Vigor Tonic	*78¢*
Aspirin tablets	*98¢*
Postage stamp	*2¢*

April 12, 1926

Another day of hills and sheeting rain. Another day of Maryland. E's had to get out twice in galoshes and slicker to push us out of mud. She told me all the jokes she could think of to keep my nerves steady. (Did you hear the one about the showgirl and the trombone?) So much rain it's been snaking in under the flapping side curtains. The bologna sandwiches I'd made in the morning were so drenched we lost our appetites.

Between the ups and downs and stops to stretch my fingers, only made it as far as Flintstone today. Campground is a stew of mud, but they had provisions. E's limping, but won't say a word about it.

Tuesday

. . . .

Sore ankle and drowning rain. Wet socks. Too many sandwiches. Parson's Vigor Tonic hardly helping.

Wish I was back at home, tucked into the easy chair with AL and a pair of books. Would even let her read a Western.

Feeling almost fragile today. A bolt of lightning and I might fall. If it weren't for F, I would.

Supper: Peanut butter, two spoons.

Hotel Auld, 1 night (European plan)	*$2.00*
Gasoline	*$1.50*
Peanut butter, tin	*25¢*
Postage stamp	*2¢*

April 13, 1926

Woke to a steady leak straight onto my left foot. As exhausted as E was yesterday, I don't think she slept a wink. She looks awful this morning. I saw her swallow a palmful of aspirin with her mug of cold coffee. Packed all of our soggy things up as best I could while she tried (and failed) to beg a plate of something hot. After a while we gave up and ate plain bread, quickly, before it got wet. As I tied down the roll of canvas tent, she sat on the running board wrapped in a slicker, tapping a box of Sweet Caporals against the heel of her hand. I've never seen her smoke, not once. I wonder what else I've missed over the past seven years.

Later

Stopped for lunch and a stretch, though it was too drenched outside to leave the flivver. We ate peanut butter sandwiches and pickles hunched in the steamy car. We haven't dried from last night and it's awful in here, everything damp and clammy. I hung my socks on the back of the seat. The car smells like a sodden sheep.

Can't see much through the side window flaps, but what I can see is pretty. Everything soft and blurred, like a Monet landscape. Lots of green and brown, spots of reds and yellows where tulips are popping up. I'm sure Pennsylvania has much to offer apart from rain and twisting roads. E kept exclaiming as we drove all morning. I wouldn't look anywhere but straight ahead.

Later

We rolled down a hill, backward, and into a tree.

I bumped my head, but poor E! With a shriek, she fell straight out the door into the rain. I ignored my throbbing head and crawled out after her. She was sprawled in a puddle, shaking like a kitten, but unhurt. I heaved her up – of course she was limping again – and put her behind the wheel to steer while I pushed the flivver back onto the road. It started rolling forward and I dove into the front door just before it picked up speed. E slid over and let me take the wheel. She sniffled all the way to Lincoln Hill.

The camp here was just as soupy as last night's. Mud clinging to everything. When E opened the door, her blue hat, the one with the fan of feathers, blew out and landed in the sooty, waterlogged remnants of a campfire. I couldn't help it, I started crying.

I feel silly about it now, of course, but at the time I didn't know what else to do. I was wet, I was cold, I was sore, and this whole thing seemed ridiculous. I told her I was sorry, that if it wasn't for me and my overloaded Model T she could be back at home in Newark right now, warm and dry and with a perfectly intact hat.

She stomped through the puddles to retrieve the hat. I insisted, she said. You had no choice. Despite the galoshes, she was muddy up to her knees. Anyway, what's back there? An empty house.

We sacrificed a proper dinner in favor of a hotel room a few miles back. I spread our wet skirts and blankets to dry while she rinsed out our socks in the bathroom. Sitting on the bed in two pairs of my Chinese pajamas, we ate peanut butter directly from the tin. She fell asleep first, curled up on one half of the bed. I waited until she started quietly snoring, on the pretense of writing this all down. But now that she's asleep, it's my turn. There may not be a separate tent, but the room has a rug. She doesn't have to know.

Wednesday

· ·

NO RAIN ALL DAY. First day I've woken up with dry eyes. Hard to wake up otherwise with a rainbow hanging over the town.

F left me alone this afternoon. Struck me just how alone I am. C and AL gone. Am going after them, but what if they don't want to come back?

Supper: You've guessed it. Sandwiches.

National Trail Camp	*25¢*
Gasoline	*44¢*
Postage stamp	*2¢*

April 14, 1926

We took advantage of the sunshine and stopped early today, deciding that our damp canvas could really do with a day drying out in the sun. E insisted on setting up the campsite, so I left her there and drove in to Wheeling. It was a big enough city that I found a place to buy a second tent, folding aluminum cot, and extra set of bedding. The way E limped every morning, I knew her makeshift bed in the backseat wasn't doing her any favors.

I also bought her a surprise. In the evenings, when I'm scribbling away in this notebook, E's just so quiet that I wonder what else she'd rather be doing. I asked her once, whether she spent her evenings reading magazines, doing crossword puzzles, playing solitaire. She just shrugged. Cleaning up the supper dishes, planning tomorrow's menu. Tucking AL into bed with a song.

I knew that couldn't be all. I knew Eth was more than a mother and housewife. Supper menus and lullabies? Once she'd been the most interesting girl on the block. She painted, she swore, she mimicked, she sang like Fay Templeton. She danced the cakewalk as well as any vaudeville performer. No one could resist her energy. She'd step from her front door and light up the street like a Roman candle.

That's why I convinced her to take a job with me at the radium company during the war, painting watch dials. She'd sing while we all worked and tell the most awful jokes. She was effervescent. Where did that all go? Marriage must be a more effective damper than I thought.

So I bought her a surprise. It isn't much. Maybe silly, even. I bought her a paint set, one of those kids' sets in an aluminum tin covered with bright yellow stars. Maybe she'll laugh, maybe she'll put it in her suitcase and never take it out, but maybe, just maybe, it'll remind her of who she used to be. Maybe it'll remind her of herself.

Thursday

Reread what I wrote yesterday. It's true, maybe C won't ever come back. Maybe I'll be the divorcée, the woman everyone avoids. Maybe I'll never have answers.

F gave me a paint set. A little gesture, and maybe she

91

didn't mean much by it, but it made me smile, really smile. I keep thinking of myself as "discarded wife" or "unneeded mother," a woman suddenly out of a job, when all along she still sees me as just Ethel.

Supper: REAL FOOD to strengthen our blood. Ham, gravy, baked potatoes, pudding. F in ecstatics.

Camp Summerford	*25¢*
Gasoline	*$1.60*
Eggs	*30¢*
Milk, pt	*10¢*
Butter, 1 lb	*49¢*
Flour	*6¢*
White vinegar	*11¢*
Mazola oil, qt	*47¢*
Hershey's bars, 3	*15¢*
Potatoes, 8 lb	*25¢*
Navy beans	*9¢*
Kidney beans	*11¢*
Rice	*15¢*
Ham, 4.8 lbs	*84¢*
Postage stamp	*2¢*

April 15, 1926

Ethel bought eggs from the camp store and boiled them up in the coffeepot. I really should get an actual pot at some point if she's going to keep cooking things like eggs. She said they were to give us energy to tackle Ohio. The men at the next campsite, seasoned travelers, nodded sagely and said that one needed something to get through Ohio.

Now that we have the second tent, I should, for posterity's sake, capture on page this little campsite of ours. I'm rather proud of it.

The two canvas tents are low lean-tos that tie to the top of the car. We use the car, sandwiched between each tent, as a sort of dressing room, and then slip out the two doors into our own "bedrooms." In each tent is a folding aluminum cot, a stack of blankets, and an electric lantern. We don't have much else apart from a pair of camp stools, which, around the fire, make up both parlor and dining room. We eat off tin plates on our laps. A washbasin for both dishes and laundry. Our little kitchen is nothing more than a folding cooking grate with detachable oven and windshield, frying pan with a foldable handle, and the coffeepot. They all came together, helpfully, in a single kit. E's been eyeing the frying pan. I wonder if she can make bacon.

Later

E asked me to drop her by the grocery in town while I went ahead to set up at the auto camp. Said she wanted to get provisions. We have plenty of bread and bologna and pickles, a full can of coffee, and a little peanut butter, so I'm not sure what else we need.

I thought maybe she'd come back with something lively like jam to go with our peanut butter, but she returned staggering

93

under a bottle crate with an eight-pound sack of potatoes dangling from one hand. She didn't show me what she bought, but shooed me and my notebook away to speculate.

Later

Oh, a real supper tonight! Sliced ham fried up nice and crisp on the edges, with a little pan gravy. Potatoes baked in the coals and served with mounds of butter. And if that wasn't enough, a little pot of chocolate pudding! E fussed around our makeshift dining table (really, the lid of the food box, balanced on a stump) and "apologized" that it wasn't much, but the best she could do on short notice. I saw new pots and pans clustered around the fire and blushed to think what E must've been thinking of my endless stream of cold sandwiches.

I ate and ate until my stomach hurt. I don't know what I did to deserve a proper meal (and warm pudding!), but I won't complain, not a bit.

As we washed up the pans, I spotted another new addition to the campsite. A scrap of wood, torn from the side of a crate and rubbed smooth, was propped up in the front window of the flivver. On it, in cheery block letters, was painted "Home, Sweet Home."

It almost feels that way.

Friday

Sunny. F woke up just as bright. More of Ohio today,

which would dampen anyone's mood. Planned a little surprise for lunch.

Supper: Baked beans and ham. Somewhere between there and here, F lost her appetite.

McDonald's Camp	*40¢*
Gasoline	*$1.41*
Postage stamp	*2¢*

April 16, 1926

Just when I was getting tired of Ohio (and it's only noon; says something about the state), E called for a lunch break and pulled out such a spread. Ham sandwiches. Potato salad made with one of those hard-boiled eggs and a dill pickle, chopped fine. She even had warm coffee in a towel-wrapped jar. She spread out a blanket over the grass at the side of the road and laid it all out. It was much more elegant than my usual peanut butter sandwiches eaten hunched in the front seat. She even pulled a sprig of blossoms from a cherry tree and dropped it in the center of the blanket. It was so sweet – I'm not sure anyone had ever been that sweet to me – that I blurted out, It's like you're taking me on a picnic.

I immediately blushed and she got quiet. Picnics were for sweethearts and families. Carl had probably taken her on dozens of them. She divided up the potato salad and wiped off the spoon while I wondered why I'd spoken without thinking. Especially when I'd spent my life being so very careful.

Though the spread deserved more, I ate quickly. I just wanted to be back on the road again, where I could blame the silence on concentration.

As E shook out the blanket and rinsed off the forks and plates, I stole a moment to write this all down. Somehow, seeing it reduced to nothing more than words makes me feel better.

Later

We were only a few miles down the road when she said, Carl never took me on a picnic. It broke the silence. Not never, not even when you were courting? I asked. I didn't remember any courting with them, no dances or nickelodeons or walks along the boardwalk. My eyes were on the road, but, from the corner of my eye, I saw a little shrug. Maybe she didn't remember any courting either.

It had all seemed so sudden, as I recalled. One minute Eth, Carl, and me were the Three Musketeers, loyal and inseparable. The war years were a quick tangle. Carl was Over There, Ethel and I here, at the dial-painting factory. I had her to myself. I didn't anticipate his return as much as she did. But then he was back, she was happy, and, a handful of weeks later, they were engaged.

She'd brought the branch of cherry blossoms in the car and spun it between her palms. Remember when we'd see all of those couples at Branch Brook Park, she asked, sharing cold chicken and chocolate cake, sitting far too close? And we'd tell each other that, someday, we'd be old enough to be invited. Young men *in boater hats, summer days, falling petals, first kisses. Do you remember imagining all that?*

I remembered those walks with her through Branch Brook Park, those falling petals from the cherry trees, those girlish wishes, but the young men in boater hats, the picnics she talked about, they weren't what I imagined. Not then and not now.

But ham sandwiches and potato salad, a plaid blanket on the side of an Ohio road, well, that was a start. At least I could pretend.

Saturday

· ·

Mothers are not above bribery. Have bought chocolate to ease the dreariness of the Midwest. Who ever knew it was so *long*? Mostly, though, bought it to see F smile. Yesterday she was too quiet.

Supper: Bread and butter. F didn't eat.

Camp	*25¢*
Gasoline	*$1.17*
Hershey's bars, 4	*20¢*
Restaurant lunch (steak, French	
fried potatoes, salad, biscuits, coffee)	*40¢*
Postage stamp	*2¢*

April 17, 1926

Indiana today. Soon after we started driving we realized it wasn't one bit more interesting than Ohio and resolved to do away with the whole state in one fell swoop. To help, E bought a stack of Hershey's bars. Her rule: a square broken off for each town we passed. Halfway through we just gave up and ate the whole lot to cheer ourselves. Some things haven't changed, she said. You still have a sweet tooth.

I have sore teeth more than anything these days. If she knew about the dentists, the appointments, the diagnoses . . . But I'm not going to say anything. Not to her, not to myself. I'm not going to spoil this golden little stretch of time.

Ethel was still talking about my sweet tooth, all of the sticks of penny candy and taffy and butterscotch drops we'd share on the walk home from school when we had a spare penny or two. Of course there was the time you lifted that chocolate bar, she added, and I was so startled I almost swerved off the road.

My single attempt at shoplifting and Ethel, of all people, had seen. We were eleven and I was instantly mortified at what I'd done. I couldn't eat the chocolate, not with the newfound guilt it brought along, so I gave it to Eth as a gift the very next day. She never said a word about having seen me swipe it. You saw that? I asked, hoping she hadn't, that it was really just a lucky guess. She gave me a funny look then. I always paid attention to everything, Flor, she said. I never wanted to miss a single moment with you.

As I sat, my flush of embarrassment turning warmer at her words, she suddenly straightened and licked her thumb. You have just a bit of chocolate here. She reached across and I felt her thumb brush damp against the corner of my mouth. Without thinking, I turned my head. My lips were against her thumb. I could've whispered into it. I could've kissed it. She *was looking straight at me. There, she said, and pulled her thumb back. Got it.*

She'd likely wiped mouths dozens of times. For a mom, it was probably a gesture scarcely thought about. But I thought about it. Too much. I drove the rest of the way to Indianapolis still feeling her touch.

Later

Ethel's finishing up her lunch. I told her I didn't feel well and wanted to lie down in the car before we set off again. Really, I just lost my appetite.

We arrived in Indianapolis. She said she'd treat me to a real restaurant lunch and left me to find something that didn't cost more than fifty cents. I found a place, with a fancy name and a lunch special on fried steaks. When E reappeared, it was with a small stack of envelopes and a hopeful expression. They wrote, she said, fanning them all out. Carl and AL, they wrote to me here.

All along, she's been sending them letters and asking them to write to her at the general post office here. Every day she drops envelopes by the campground's office, to go out with that morning's mail. Every day. Between all the picnics and recollections and thumbs on my lips, she's writing to her husband. I was a fool to think that anything was, well, anything.

BERYL

Who comes to Nevada anyway?

FRANCIE

Sinners and prospectors.

BERYL

Aren't those the same thing?

FRANCIE

If I meet a prospector, I'll let you know how we get along.

—Excerpt from the unproduced screenplay
When She Was King

Chapter Six

1952

Driving up to the entrance of the Prickly Pear Ranch gives Louise goosebumps.

She has no reason to remember it, this faded, crumbling dude ranch out in the middle of nowhere. There isn't even a real road leading to it. Just a dusty track that leaves her red Champion rattled and pale brown. She unpins the hat from her head and steps from the car.

It isn't much, this ranch hidden way back here. Certainly not the "oasis" she remembers from the sign. A sloping fence marks a property scrubby with weeds. A few low, white buildings crouch cramped around a central courtyard. In the middle is a rustily sputtering fountain. She can see the dip of a pool beyond, empty, tiles edged in green. She knows there must be stables and she slips off her sunglasses and shades her eyes until she spots a slanted wooden structure, half a breath from falling down. She pities any horses inside.

A lizard scampers up the side of one of the bunkhouses. A man steps out, and Louise puts her sunglasses back on. He's a cowboy, and not the fringed and embroidered Hollywood version. He wears a snap-button shirt and blue jeans so well-worn that one pocket is torn. He's maybe fifty years old, maybe sixty. Hard to tell. He stops on the porch, scratches his head, adjusts his belt buckle. Beneath the battered brim of his Stetson, his eyes are bright blue.

He notices her, because he pushes back his hat and blinks. "I didn't know we had anyone arriving today." He throws a cigarette butt over the railing.

She tosses her hat on the front seat of the car. "I'm not."

"Arriving?" He raises his eyebrows. "Not anymore."

The courtyard is deserted. She hears nothing but the wind and the wheezing gurgle of the fountain. She doubts that anyone has arrived in quite a while. "I'm just here to look around, if that's okay. I'm not staying."

He coughs and lights another cigarette. "Don't know why."

"Why I'm not staying?"

"Why you want to look around." He picks a piece of tobacco from between his teeth. "But suit yourself."

His accent isn't western. It doesn't sound like long days in the saddle, like bonfires, like moonshine and cattle and lariats. There's something more refined in it, maybe even a touch foreign, like he's a Prussian count slumming it on the range. If you believe the movies (and who doesn't?), dude ranches are for the elite, the wealthy city folk seeking the wild roots of America. Maybe his way of talking is deliberate. Part of the atmosphere. She knows a restaurant in LA that only hires waitresses who can fake a French accent. Very chichi.

She picks up her purse. She's not dressed for a dude ranch, not in her white dress and cork sandals. She's not dressed for the desert, period. She slings the purse up into the crook of her elbow and works her way across the weed-choked lawn to what remains of a flagstone path. Her heel catches, and she feels ridiculous. The old cowboy leans against the porch rails, smoking and watching her. She wishes he'd go away.

She walks past the long white buildings to the fountain huddled low in the dirt. It looks far too grand for a crumbling dude ranch, or at least might have been once upon a time. Up close, she can see it's only cheap plaster. Neptune with his trident sits amid halfheartedly spurting water. The tip of his nose is broken off.

She crosses the courtyard. She can see the pool tucked behind. It's dry and missing more than a few tiles. Deck chairs are stacked like driftwood.

The cowboy follows her, walking along the bunkhouse's long porch. "This place used to be nice," he says.

She doubts it. She's seen *The Women*. She's flipped through *Town & Country* in the dentist's waiting room. Manicured lawns, turquoise swimming pools, cherry-garnished cocktails served by rugged bartenders in leather boots. She knows that dude ranches are only one sandy step from the East's lush resorts. Even when this place was brand spanking new, it was an imitation.

"How could it be nice with only one tennis court?" she asks flippantly.

103

He regards her beneath the brim of his hat and finishes his cigarette.

The bunkhouses all have their doors thrown open. Inside, curtains are drawn, beds are unmade, dust lazily drifts across the doorways. The place is deserted, at least as far as she can see. The old cowboy might be the only occupant of this whole disheveled ranch.

"You know, movie stars used to come here." He blows a lazy smoke ring, one that floats up to the sagging roof of the porch. "You look like a movie star."

"I'm not." She tilts her head down. "I've never been here."

"Liar," he says.

She looks up.

"You can't see the tennis court anymore."

She takes off her sunglasses then and drops them in her purse.

"Glass of lemonade?" he asks.

She nods.

"Or whiskey." The cowboy tosses the cigarette butt off into the dirt. "Whatever the customer wants."

The lemonade is tepid, but deliciously sour. She doesn't take him up on the whiskey, not yet.

"I grow the lemons myself," he says. "Also chili peppers. Do you like Spanish omelets?"

"I've already eaten lunch."

"I haven't." He sets down the tin pitcher. "Juana!" he calls. "We have any tomatoes?" He disappears into what she guesses is the kitchen, leaving her alone with her lemonade and a terrifyingly taxidermied bobcat.

104

He'd called it the mess hall, like they're in the army, this central room with long slab tables and antler-bedecked chandeliers. It's both dining hall and lounge area, with tooled leather couches around a wagon wheel table at the other end. A small bookcase holds cast-off copies of popular novels. *A Tree Grows in Brooklyn. Frenchman's Creek. The Ides of March. The Grapes of Wrath,* which she hasn't read in a decade. Things to read on the porch with a big glass of iced tea. She picks up the dog-eared copy of the Steinbeck and thumbs through it.

Perched along the top of the bookcase are Gurley candles, the same collection of kitsch that her father pulls out every Christmas. This display boasts a red-steepled church and an alarmingly large host of choirboys on a rectangle of batting. This dry bit of Nevada has probably never seen snow, but the little bunch of choristers stand ankle-deep in it to sing. There's no Christmas tree, not here in the desert, but a potted cactus is strung with blue lights. And to add to it all, the stuffed bobcat wears a jaunty Santa hat.

The mounted head of a bighorn sheep presides over the room. She tries to imagine guests in times past sitting on these benches, eating barbecued chicken or cornbread or dripping slices of peach pie. With the windows open and a hint of a breeze pushing through the room, it's halfway pleasant. If it weren't for that bobcat, that is.

Almost every square inch of the walls is covered with framed photographs, mostly of horses. There are indeed a few photos of Hollywood types – he wasn't lying about that. Some actors from B-list Westerns, a has-been actress she knew from the Studio Club, a pair of lowbrow comedians, and one furiously macho director she once had the misfortune to work with. The photos are autographed and addressed to "Steve" or "Marjorie" or just "the Prickly Pear."

She hears footsteps. Without knowing why, she slips the battered copy of *The Grapes of Wrath* into her purse.

The cowboy reappears with a bowl of biscuits. "She's making up something small. It's too hot today to cook much of anything."

Louise slides onto a bench with her drink. "Really, I'm not hungry."

He takes off his Stetson and hooks it over the horn of the bighorn sheep. "Do you want more to drink?" He plugs in the cactus's lights.

She shakes her head. She's seen the rest of the ranch. She'd like to avoid the bathroom.

"Are you Steve?" she asks, nodding toward the pictures.

"It's as good a name as any," he answers, which isn't really an answer at all.

She's worn a fake name for the past dozen years. Maybe "Steve" isn't his real name either. Out here, he could be a washed-up actor, he could be a lunatic, he could be a fugitive. Maybe all three. She inches her purse closer to her.

He notices, and grins wolfishly. It doesn't make her feel better.

He shrugs and says, "I came to work the mines in Searchlight after the war."

He looks too old to have been much help in the last one, so she asks, "World War I?"

"As you Americans call it," he says, and she hears that little accent again. It's hardly noticeable, but she deals in the spoken word. Maybe he really is a Prussian count in blue jeans.

"My father fought in it."

He pours out a lemonade of his own. "I know."

It's said with a sly confidence. She mentally sorts through Louise Wilde's official bio, but she doesn't remember there ever being anything about her dad's army record. Maybe a publicist let it slip. Maybe she did.

"I've been to Searchlight," she says. "It's not much of a destination."

He straddles the bench, keeping one eye on the kitchen door, one on Louise. "I was disinherited. What's a boy to do?"

"There have to be easier ways to find fortune."

"You think it was all really about the fortune?" He's suddenly serious. "I'm not the first person to wander into the desert in search of peace and absolution."

She quiets, just as serious. "Did you find it?" she asks. "Absolution?"

He picks up a biscuit from the bowl, tosses it back and forth between his hands. "As much as I could."

From the kitchen, a woman sings in Spanish, in a voice as light as feathers.

He runs a hand through his faded hair. "Is that what brought you way out here?"

"I was driving past," she says, as if that explains why she'd be on that stretch of 95 in the first place. "Driving past, and I recognized the sign."

He has to know the sign is unreadable. That there's no way it could direct anyone down his rut of a road. But he nods as though it all makes perfect sense.

"I don't know why I'd remember this ranch out in the middle of nowhere. The road isn't even on the map. I don't know why I'd remember a tennis court that doesn't exist."

"I once passed a church in New Mexico I could've sworn I'd seen before. I could even tell you what color the baptismal font was. Juana said I must've been there in a past life."

She looks around the mess hall, with its glassy-eyed animals, and can't think of a place she'd want less to have spent a previous life. "You don't really believe that, do you? That I was here in a past life, of all things?"

He snorts. "That bullshit? No, I don't." He takes a long swallow of his lemonade, his throat rippling. "I recognize you. You were here in *this* life."

But he doesn't explain further, because the door to the kitchen swings open and a woman appears, holding a plate in each hand. She's swaybacked and not particularly pretty, with a gap between her front teeth and hair dyed an orangey shade of red. But at the sight of her, something settles in Steve's face. He goes, in an instant, from watchful to content.

She sets the plates down on the table and takes a pair of forks from her apron pocket. Steve touches the back of her hand, just once, just for a moment, but it's enough to bring a smile to the woman's face.

Louise waits until Juana leaves, until Steve blinks and pulls that mask back up, that tough-as-nails, cool-as-cucumbers cowboy mask. "You said you recognized me," she prompts.

He nods and pulls one plate closer. Juana's added a sliced sausage alongside each promised omelet. "You're that actress, the one who does all the song-and-dance pictures."

Her hand creeps toward her purse, where her sunglasses are. "No, I'm not."

"You were in that cowboy one where you tap-danced along the edge of the horse trough."

"I'm sorry, that wasn't me." She fiddles with the clasp.

"And you were on the cover of *Life* in a dress made of feathers."

That awful thing had molted with every step she took.

He shakes salt over the whole deal, the omelet and the sausage. "You should try this. I remember you liked eggs."

She used to, back when she was allowed to eat them fried in butter, drizzled in hollandaise sauce, layered with cheese. "Wait, what do you mean, 'remember'?"

"I told you." He cuts into his omelet. "You were here once upon a time."

"You must have me confused with someone else." She waves away his words. "I've never been out this way. Filmed on location in Bakersfield once. Never in Nevada."

He chews through a mouthful of eggs. "You were little, but I didn't think you'd forget. You were here with your father."

There was a train trip with Dad, ages ago. She was young enough that she still wore bangs and had baby teeth. She didn't remember much beyond the clatter of the tracks, the postcards Dad let her buy in each town, the one time he let her finish his cup of coffee.

"You know my dad?"

"Marjorie – she owned the Pear back then – was always trying to convince one of her nephews to come out West and visit. Carl was the only one who ever did."

"And I came too?"

"Don't you remember?"

She shakes her head, but she's not so sure anymore.

Fork in one hand, he lights up a cigarette with the other. "I was head wrangler then. Would take you and your dad out riding, fishing, chasing lizards along the wash. You loved riding. A regular dudine. You insisted on going out even in the rain. We couldn't argue with you." He chuckles and wipes his mouth. "You called me 'Mr Steve.' And I called you 'The Empress.'"

The Empress. He says the name like it's something. Like she should *know*. And suddenly, just suddenly, she can feel it.

Sunburns and scabbed knees. Too-big denim overalls. The sun on her bare head, the warm saddle against her legs, her fingers tangled tight in a white mane. "I rode a horse called Odin."

He smiles crookedly and forks up another bite of egg. "Nothing tamer than the god of frenzy for you."

Eating whole lemons fresh from the tree. Catching lizards and pocket mice. Bonfires and prickly pears and sand caught between her bare toes. "How young was I?" Young enough, apparently, that the trip comes back only in sensations, in tastes and smells.

"Six? Seven?"

The images quiet. "When my mom died."

Now all she can taste are tears at the back of her throat.

Steve finishes chewing. "A hard summer."

Louise stands, leaves her purse and lemonade, and crosses to the window. It was. Unbearable. "She was young. Younger than I am now. And he loved her. It broke him in half when she died."

Outside a goat stands listlessly in the yard. Beyond the goat, she can see a single, crooked acacia tree. The bench creaks, but Steve doesn't get up.

"But we came out here before she died, not after. I remember sending her letters. Drawing pictures with crayons that were always half-melted." She sifts back through those mental snapshots. The train station postcards, the horseback rides, the lizards and lemons. Sitting on Dad's lap by a bonfire. Drinking his coffee on the train. Mom never would've allowed that. "She didn't come out here with us."

"No, ma'am," he says. "She didn't." He's done with his omelet and sits smoking. "She arrived later."

"In an old Model T." And suddenly it makes sense. Their two trips – one by train, one by car – intersecting at this Nevada ranch. She knows Aunt Marjorie from family photos, a brassy-haired woman with an ample bosom and painted fingernails. "She didn't stay long, though, did she?"

Smoke curls around his fingers. "No, she didn't." He's watching her closely.

She remembers being in the Model T – in her nightgown?

– with the smell of the warm leather and horsehair. Lying tight against Mom in a big bed tangled with blankets. Sitting in the yard with a lapful of evening primroses, tying them into a crown. "I remember so little."

"You were young. Besides, adults never tell kids the whole story."

The window is cold, or maybe it's her. "What else is there to the story than a dad bringing his little girl to ride horses for a month?"

"I know you saw him as your dad, but he was no different from anyone else who stayed at the ranch." Steve stubs out the cigarette on his empty plate. "Your father came to Nevada to get a divorce."

"Excuse me?"

"You didn't know about the divorce?"

Louise sinks onto the sofa. "I think I'll take that whiskey now."

He nods. "I think you'll need it. You're white as a ghost already."

"All these years, Dad's never said a word about a divorce. You're lying."

"If it makes you feel better, he didn't go through with it in the end."

She wants to believe in a happy reconciliation, but she's seen too many Reno-vations among her friends. Pulling out just before establishing residency – it didn't make sense. "Why?"

Steve scoots back his bench and stands. "Maybe I should fetch you that whiskey."

He disappears into the kitchen.

112

She doesn't need whiskey. She doesn't need stories. She doesn't need more reminders that she never really knew her mother. What she really needs is her dad.

Without waiting for Steve to return, Louise retrieves her handbag and leaves.

BERYL

Sometimes I wonder if ignorance isn't bliss after all.

FRANCIE

His letter?

BERYL

His letter.
(looking at envelope in hand)
You think a person is happy, you learn they're miserable. Now you both are.

FRANCIE

There are things I wish I didn't know. But ignorance is ignorance. I might still be in New Jersey if I didn't know.

BERYL

And I might be putting mashed potatoes on the dinner table.

—Excerpt from the unproduced screenplay
When She Was King

Chapter Seven

1926

Sunday

· ·

Stack of letters from C and AL. It's like Christmas morning!

Both wrote, but mostly AL. Scores of pages filled with big, round letters and optimistic spelling. She told me all about the mountains and deserts, about riding horses with the "dood ranglers," about eating chili con carne until her tongue burns. She sounds so *happy*. It makes me happy. I think.

C's letter was shorter. He apologized, mostly. And if that isn't a hopeful sign, I don't know what is.

Supper: Ham and eggs, stewed prunes, coffee.

Camp	50¢
Gasoline	$1.40
Postage stamp	2¢

April 18, 1926

I didn't know she was writing to them. Honest. But I should have. Of course she misses her girl up and down. Of course she'd write letters, even unanswered, if only to feel near to AL when she's not.

But Carl? She hardly ever talks about him. Every now and again, but not with the hurt and longing and great sobs that she did on that very first night. I'd kidded myself that she wasn't thinking about him. How stupid I am. How stupid to suppose Ethel's thinking about anything or anyone but the husband she's going after.

Later

Only lunchtime and already today is too long. E kept up chatter the whole drive this morning, all about AL and her horses, all about C and his apology. I haven't seen the letter, but to hear her talk, C's is as touching as any of Abelard's. He regrets leaving the way he did, she said. And regret brings people back.

I know regret. It pierces you right between the ribs and doesn't budge. I felt it the moment E told me she and Carl were getting married, felt it when she walked into that courthouse in a dress of baby blue crepe, have felt it each and every day since.

Regret for years of things unsaid. But it just gnawed at me all those years. It didn't bring me back to her.

We stopped for lunch. She'd made cheese sandwiches, buttered on both sides just the way I like them. But I couldn't eat, not with her sitting there so happy and hopeful. If this works out, she told me, and I get Carl back, it'll be all because of you, and I had to walk away. A good friend wouldn't sulk. A good friend wouldn't let anyone see what was really in her eyes.

Later

Couldn't concentrate on driving, couldn't concentrate on E. Feigned a stomachache as an excuse to stop early. I deserved a stomachache, the way I sat there begrudging E her happiness. After a while, I began to believe it myself.

E made me lie down in the car while she set up the tents. While she was outside, I lifted C's letter from her purse.

I don't know why I did it. I really don't. Maybe it was to tear it into a million pieces. Maybe it was to see what he had that I didn't. Maybe it was to catch a glimpse of the address so I could send a letter of my own. Maybe all three. But I read the letter and I suddenly didn't know what to do.

"Dear Eth," it said, and it was brief. "I shouldn't have left like I did, with nothing but a note on the table. I regret that. I should've waited for you to come home, told it to you straight, but I'm a sap and a coward. Anything I said would've been feeding you a line. Eth, I'm just so balled up and needed to escape. Away from you, from our house, from our life. Away

from everything but Al. These days, she's the only part of me that feels honest." Like I said, it was brief.

It's certainly cryptic. C always knew how to talk circles around what he really wanted to say. But it wasn't the apology E made it out to be. It wasn't begging for forgiveness or promising to make things right. Did she not see that? Or maybe she did, but tried to convince herself otherwise?

I don't know if I should tell her what I think. It would crush her. And, to do so, I'd have to admit I'd taken the letter from her purse. Is there anything wrong with a bit of hope? I don't know. Until yesterday, I thought maybe I'd had some.

Monday

· ·

F restless today. As kids, she used to get like this. Fidgety and impatient. Always whenever she had something to talk about that she didn't want to. When her dad lost his job. When her family moved too many blocks away. When I told her C and I were getting married. She never did talk about that last one.

Supper: Peanuts and gin. Dinner of champions.

McCracken's Camp	*25¢*
Gasoline	*$1.20*
Postage stamp	*2¢*

April 19, 1926

Tonight E forgot to make dinner.

118

She went into town to buy a chicken, but instead came back with lipstick, a pot of kohl, and the news that there was a speakeasy nearby. It almost made me smile, to hear her talk as though she were a flapper instead of a housewife, as though middle-of-nowhere Illinois was all that interesting. But maybe there is more to E than I know. The way she bee-stung her lips – garnet red, like Clara Bow's – and rolled down her stockings, she looked like she went to speakeasies every day of the week. She waved me into a seat, pulled a tiny brush from her paint kit, and did up my lips and eyes without even asking. It was so much like the old Ethel – sparkling, dynamic, assuming – that I couldn't resist.

She made me close my eyes, but she was near and warm. I heard her inhale and knew her tongue was caught up between her teeth, the way it always was when she was concentrating. Her breath smelled like Sen-Sen. It was like we were back at the watch factory, painting each other's lips and eyelids with the paint meant for the luminous dials. I always wore more. It was the only way I could glow like Ethel always did.

I reminded her of that, of those days painting at long tables in the factory, washed over in sunlight and her singing. I thought to make her smile with my reminiscing. I'd feel the Sen-Sen laugh on my face. But she didn't laugh. She stopped and sat back. Though my eyes were still closed, I could sense it. The air felt empty. I opened them and she was looking at me. She was so serious, so quiet, with nothing showing except in her eyes. The corners were pinched in panic.

I knew then that she knew. That she was dying too. And that she was terrified of anyone finding out.

I wondered how long she'd known, how long she'd kept the secret from C and AL, how long she had left. Though I'd been going to dentists for months with loose teeth, blinding headaches, a sore jaw, I'd only known for two weeks. In the end, that might be all I had left. I hadn't told E about the two teeth I'd lost just since we set out or the pain that had spread down to my shoulder. I hadn't even admitted it to myself.

She blinked, and the panicked look fell away. I've done your eyes up all wrong, she said, and there was something thick and sad in her voice. You look like a corpse. She reached up with a handkerchief to wipe away the kohl from around my eyes, but I caught her hand.

Forgetting the pain, forgetting the picnic, the letters, the chocolate on my lips, I pulled her tight against me. She felt like a daffodil stem, bending, green, impossibly thin. For that moment, I didn't care what she thought. I didn't care what anyone thought. I just wanted to hug her the way I used to, back before we grew too old, back before it became more than a schoolgirl crush, back before I walked away from our friendship. I wanted her to feel me, to know that I was here, that I would be, no matter what she needed. To stay with her until the end, or only as far as it took to bring her back to her family.

I held her for maybe a moment longer than I should have, a moment more than was friendly, held her until she tensed up in my arms and I let go. That's when she finally gave a little laugh. Gee, Florrie. I forgot how fierce your hugs always were. She turned to fuss with her makeup and I pushed my hands against the canvas of my seat. Because, oh, they were shaking.

I hadn't done that in years. Hugged her. Touched her, even. Not even a brush on the shoulder. I used to, the way schoolgirls did. We'd been friends for eons. We walked with linked arms, touched fingers across the aisle between our desks at school, lay hip-to-hip on the sidewalk looking up at the clouds. But then one high school day, at a football game of all places, she called my name across the crowded bleachers. She was wearing a cherry-red scarf and her cheeks were pink. I'd only just arrived and was searching for an empty seat. She called my name, she waved, and my heart flipped. In that moment I knew. It wasn't an empty seat I was looking for. It was, and always had been, her.

My heart did that flip again, as I sat on my shaking hands and E fiddled with the makeup. I swallowed it down and said, Let's get zozzled.

Later

E's fast asleep in her tent and I'm still out here, sitting by the fire. We didn't go to the speakeasy after all. I bought a jar of gin off the fellas a couple of campsites over. At least they called it gin. I'd been to a juice joint or three. I'd tasted hooch. This was gin of the most literal bathtub variety. They charged me forty-five cents for it, which just about made Ethel spit, so he said he'd give it to me for forty and a kiss. The very idea made me blush. As cool as a cucumber, I handed over two quarters and told him that real ladies never shop the sales. It was worth it just to see E laugh.

So we stayed in, just the two of us and our jar of moonshine. We sat in E's tent, with the side rolled up, and played rummy by lantern light. E won fifteen times in a row. I didn't mind one bit. I've never done this before, she confessed. Drink moonshine? Play rummy? Visit Greenville, Illinois? All of that.

After a while, the two fellas from down the way stopped by. From their grins, they'd had a fair amount of moonshine themselves. The speakeasy hadn't been worth the trip, they said, and anyway, we were probably better company. I was half under myself and cheerfully dealt them into the next hand. Dale (the one with the mustache) gave me my ten cents back, no kiss required, and Boyd (the one without) gave us a bag of peanuts. Which was perfect. We'd forgotten dinner, after all.

They asked how long we'd known each other. Eighteen years, we said at the same time. It was a silly play I'd written, I said. Wonderfully silly, she agreed. I told them, Ethel played the part of King Henry, and was rewarded with a blush.

They stayed to play three hands of rummy. Dale did a lot of winking at me from across the table. I'd drunk enough that I was halfway flattered. I wondered if he'd ask to kiss me again. Not that I'd let him. But it's still nice to be asked. E stopped talking and she stopped winning. Just played quietly and twisted her wedding ring around her finger.

After Dale and Boyd left, we ate peanuts and listened to the fire crackle. E tossed a shell into the fire and asked why I hadn't just given Dale a kiss. I laughed. I didn't answer. The whole idea was too absurd. Didn't she see that? She drank another swallow of gin, even though her cheeks were already flushed pink. She

*asked, softly and suddenly, why I never married. You've never
said. My hands started shaking again at her question. Had she
been wondering? I pushed them into my pockets. She watched,
at me fidgeting on my camp stool, at my hands balled up in my
pockets. Why didn't you marry?*

*I didn't answer. I couldn't. She stood and brushed peanut
shells from her lap. I thought I knew, she said. Maybe I didn't
after all. She crawled into her tent, leaving me alone out by
the fire.*

Tuesday

. . . .

Awful, bumpy, queasy ride. Last night was perhaps not the
best of plans. Ankle aches besides. All the way up to my
hip. Been forgetting to take my Parson's Vigor Tonic. Every
day, Dr Glass said, to help with the anemia. At St Louis, we
decided to stop over and make a day of it.

Found the general post office. Only one letter waiting from
AL. None from C.

Supper: Stew, biscuits, quick custard.

Bungalow Auto Camp	*50¢*
Gasoline	*$1.00*
Frankfurters	*2 for 5¢*
Lemonade, 2	*10¢*
Movie tickets, 2	*10¢*
Popcorn	*5¢*
Postage stamp	*2¢*

April 20, 1926

E was quiet all morning. Not that I knew what to talk about today, not after last night. Maybe she didn't either. She sat still, staring straight ahead at the road and not saying a thing.

I worried, of course I worried. My night hadn't been so drink-clouded that I didn't remember the moment I mentioned the radium paint and her eyes tightened in panic. I hadn't forgotten. I understood that look. I knew she was sick too. So to see her so still and quiet in the car, right hand clutching the edge of the seat where she didn't think I could see, I knew. Something wasn't right.

I wasn't feeling my best either. I had a sore molar and knew I'd lose the tooth soon. Impromptu meals of peanuts and chocolate probably weren't helping. I wondered if E noticed me cutting up my food into the tiniest of pieces, if she noticed me taking aspirin after aspirin.

But I remembered, now, her surreptitious handfuls of aspirin, her limps in the morning, her occasional cold compresses in the evening. There'd been signs all along that something wasn't right with her. I'd been too worried about my flighty heart to take it all seriously.

Do you want to stop at St Louis? I asked. We'll be there by lunchtime.

It might be nice, she said, to see people and streetcars, to sit on a park bench, to go into a real store. She let go of the car seat. Yes.

We reached the city and found a bench in a leafy park. E said she wanted to just sit still for a moment with her eyes closed, listening to the birds. I left her there cradling the jar of our leftover breakfast coffee and walked into the city.

I found a druggist and restocked on aspirin. I asked if he had anything stronger. He did, of the back alley variety, so I bought some of that too. E seemed happy enough with the hooch last night, and I knew it just might help when the aspirin didn't.

Truth be told, I was feeling a bit delicate this morning, in a way that had nothing to do with the radium lingering in my bones. It had been a while since I'd drunk that much. But I couldn't admit that to E.

Last night she'd said that it was her first time drinking moonshine. I suppose in all those years she'd played housewife, I'd done more. I'd had a string of jobs after the watch dial factory. Rubber factory, department store, florist's shop, newspaper office, lunch counter at the five-and-dime. I had my very own apartment, a cold-water flat the size of a hatbox. I ate from lunch carts and pushcart vendors. I took the train into New York when I had a little left over at the end of the week. Twice I'd been to the sorts of speakeasies in the city that had nothing but women.

I tucked my purchases in the car; it wouldn't do to be caught walking around the city with booze. E was leaning back on the bench with her hands on her lap and her eyes closed. I bent close, close enough that I could smell the cocoanut oil that she puts in her hair, but her breathing was regular. She'd just dozed off.

I left her napping on the bench by the car and went to find the general post office. There were two letters waiting *for Ethel Wild, one in Anna Louisa's round handwriting, the other in Carl's. I'd half been hoping that he wouldn't write again. I tucked them both in my pocket and went back to the park.*

She was awake, her hat off, repinning her hair. The jar of coffee sat empty beside her on the bench. The sandman snuck up on me, she said, smiling. Where did you go?

The post office, I said, and slipped my hand in my pocket.

She straightened on the bench, suddenly looking so bright and hopeful. Oh! Were there any? Florrie, were there any for me?

From AL, I said, and took one of the envelopes out of my pocket.

Oh, my little dear! She took it, touched all four corners, as though reassuring herself that it was real and it was here. She flipped it over and back, then looked up at me. But none from Carl?

In my pocket, the other envelope crinkled, betraying me, but she didn't seem to notice. No.

I tried to convince myself that what I saw in her eyes was a smidge of resignation. Of relief. Of satisfaction. But I knew that's just what I wanted to see. I knew that what was really there, what she really felt, was disappointment. And all it would take to dispel it would be the envelope hiding in my pocket. But I said, No, I'm sorry. It was horrible, but that was that.

She looked down to the one in her hand, turned it over, and then sighed. When she looked up again, it was with a smile. At least I have this. At least one someone is thinking of me.

More than one someone. I hope she knows that.

We lunched on frankfurters bought from a gent with a street cart (I've never done this either! she said) and then splurged on a movie, like the old days. That's My Baby, with Douglas MacLean and Margaret Morris. E roared through the whole thing. We shared a nickel bag of popcorn, smuggled into the theater inside my umbrella.

Later

Whether it was the nap in the park, the letter from AL, or the movie and popcorn, something revived E for the afternoon's drive. With our long stop, we only got as far as St Charles, but the camp was clean and cheerfully crowded. The next campsite had five young women sleeping like canned sardines in a wall tent. They had a great pot of mutton stew that they were happy to share. E made a batch of pan biscuits and a quick pot of custard to add to the spread.

It was nice to have a tableful of conversation. E was livelier than I'd seen her in a while. When one woman said that she was headed back home a new divorcée, they all cheered. E bit her lip, and I wondered if she was going to say something about Carl, about Nevada, but she didn't. They all started singing "Wild Women Don't Have the Blues." When they got to When my man starts kicking I let him find another home, they practically shouted the line. Though I'm sure E had never heard it before, she joined in for the second round.

FRANCIE

There it is.

Both step close to the edge of the Grand Canyon and look down.

BERYL

I didn't know anything could be so big. Makes my problems seem rather small, doesn't it?

FRANCIE

You're not a canyon.

BERYL

Some days I think my worries could fill one.

FRANCIE

And your happiness?

BERYL

Some days.
(still gazing down into the canyon)
I could wake up to this every morning.
(impulsively)

We should move here.

FRANCIE

We?

BERYL

Why are you blushing?

FRANCIE

Because Arizona's too hot.

—Excerpt from the unproduced screenplay
When She Was King

Chapter Eight

1952

Louise drives too fast. She doesn't know what the speed limit is out here. She doesn't care. Desert whips past. She wants to get out of Nevada. She wants to get away from what she's heard.

She's left the top down, and the wind lifts her hair. Curls defiantly uncurl. She hasn't put her hat back on. She hasn't tied on a scarf. She doesn't know if she cares.

She knows about divorce ranches. Who doesn't? She's seen *The Women*. She's seen *The Road to Reno*. She's seen all of the news items about this celebrity or that waiting out her six weeks amid cowboys and endless Manhattans. Hollywood makes it seem almost glamorous. Easy. Lord knows, Hollywood is all about easy. Girdles and pancake makeup can hide a multitude of regrets. So, in Nevada, can a divorce.

She turns up the radio. It's Doris Day, singing like a breeze. She pushes her foot down on the pedal. Mountains whir past.

Divorce is for bored housewives. For cheating husbands. For young girls, for rich ones, for ones so impulsive they can't settle down. It wasn't for her dad, so quiet and steady. It wasn't for her mom, dead before she'd gotten far in life. And – not that anyone asked – it wasn't for her.

Louise finds a diner in Needles with a pay phone. She places the number with the long-distance operator and perches on the stool in the booth. While the call is being routed, she straightens her stockings and brushes dust from the toes of her shoes. Catching a glimpse of her reflection in the diner's windows, she begins to regret not having worn a scarf in the convertible.

Operator rings operator rings operator. She imagines them lined up across the country like beads on a necklace. She runs her index finger over her lips and can't remember when she last reapplied her lipstick.

In the restaurant, a man sitting at the counter watches her. She pats down her hair. She wonders if he can recognize her through the glass of the phone booth, with her dusty dress, her wild hair, her determined face. He pushes back his fedora and continues staring over spoonfuls of chili. The Newark operator announces, "It's ringing," and the line connects with a click.

She hears, "Hello?" The word sounds small all the way from New Jersey, and she pivots away from the diners.

"Phone call from Needles, California," the long-distance operator says.

"Needles?" the man asks on the other end of the line. "Well," he says, "I guess so."

"Daddy?" she asks, her voice suddenly just as small.

She forgets her bare lips and matted hair. She hunches her shoulders down, closing herself in on this one phone call. "It's me." As though anyone else would be phoning and calling him "Daddy." She says, "It's Anna Louisa."

The line crackles. She's not sure if it's the connection or if Dad's dropped the phone. But it clears. "Al," he says, more loudly than before. "What are you doing calling today? It's not Sunday."

"Oh, Dad, yes it is. You're just playing hooky from church again today, I bet."

He gives a dry laugh. "I've had pneumonia. If that doesn't get a free pass from the Almighty, I don't know what will."

"You still run-down?"

"Oh, I'll get by." He coughs, but he sounds better.

"You know where no one gets pneumonia?" she asks. "The desert. If you came out this way, like I keep saying . . ."

"Oh, hush. You know I need to be where it snows and rains and turns orange every autumn."

She crosses her legs. "I just worry about you, Daddy."

"And I worry about you, Al. You didn't call last week."

"You know how things get when we're finishing a picture. It's been an absolute hive." She slips her heel out of her right shoe and rubs it with a thumb. "And we're already getting ready to start the next." She hesitates. "It shoots in Vegas."

"Like that Jane Russell picture?"

"*The Las Vegas Story*? Less drama, more tap dancing."

"Hmph."

She doesn't mention that this is the second time she's

found herself driving away from Las Vegas instead of toward it. That she has to be on set tomorrow morning and hasn't even checked into her hotel. That more than the film, more than the script, more than the ultimatum, it's Nevada itself she dreads.

If she checks in to the Flamingo, walks in and out of its doors for six weeks, what happens at the end of it? When all she has to do is walk into the courthouse and, minutes later, walk out with a divorce in hand. She doesn't want to stay long enough to let herself think of that. She doesn't want to allow that to be a possibility.

"Is that why you're calling from Needles? It's been a while since you've shot on location. On your way there?"

Out the window, cars stream past. People heading off to adventure. People looking to see how far the country stretches. She thinks of her mother's ledger and Florence Daniels' diary, both tucked in the brown envelope back in the apartment. "I don't know."

The line crackles again. "I'm sorry. What was that?"

She knows this phone call is costing a fortune. But these weekly phone calls with her dad are worth all the gold in the Yukon. "No," she amends. "Well, not right now." She tugs on the phone cord with her pinkie. "I thought I'd come home for Christmas."

As she says it, she can almost smell snow and pine trees and hot gingerbread. A lump works its way down her throat.

"Home?"

Though she hasn't been back in years, though the word has been redefined a half-dozen times – from apartments and hotels to the little bungalow on Rodeo Drive – right now, all she can think about is a black-shuttered house with a crooked elm in back. "To New Jersey."

Christmas had always been her favorite time of year. Carols and snowmen and too much to eat. Popcorn over the fireplace. She can almost taste it. Until this moment, she hasn't realized how much she wanted to be there.

Her dad is quiet for a moment. He muffles another cough. "You're not going to fly, are you?"

After three crashes in the past year, Newark Airport had been closed. Every Sunday night call with Dad had been full of news. The third plane had narrowly missed an orphanage.

"Is the airport still closed?"

"It's open now, but Al, you shouldn't . . ."

"I won't." She fingers the car key sitting on the ledge by her purse. "I'm driving. I have a big red Studebaker, Dad, as bright as a maraschino cherry."

"That's a long way to drive."

"I have a map of sorts."

Dad coughs again, and she hears a voice murmuring in the background. She wonders if Hank still comes over for Sunday dinners. She wonders if he still brings meringue-topped cream pies.

"Al, this is probably costing you a mint."

"Okay, Dad." She tucks her hair behind her ears. "I'll see you in a few days."

He says, "I love you . . ."

". . . as big as the prairies," she finishes.

It's their usual sign-off. The way they've always said

goodbye, good night, be right back. It's theirs and theirs alone.

She stands, ready to hang up the phone, but she stops. "Dad? You still here."

She hears scrabbling on the other end. "Al? Everything okay?"

"Did . . ." She hesitates. "Did Mom love me too?"

There's no hesitation in his voice. "Every moment of every day."

Though she thinks she knows the answer, she asks, "Then why didn't she take me with her? When she went on that road trip to California, why didn't she bring me along?"

She wonders if he'll tell her. About the trip in search of a divorce, about Mom's trip in search of them. He's quiet. Maybe he will.

But when he speaks, it's to say, "Sometimes we have to leave behind those we love, Al. Sometimes we have to do what we think is right for ourselves and hope they understand."

She doesn't know if he's talking about Mom or if he's talking about himself. Or maybe he's really talking about her, driving off and leaving Arnie alone in Beverly Hills. She hangs up, without repeating the sign-off. She doesn't know how to respond.

She leaves the booth and orders a cup of coffee. It's burning hot, but she drinks half of it quickly. It's easier than thinking.

She knows what she has to do. She thinks she's known it since leaving the house yesterday, maybe even since leaving

135

the studio meeting where they gave her the new script and the ultimatum.

She goes back into the booth and places a call to the studio. She really should've called Charlie, her agent, but she knows he spends Sundays napping on the hammock in his backyard. Charlie's a friend. She won't make him put down his beer to come to the phone.

While she waits for the call to be routed, she sips her coffee. Through the glass of the booth, the waitress glares. She should've left her mug on the counter. The long-distance operator connects to Los Angeles and the studio switchboard begins ringing. The studio should be empty, with everyone home ready to tuck into Sunday dinners. She can leave a message. She can be well on her way to New Jersey before they get the message that she's not going to Las Vegas after all.

Of course she's not as lucky as that. Of course the head of production is working through the weekend, and is happy to take her call. She really should've called Charlie.

He's irate. She could've guessed that he would be. She wishes there were whiskey in her coffee. "What are we going to do now?" she hears, and, "Who do you think you are?" She's past caring about the answer to the first question, and starting to get an inkling about the second. She puts the receiver down on the ledge, the yelling reverberating through the little booth, and reapplies her lipstick. She drinks more of her coffee, leaving a red mark on the rim. When the phone calms down, she picks it back up. "Suspend me if you want. When you're ready to talk about a new contract, call Charlie." She drops her lipstick in her purse and snaps it shut. "I have to do what I think is right for myself."

She places one more call to LA. Though it rings and rings on the other end, Arnie doesn't pick up.

Leaving the empty mug on the counter along with a nickel, she heads out.

She drives as far as Williams, Arizona, before realizing she needs to look at something other than endless black pavement. The sun is low and as orange as a pumpkin. She checks into a motel, which gleefully boasts steam heat and knotty pine interiors. Steam heat? She's spent the day shut into a car. She sheds her cardigan. With the window open, she turns on the radio and stretches flat on her back.

It's that new song "I Saw Mommy Kissing Santa Claus." Every ten minutes, it seems, it's on, Jimmy Boyd whining his way through the song. She contemplates changing the channel, but doesn't. That would involve getting up from the bed.

Cool and still beneath the music, she dozes off.

When she wakes, Gene Autry is singing "Rudolph the Red-Nosed Reindeer." She rubs at her eyes with her thumbs. How long has she been asleep? Through the window, the sky is indigo. She washes her face and heads to the motel's cocktail lounge, where, feeling adventurous, she orders fried rice with chicken. It comes sprinkled with almonds and is delicious.

There's a phone at the bar, nestled next to an overzealous

poinsettia. The bartender slides over an old-fashioned on a paper napkin while she dials the operator. She tries calling Arnie, again, but there's no answer, again. She leaves some change on the bar next to the phone and takes the drink back to her table.

When the waitress comes by with a second old-fashioned, she asks, "Heading there tomorrow, or have you already been?"

Louise drinks the last swallow from her first glass. "Pardon?"

"The Grand Canyon."

The new drink has two cherries in it instead of one. "Is that around here?"

As soon as she asks, she knows it's a mistake. The waitress snaps her fingers and disappears. Louise hurriedly gulps, knowing she'll return with some of those damned brochures.

Indeed she does, handfuls of brochures printed in red and blue, showing canyons, rivers, mule tours. "Most people think two days is enough, but there's really so much to see." She moves Louise's empty plate to make room for the brochures, which she spreads open. "What you've seen in the movies is hardly anything."

Louise pulls a brochure closer. The photo is striking, more so than the monotonous landscape she's been driving through. "There have been movies filmed there?"

"Oh, sure." The waitress stacks fork and knife on the empty plate. "*Grand Canyon,* of course. *Family Honeymoon,* with Fred MacMurray. Oh, *Thief of Bagdad.* I'll never know for sure, but I swear Sabu came in here for a drink while they were filming."

Louise is certain a star like Sabu never ventured to Williams, Arizona, just for a cocktail. But, then again, she never would've thought she'd be sitting here having one herself. "Can I take the drink up to my room?"

The waitress looks almost relieved. Louise is the only woman alone in the lounge, and the only one with a drink. "Please do." She takes the bill from her apron pocket. "But you really should think about stopping at the Grand Canyon." She shrugs. "If for no other reason than to say you've seen it."

It's as good a reason as any. The next morning, after she checks out of the motel, she drives to the center of town, and then turns north. The map she has says it's only sixty or so miles to the Grand Canyon National Park.

The day is blue and warm with wispy clouds high above the desert. She wears her white dress again, this time with her gray pumps, matching gloves, and a dove-gray hat with a spray of arrow-tipped feathers in front. As she drives, they brush the roof of the car. She fiddles with the radio, but way out here, she can't find a station she likes. Anyway, she's too keyed up for music.

Before she left the motel this morning, she called Arnie. It rang for a full minute and a half before she gave up. Maybe he'd been asleep. Maybe he'd been in the bathtub. Maybe he'd been sitting at his dusty desk, watching the curved black phone ring and not caring.

She also made another phone call, to her agent. It's Monday now. He's always at his desk by six-thirty Monday mornings, just in case. It was early enough in the morning

139

that the call went through quickly. Charlie answered on the first ring.

"Charlie," she began, "I know what you're going to say."

"Do you have any idea the messages I had on my desk this morning, LuLu?" His voice was graveled from decades of chain-smoking. "You'd think you'd assassinated Truman."

"Not showing up on set? No, *that's* treason."

He coughed. She could hear the snick of a lighter. "So you deposit this mess in my lap and head off to . . . Where are you going?"

"The Grand Canyon."

"Why the hell are you doing that? You do know that's outside, right?"

Only Charlie could get away with that, both the "hell" and the teasing. "Which of the two of us knows how to ride a horse?"

"If I climbed on a horse, that sucker would fold beneath me like an accordion." There was a muffled "damn" and the clatter of the phone hitting the desk. When Charlie came back on the line, he said, "Spilled my coffee."

"Tell me what else is new."

"So why are you calling?" She could picture him frantically mopping at his tie with a handkerchief. There was a reason all of Charlie's ties were brown. "This is costing a fortune."

"Well, Charlie, who else would I call?"

"You mean, who else would deal with your messes."

She tried to put a wheedle into her voice. "No one can fix them as good as you."

"That's because you pay me buckets." He saw straight through her little-girl voice. He always did. "LuLu, what do you want?"

"You know what I want. A better contract. Better scripts. Better roles, that *don't* involve tap shoes."

"We can work on the studio," he said. "But not if you're suspended."

"They won't suspend me. They don't want to lose me."

"They're going to know you're bluffing. That, after the holidays, you'll be back at the studio door with your palms out."

"Who says I'm bluffing?" she said evenly.

He didn't answer. She wondered if he was just sitting there puffing on a cigarette. She wondered if he had hung up.

Over the line, she heard a slurp of coffee. "Well," he finally said, a creak of a word. She held her breath. "I have a mean poker face. What do you say we ante in?"

She wondered if he could see her smile. "Charlie, you're a sweetheart."

He sighed. "You need anything else, LuLu?"

"Could you wire me some money here in Williams, Arizona?" She could see a squat bank right across the street. "I'll stop back after seeing the Grand Canyon. Should be enough time for it to get here."

"Sure thing."

"And Charlie?" She hesitated. "Could you swing by the house? Not today, but . . . Well, if you could just stop by. It's been a while since Arn's seen you, and—"

"LuLu, honey. Consider it done."

As she drives to the National Park, still glad that she'd gotten Charlie on the phone, something eases in her shoulders. Her agent never looks like he fits in to Hollywood, with his cheap suits, his food-spotted ties, his overflowing paunch, but he's sharp as nails and tough enough for even the movie business. "Consider it done," he always says, and she always knows it will be. That quick phone call had cost almost three dollars, but had left her feeling immediately relieved that the studio, her money, and Arn were all in Charlie's competent, nicotine-stained hands.

She pulls into the park, following the road past a log-cabined visitors' center, past a souvenir shop, a garage, a railway station. She'd left the brochures back at the motel and couldn't be bothered to stop at the visitors' center, already crowded with camera-toting men and women in plaid shirts. A lot in front of a long, low building glistens with cars, and she parks.

It's a hotel, the El Tovar. She vaguely recalls mention of it in one of the brochures. It's part Victorian resort, part Swiss chalet, part desert lodge, all peeled pine and limestone and wide verandahs. A woman in a pink cotton dress leans against a porch rail, lazily fanning herself. She blows a kiss to a man walking past with a mule.

The lobby looks like a hunting lodge, with antlers and rough-hewn beams. Pine boughs swing between the beams and along the stone fireplace. There's a line of people waiting to place calls, so she leaves the number with the desk and orders a coffee, black. While she waits, she wanders across the reception room. Through the windows, she can see the back terrace and realizes that the hotel is perched straight on the rim of the canyon. It's a terrifying thought, this expensive hotel teetering on the edge of the wilderness. The fact that it has been doing so for half a century doesn't make her feel any better.

"Miss?" A uniformed man waits patiently to be noticed. "There's no answer at the number you gave us. Would you like us to try another number?"

She thinks for a moment of calling Pauline next door and asking her to check on Arn, but she doesn't know Pauline's number.

"No." She shakes her head. "No, thank you." She sets the coffee on a table next to a lamp and drifts out onto the terrace.

It's cold here, seven thousand feet above sea level. Cold enough that she wishes she had a sweater on. The other people scattered on the terrace, sipping cocktails or steaming mugs of coffee, are dressed in turtlenecks and soft jackets and wool trousers. One woman even wears chocolate-brown earmuffs, like she's at a ski resort.

They don't belong, in their resort wear. She doesn't even know if she belongs, in her white dress and heels. She doesn't know how any of them do, because, right there, straight ahead, is the real, wild world.

The curved terrace is edged in wooden rails, but they don't keep the nature out. The rim of the Grand Canyon is a handful of yards away. Oranges and browns and spatters of white that might be snow. So close that she could throw a penny into its yawning, breathless emptiness. She walks straight up to the rail and leans against it, wondering how far below she can see. A stone-bordered path winds down into the canyon, dotted with a few distant mules and riders, but they're far enough away that all she hears are faint jingles from the mule bells. Even the conversation behind her on the terrace, the clinking of teacups on saucers, fades.

She leans and she breathes and, in that cold inhale, she forgets for a moment everything she'd driven to escape and everything she's driving toward to uncover. It's just her and the impossible depth of the canyon, the impossible height of the sky.

For a quick, wild moment, she imagines jumping. Not to find the bottom, but to find the air in between here and there. She pictures her white dress billowing, her hair streaming. She pushes her shoulders out over the railing.

"First time, Louise?" a voice asks, and she jumps back.

It's Duane, of the freckles and the sedan and the impending divorce. If she's surprised to see him here in Arizona instead of in Nevada, she doesn't say.

"Obvious?" she replies.

"Want to go down to the bottom?"

Whether he means on foot, on mule, or floating in a weightless billow of white, she doesn't care. She just nods.

He offers his hand. He pulls her back from the edge of the railing.

The El Tovar is an enthusiastic blend of rich and rugged, of East and West. Louise unabashedly loves it. She's already mentally redecorating her house, adding a moose head to her space-age living room, a Navajo rug to her bedroom.

She and Duane eat lunch in the dining room. The furniture is almost Arts and Crafts in its clean lines and in its chairs and tables that wouldn't be amiss in her dad's house. Above are hewn beams, yellow hanging lights, and far too many Christmas garlands. In this rustic room, they look through menus elegant with hearts of celery, shrimp Louis, stuffed avocado. She knows she should have the fruit bowl with cottage cheese, or maybe the turkey salad, but at the same time as Duane, she drops a finger on the Harvey House hamburger.

"Are actresses really allowed to eat that many hamburgers?" he asks.

It takes a moment before his comment sinks in. Earlier, she realizes now, he'd called her Louise. "You know I'm not Anna, don't you?"

He waits until they order to answer. "I should probably say that I watch nothing but monster movies or macho Westerns. But" – and here he leans closer, whispering across their coffees – "but what I really like, when no one is looking, is a good musical."

She's sure he's making fun of her, and takes a scalding sip to avoid a retort.

He pushes her sweating glass of water closer. "What, can't a man enjoy a good song-and-dance number?"

"Not a man like you," she says. "At least I don't think so."

He gives her a wide grin, and suddenly she doesn't care if he's teasing or not. "Really, though, I've seen all of the Betsey Barnes movies. Even that god-awful last one." His eyes widen. "Oh, I'm sorry."

"Me too. It *was* god-awful." She takes a more careful sip of coffee.

"What do you think we all watch out there in Korea? The guys like to see a pretty face." He folds and unfolds his napkin. "I recognized you right away."

"Then why'd you let me introduce myself as Anna?"

He shrugs. "I figured you had a reason."

The waitress sets down a sloshing cup of vegetable beef soup in front of Duane. Louise ordered a chilled fruit cup to start, to make herself feel better about the hamburger and French fried potatoes to follow. As she spears a chunk of soft pear, she says, "You're not in LA, so you didn't go home to kiss and make up."

He shakes his head.

"But you didn't stay in Nevada." She eats the pear and fishes for a peach slice. "Does that mean that Mavis and her marital bliss are safe for the moment?"

He grins. "For the moment." He breaks a saltine into the soup and stirs. "No, it's what you said, about not knowing which battles were worth fighting at home. It made a lot of sense." He leaves the spoon in the bowl. "Mavis isn't the enemy. It's just battle weariness that's got us both. It wears you down until you can't see straight. You know?"

She does.

"Anyway, I convinced her to come out here and meet me. A little holiday vacation. A rendezvous between jobs." He slurps a spoonful. "Well, she said yes. She's on her way to the Grand Canyon." Through his mouthful of soup, he manages to grin.

"Oh, I'm glad," she says, and means it. "But what about

the dog?" She's just realized that his cheerful beagle isn't there, waiting for a bite of hamburger.

"The what?" He winks. "Joking. He's my brother's. They're on their way back to Comstock." He eats another spoonful and wipes his mouth. "So what about you?" His eyes are back on his bowl. "Last I saw, you were headed to Vegas. If you don't mind me saying, you've gotten a little off course."

"I'm driving home for Christmas," she says.

"And where's home?"

A year after moving out to California, she was already calling that "home." Her room in the Hollywood Studio Club, her booth at the diner down the street, her "accidental" run-ins at the Wilshire library with a cute writer named Arnie. But now when she says the word, she's thinking of snow, carols on Dad's piano, ham and overcooked potatoes. Unquestioning warmth. Home. "Too far away."

"Home isn't with your husband?"

She shifts and tucks her hands on her lap. "I didn't say I was married."

"You don't have to. I read the Hollywood rags." At her raised eyebrow, he qualifies. "The good ones."

"It's not as though Arnie is a secret."

"Is that his name?"

"Arnold Bates."

"I don't remember. Film editor?"

"Screenwriter."

"And it's been four years."

"Ten!"

He coughs on a mouthful of soup. "Ten, eh? I guess it's not surprising that things are on the outs after that long."

"On the what?" She sets down her fork.

He waves the soupspoon. "Hollywood rags, remember?"

Arnie reads them – he used to write for them, after all – but Louise gives the gossip magazines and newspapers a wide berth.

"The past year or so, you've been seen with Don Jensen. The papers all show it. All the premieres, all the parties."

"What?" She's outraged. "Donnie's a good pal." A good pal in need of a girl on his arm, at least for the photos. Not that the papers know *that*.

"And he's been your constant escort. The papers have had a field day."

She pushes the cup of fruit away, suddenly not hungry. "I didn't know," she says. "I don't read them."

"Well, if you're bringing Don instead of Artie . . ."

"Arnie."

". . . then what are we supposed to think?"

She wonders what else he's seen in the papers.

Their plates arrive, the meat and bun piled artfully with sliced onion, tomato, dill pickle, and a dainty spoonful of slaw. A pile of French fried potatoes, golden brown at the edges, nestles up to the hamburger. Duane busies himself with salt and ketchup, giving her a moment to think.

"He was in Korea," she says. "Arnie was." She takes the onion from her hamburger and separates it into rings. "He's only just gotten back."

148

Duane looks up from his plate. "Why didn't the papers say that? A Hollywood type taking a break from pictures to enlist. They'd eat that up. It sure makes a change from the headlines these days."

She drops the rings of onion in a scatter on her plate. "He didn't enlist, okay? Bum ticker. 4-F. He was there as a war correspondent, this war and the last."

"That's it!" He snaps his fingers. "I recognized the name from more than the Hollywood papers. I was stationed in Tokyo. I remember his articles. He interviewed me once."

Louise straightens. "He did? Wait, you knew Arn?"

"Skinny kid with glasses? Fondness for bow ties? After you buy him a few drinks, he starts singing 'Skip to My Lou'?"

She leans over the two hamburgers, takes Duane's face between her hands, and kisses him soundly on the forehead. He doesn't need to ask if he's got the right guy.

But they've just begun applying themselves to their hamburgers when Duane asks something else. "If everything's good and you're not on the outs, if he's there, back in LA, well then, why are you here?"

She wipes coleslaw from the corner of her mouth. "Sometimes things aren't as easy as that."

"Yesterday, when you were giving me a dressing-down over running off on Mavis, you made it seem that it was exactly that."

"Easy?"

He nods.

She folds her napkin as tight as it can go. "Sometimes

problems are more than marriages and work and busy little households." She squeezes the cloth between her hands. "Sometimes they're about how much of life we can handle. Every once in a while, it's more than fits in our hands."

FRANCIE

Beryl, what would you say if I apologized?

BERYL

(yawning)
For what?

FRANCIE

Oh, I don't know.

BERYL

Can't it wait until morning?

FRANCIE

Maybe.
(waiting for one, maybe two minutes while crickets chirp)
No.
(rolling over on her cot)
I haven't told you the whole truth. About . . . a lot of
things. About important things. And maybe I never
will. But can you forgive me for all of those things
unsaid? Can you trust me on that? . . . Beryl? Beryl?

BERYL

(snoring)

Chapter Nine

1926

Wednesday

. . . .

Lucky I wake up before F every day. I was up at five and in the bathhouse. Sick to my stomach over and over and then just sat on the floor next to the toilet crying until I had nothing left.

I feel wretched and all I want is my C and my AL. Reread his Indianapolis letter forward and back. Why offer all that and then say nothing? Why has he turned my world on end?

Supper: Fried chops and potatoes, bread pudding. (Still galls me to pay for meat of all things.)

Camp Columbia	*25¢*
Gasoline	*$1.52*
Milk, pint	*7¢*
Butter	*49¢*

Eggs	25¢
Bread	71/2¢
Pork chops	541/2¢
Postage stamp	2¢

April 21, 1926

Guilt can be a demon sitting on your chest. I could scarcely breathe last night, thinking about that envelope tucked in my duffel. I don't even know why I did it. I'm not a thief (that long-ago chocolate bar notwithstanding). But I am a liar. I've had years of practice in that. The very fact that I'm writing these words, that I'm swearing I have no idea why I took the letter, that, right there, proves it. Liar.

I didn't sleep last night. I lay in my cot, feeling breathless and heavy and angry and sad. When it got to be too much, I wrapped myself in my blanket and left the tent. I walked, to the edge of town and beyond. I walked until the first fingers of dawn touched the edge of the horizon. I walked until my legs ached and my head felt lighter. I knew I had to give her the letter. No matter that I wanted her to stop thinking about C. No matter that I wanted her to look out the window, look at me, look anywhere but back toward Newark or ahead to Nevada. I had to.

When I got back to the campsite, my skirt and stockings were soaked and E was gone. I changed and brought my journal out to a log by the campfire. The envelope was tucked inside. But E didn't come back. It was early, but other campsites were starting to wake up. I watched the door of the bathhouse, wondering what was taking so long. It could be nothing, but it could be Ethel stretched on the floor beneath the sinks. I was up and ready to head in there after her, when she came out so pink and scrubbed and smiling that I couldn't help but smile back.

I've decided there's no sense in spending the trip worrying about all and everything, she said. It's about the journey, not the destination. She sat right there on the log, so close I could smell the soap she'd used. I'm sorry for being such a Gloomy Gus. She said more, lots more, but I don't remember it all. It didn't matter. None of what she said mattered. She nudged my shoulder and touched my arm and gave me silly apologies.

And just like every time she's near, I couldn't think straight. All I could think about was her.

It's why I left all those years ago. She was marrying Carl and I didn't want to be the friend who would be invited by for baptisms and birthday parties and cold chicken luncheons. Carl would kiss her on the forehead, she'd have a baby on her knee, they'd both offer me another slice of cake. But cake wasn't what I wanted. I'd have to sit across from her at the lace-topped table, sit next to her on the sofa, sit right there and know that what I felt meant absolutely nothing. At least to her. To me, it meant the world.

Thursday

What a day. It made me, for the first time, wish I'd just taken the train to Nevada.

Though that would've meant no F. And I'm not sure if I'd have been willing to give that up. There have been too many years without.

Supper: Fried chicken, scalloped corn, chocolate pudding.

Camp	*50¢*
Gasoline	*44¢*
Chicken	*72¢*
Wrenches, set of 5	*$1.45*
Spark plugs	*47¢*
Tire iron	*59¢*
Tire	*$7.95*
Inner tube	*$1.50*
Tire jack	*$1.55*
American Junior pump	*$4.00*
Johnson's Hastee Patch tape	*50¢*
Tire pressure gauge	*$1.25*
Valve caps	*40¢*
Postage stamp	*2¢*

April 22, 1926

Into the best-laid plans, a wrench appears. In this instance, a literal wrench – and chicken wire and a pump and jack and tire tape, as I've had to buy all of those today. This morning, as we drove, eating our breakfast, we heard a loud bang. The car jolted and lurched off the road. E gave a little shriek and I dropped my biscuit clear down my blouse.

We figured out soon enough what the problem was (apart from crumbs in my brassiere). We'd had a blowout, our very first. Three boys driving a "bug" pulled off to help. They were amazed that we'd made it all the way from NJ with no tire troubles. To hear them talk, they patch a tire at least every other day. They ticked off a terrifying list of things that could (and would) go wrong with our flivver. Tire punctures or blowouts, blown spark plugs, dead batteries, burned-out brake bands and bearings. They took us to task for not maintaining our poor Lizzie. I was in a cold sweat, thinking of all those lonely roads we could have been stranded on.

They gave us a lift to the next town. While I went with them to the hardware store to ferret out wrenches and mallets and whatnot, E went to the grocery for a fryer chicken. Back at the car, the boys helped us fix up the tire. They also cleaned out our spark plugs, tightened our brake bands, and generally gave the flivver a once-over. They followed us ahead to the next campground and E made fried chicken and corn by way of a thank you.

E seems fine as apple pie, but I couldn't go to sleep. The whole thing's shaken me so much. I don't know what it was. Being stranded. Being at a loss. Being beholden to someone else. I've gone through so many years without once owing a man anything. Even a chicken dinner. And yet, today, a whole carful of them needed to swoop in and save us. White knights in a jalopy. It's infuriating, yet more infuriating to see E standing on the side of the road, not knowing when I could get her to a campground. As much as it galls me, as much as it'll keep me up, am glad we limped on ahead. Am glad I know how to keep it from happening again.

Friday

. . . .

Hard driving today and we made it to Kansas City. F has been nervous as a fawn since yesterday's mishap and

157

wanted to find a garage to give the Lizzie a sound checkup. In the meantime I replenished our larder.

She came back with a pint of hothouse strawberries, the name of a good campground outside of town, and two letters from AL. One has a crayon drawing of a spotted pony. If I hold the letters just so, I swear I can see her little fingerprints.

Supper: Salmon croquettes (slightly charred), creamed peas, strawberries with sweet cream.

Camp Hickory Grove	*35¢*
Gasoline	*$1.61*
Celery!	*18¢*
Onions	*17¢*
Peas, four No. 2 cans	*40¢*
Corn, four No. 2 cans	*64¢*
Tomatoes, four No. 2 cans	*28¢*
Salmon, two cans	*64¢*
Postage stamp	*2¢*

April 23, 1926

Made it to Kansas City today. I told E that I wanted to stop at a garage (true), but really I wanted to stop at the post office (truer) before she did (the truest).

The whole drive here today I kept arguing with myself. No, I shouldn't have hidden that letter from Carl back in St Louis. No, I shouldn't keep it in my duffel. No, I definitely shouldn't do it again.

But then, there I was in the Kansas City post office, asking for general delivery for Mrs Carl Wild, and not feeling nearly as awful as I should. There were two each from C and AL. The ones from AL went straight into my pocket, but I stood a moment looking at the two from Carl. He'd learned the same Spencerian script that Ethel and I had in school, but these were addressed in block handwriting, like the sort a butcher would use in lettering signs and price lists. I stared at the envelopes, at the black-inked name and address, and wondered what else was there. Did he pen her name with a sense of wistfulness? Think of her as he formed each E and L? Or were they written with determination, resolve, finality? Hoping that it would be the last time he'd ever write that name again?

When she'd gotten that first letter from him, the one that set her fluttering with hopefulness, I knew she was reading them with rose-colored glasses perched on her nose. I'd read Carl's letter. E was infusing it with a promise not warranted.

What if these were the same? These two in Kansas City and the one I'd pocketed in St Louis. What if they were blunt enough to shatter her illusions? Or, worse, vague enough that she held on to that hope for the next thousand and a half miles, only to have it punctured the moment she stepped onto that Nevada ranch? Holding on to these letters, keeping her from whatever was inside, it was the only way I knew to protect her. It was the only way I knew to keep her heart from breaking, again, all in a rush.

After all, being gradually forgotten was kinder than one grand rejection. It was. I knew it. That's why I let myself drift from Ethel's life all those years ago. It's why I was always "too booked up" when she wanted to make plans. Why I took ages to reply (if at all) to her cheery little postcards. Why I stopped coming by as often and, eventually, stopped coming by altogether.

I was protecting my heart, but I was also protecting hers. How quickly everything would've changed if I'd said to her what I always did in my imagination. If she then said to me what I was sure she would. For our friendship to break in two in one single instant, that would have been more than I could bear.

Later

E was tickled at the letters from AL. About the lack from C, she said nothing.

Mail is cause to celebrate, she said. That, and being in a city with a real grocery store. After we set up camp, she walked to the nearest with a bag and shopping list. And I was left back in the tent with the three letters and not nearly enough guilt.

I stared at them, at that blocky handwriting on the envelope, thinking it looked far too casual for a letter ending one's marriage. Surely that required cursive. Handwriting was for shopping lists and score pads and notes passed across the aisle in school. Was he finally writing something real and intimate? Were these letters exactly what Ethel hoped they were?

Later

I broke down and did it. I couldn't sit there staring at those envelopes, wondering whether or not I was justified in keeping them, wondering whether or not there was really something to protect E from.

So I filled the coffeepot and moved it over the fire. In all the good spy novels, someone always steams an envelope open. It never sounded tricky. In fact, steaming open envelopes – to discover a secret, to stem a betrayal, to intercept a forbidden love affair – always sounded rather romantic on the page.

But it wasn't. It took forever to get the pot boiling, with me holding this sorry little envelope up the whole time. When it did roll to a boil, I burned myself. I had to go and dig through my duffel for a glove, and then both glove and envelope got somewhat sodden with steam and sputtering water. But it did loosen. The envelope opened.

I didn't know what I expected. Dismissals and denials. Apologies. Outpourings of love and regret. Pages of something. But the three letters, lined up damp on my plaid blanket, they weren't anything. They were even shorter than his first, if that was possible. Three notes that, I knew, wouldn't be any kind of salve to her heart.

But I didn't read them, not then, because she burst into my tent with her bag of groceries and excited chatter about all of the astounding deals she'd found (Tomatoes, two cans for twenty-eight cents! I've never seen prices like that in Newark. And, Flor, celery! I've only ever read about it!). I threw myself onto the blanket, across the wet letters, and hoped that the envelopes were kicked far enough under the cot.

I wondered if she'd seen, the way she froze and stopped her babble. The way she just looked at me. But I didn't mean to wake you, she said. And, Why's the kettle going?

I stretched, I yawned, I tried to make it look like, yes, she did just wake me. I was going to surprise you with coffee, I said, and hoped she believed me.

She pushed hair off her eyes. Somewhere in her walk, she'd lost a hairpin. You're always watching out for me, she said. Thank you.

April 16, 1926

Prickly Pear Ranch
Nevada

Dear Ethel,
I wish you'd stop writing so often. Write to Al, by all means, but to me? Eth, hey, it can't be good.

We never were much for letters anyway, the two of us. Remember the time you passed me that note in class, the one with a line of Xs straight across the bottom? We were in eighth grade, I remember, because it was right before I left school. I'd never once gotten a note before then and didn't again. Did you know how I wrestled with my reply? I never did give it to you. In the end, it wasn't worth much.

You wrote a few times when I was overseas. Heartsick soldiers welcome anything. But maybe, even then, we didn't have a thing to say to each other.
  Carl

April 19, 1926

Prickly Pear Ranch
Nevada

Dear Ethel,
Five more letters came from you this morning. Has it really been that long or have you been writing two a day?

You may not think so, but Al hasn't forgotten you these past couple of weeks. She talks a blue streak to the dude wranglers here about anything and everything, including you. She's been learning how to cook, if you can believe that. Fried fish, hash, slumgullion, creamed chipped beef on toast. The kinds of things a bunch of old army vets and cowboys can whip up in a wiped-out fry pan. You'd have kittens at our "kitchen."

Yours is still the best, though. Some days, I wake up thinking of your doughnuts. But, Eth, we have to have more than that. Doughnuts aren't enough. A marriage license isn't enough. I thought it would be. I thought Al would be. But seven years down the road and you dropped the mashed potatoes and I just knew it wasn't.

Carl

Prickly Pear Ranch
Nevada

Dear Ethel,
You keep writing and I don't know what you want
me to say. If I knew it, I'd say it. Do you want me to
say that I've changed my mind? Do you want me to
say that I'm coming home? I'm not. I can't. I don't
want that and I know you really don't either. That one
day, I watched you picking up all the broken pieces of
that bowl and, Eth, I knew if I stayed I'd leave your
heart in just as many pieces on the floor. You may not
believe me, but I care too much to do that.

You can have anything you want. The house on
Elm. Everything in the tin bank. My bicycle. My
Army Wound Ribbon. The painting we got on the
boardwalk. The piano. After all, you bought the
piano. You can have anything. Except, can I ask? Of
everything we've ever shared, can I keep Al?

I know you must've been in a lather when you
saw that I'd left and taken Al. You could've gone
to the police with cries of kidnapping. But you
didn't. You know me and you know Al. You know I
couldn't be apart from her even for a day. And I'm
not saying that you could either. But, Eth, hear me

out. If mothers can have their children to raise all alone, why not fathers? Aren't we allowed to love them full-to-the-top? Can't we have the chance to hold them close as long as they'll let us?

Carl

The car is stopped – dead stopped – in the middle of the road.

BERYL

Why is the expression "stubborn as a mule"?

Both women stare out through the windshield at something in the road.

FRANCIE

You're right. It should be "stubborn as a turkey."

BERYL

They're not even moving. Blow the horn again.

They simultaneously raise up in their seats to get a better look, then sit back down.

FRANCIE

I don't think they even care.

BERYL

Isn't that just stubbornness? Not giving one whit what anyone else thinks.

FRANCIE

You used to be stubborn like that.

BERYL

Are you calling me a turkey?

FRANCIE

Gobble, gobble.

—Excerpt from the unproduced screenplay
When She Was King

Chapter Ten

1952

Since leaving Newark on that one-way bus ticket all those years ago (one-way left no room for cold feet or instant regret), Louise hadn't been far out of Los Angeles. San Diego, once. Bakersfield for a shoot. That single trip across the ocean and back during the last war. That one brief, ecstatic weekend when she and Arnie ran off to Palm Springs with a pocketful of cash and a marriage license.

They'd just finished up *Betsey Barnes, College Girl*. Flush with a big paycheck, Arnie had popped the question. Flush with a renewed contract, she'd kissed him in reply. She borrowed the dress she'd worn in Betsey's last number, a mauve silk ensemble with a swingable chiffon skirt and matching beaded jacket. It was ridiculously inappropriate for a courthouse wedding, even for California, but Louise didn't care. She felt like a princess and, besides, she knew no one was going to check the costume room over the weekend.

They stayed in their hotel room, living off room service. When they finally emerged, on their last day at El Mirador, it was to a rare rainstorm. They were the only ones walking barefoot across the puddled lawn, draped on soaked canvas lounge chairs, kissing beneath the dripping archways around the pool.

She wonders why they never went back.

But the Grand Canyon is unlike anything she's seen. It's not California beach, Nevada desert, Palm Springs resort. It's certainly not New Jersey. She's always had little more than a friendly acquaintance with the Director Up There, but standing on the rim of the canyon, she sees an artistry she never knew existed. She understands the beauty that only eons of patience can bring.

Patience is something she feels short on these days.

The next day, as promised, Duane takes her to see the canyon. While she eats a broiled grapefruit half, beautifully garnished with a maraschino cherry in the center, he arranges for two places on a mule string down Bright Angel Trail.

"They say it's the best way to see it," he tells her. "Even in the winter."

She doesn't ask who "they" are. They probably had brochures.

He leaves her to finish her grapefruit and goes to change. It seems that Duane, ever the soldier, ever prepared, has a pair of cowboy boots for just this occasion. Louise isn't sure what she has in the wicker suitcase for a mule ride in December. Everything she packed is light and gauzy, California pastel, desert airy. She finally settles on a slim pair of black pants and a fitted black jersey top. It has a scoop neck, modest enough while still showing a hint of collarbone. Long-sleeved, which she hopes is warm enough.

She considers her white Keds, but they feel too sporty for her spare ensemble, too suburban for her urban chic. Instead she puts on her flats, bright red against the black of her pants. Her hair, she ties up in a ponytail. She hasn't worn a ponytail in years, at least not since her Betsey Barnes days, but it seems appropriate, somehow. Maybe it's because she's still pretending to be Anna. Maybe it's because she's far from home. Maybe it's because here, where the air stretches for miles, she feels light and young and as hopeful as she did when she was eighteen.

She keeps her makeup light. Powder, rouge, pale lipstick. Eyebrows and lashes dark and neat. A dab of Evening in Paris behind each ear. No accessories but her turquoise bracelet. No hat, no gloves, no handbag. She checks her reflection one last time in the bathroom mirror. Not a frill, not a petticoat, not a feather or bead. She looks simple and fresh. She looks as ready as she'll ever be for a National Park.

When she meets Duane out at the corral, she suddenly sees how wrong she is. The few other women waiting for their tour are wearing riding pants or men's blue jeans. They have canvas jackets over their blouses and thick-soled shoes. Plaid. Lots of plaid.

With her trim black pants and tortoiseshell sunglasses, Louise probably looks like she's headed for a jazz club or a poetry reading. She probably looks like what she is: a frivolous movie star unsuccessfully slumming it for the day. A modern Marie Antoinette. She steps back, to the safety outside the corral, and drops a hand on the wooden rail.

And she's not warm enough. As ugly as they are, she almost envies the plaid flannel and canvas hunting jackets. The back of her neck is cold. The little hint of bare ankle above her flats white and icy. She considers, for half a silly second, going back to the room for her mink.

She doesn't think anyone's noticed her – at least she hopes no one has, this girl who doesn't know how to dress for a mule ride – but Duane spots her from across the corral and waves. He's sitting on a wooden bench changing into his cowboy boots. They're magnificently tooled, with silver studs dotting the sides. He even has on a wide-brimmed hat, just like a real dude wrangler. Maybe he bought it at the park's souvenir shop. Maybe she should've bought one too.

He waves again, but she doesn't move from her spot outside the corral. "Yoo-hoo!" he actually calls.

Some of the others turn at his shout. Maybe, despite the ponytail, they recognize her. Including the guides in their fringed jackets, she counts ten others, men and women. One shields her eyes and peers in Louise's direction. Louise wants to sink into her red flats. Instead she adjusts her sunglasses, as though they hide her from the stares. Maybe they do.

Duane knots the laces of his oxfords together and slings them over his shoulder. He strolls across the corral toward her. "Mules are stubborn," he says, leaning on the gate. "They won't come to you way out here. You have to go to them."

She manages a thin smile, one that she can't keep on her face for very long. "I can't go. I'm sorry."

"Why not? It's booked and everything. No refunds, they said."

"I'll pay you back the eleven dollars."

He tosses his shoes over the rail. "What gives?"

It's funny how, in no time at all, Duane's talking to her like an old friend. Like a little sister. Like the girl next door. She tries to imagine any of the men at the studio, the directors or gaffers or set dressers, looking her in the eye and asking, "What gives?" As long as she can lipstick on a smile, they don't give a damn.

But Duane is resting his elbows on the gate. He's looking her straight in the eyes. He wants to know.

"Well." She hesitates. "I'm not dressed for it."

"They're still saddling up the rest. You have time to change."

She hesitates again. "I don't have anything else."

She waits for him to laugh. It's a bare admission. Actresses always have the right outfit, whatever the occasion. Church? Light wool suit in a muted pastel, a little curve of a veiled hat, gloves, sensible brown pumps. Premiere? Floor-length gown – Dior or Adrian, please – with just a hint of bare shoulders peeking above a stole. Beach? Pedal pushers, wrap blouse, and canvas flats. Meeting where you

173

hope to convince the studio that you're a woman with a brain? Lucky yellow scarf.

Duane must know all of this. And yet he doesn't laugh. "Who forgets to pack their mule-riding duds?" he says with a wink, and she's the one who laughs.

"They're in my other suitcase," she says airily.

"Anyway, you bring a little California to this old corral."

The ladies are still staring, but surreptitiously, over the tops of their mules' heads. Two of the men are openly ogling her leg-skimming pants. She arranges herself behind the rail fence.

"Maybe I don't want to." She tugs on her pants. They show the curve of her calf, the dip behind her knee. "You know what I wore to my very first audition? An evening dress. Big velvet rosette at the waist and everything." She gives a short laugh at the memory. "See, I've had experience sticking out like a sore thumb."

Duane doesn't even think about it. He steps out of his tooled leather boots and hands them over the gate.

She just stares. "I can't take those from you."

He's standing in the dust of the paddock in nothing but his stockinged feet. "They pinch my toes anyhow."

She's sure he's lying, but takes the boots.

They're huge, coming all the way up her calf; she's relieved that the men now have less leg for their viewing pleasure. Duane slips off his heavy socks and passes those across too. "Ball them up. Put them in the toes."

"Really, you don't have to . . ."

"How many guys can say they've given their socks to Louise Wilde?" He grins. "Take the hat too. Please." He

174

doesn't wait for an answer before reaching across and plopping it on her head.

For a moment, she remembers another hat being plopped over another ponytail.

On that very first ride, all those years ago, Mr Steve had given her his hat. It sank down over her eyes, but, astride that placid pony with her new hat, she'd felt like she belonged.

Louise's eyes are suddenly stinging, and she blames it on the dust. She ducks her head and hopes no one notices. He's not giving her the literal shirt off his back, but it's pretty close. As she adjusts the boots, Duane wipes off his bare feet with a handkerchief and puts his oxfords back on.

Then he isn't the only one by her side. A bland-faced woman has crossed the corral and untied a shawl from her shoulders. It's a stiff, plaid affair, something her Oma Wild would have worn. For a moment, Louise is embarrassed. Embarrassed for the shawl, for the plain woman, for the assumption that she needed anything.

But Duane doesn't let her be embarrassed. He thanks the woman and takes the shawl. He knots it around Louise's shoulders. It smells faintly like talcum powder. "Better?" he asks.

She always knows her lines, but there's no script for this. "Yes," she says, and clears her throat. She touches Duane's hand, tightening the knot. "Thank you."

It's been ages since she's been in a saddle, but her body remembers the feeling the moment she's on the back

175

of the soft-eyed mule. Achingly remembers. Before too long, her legs and backside are sore and itchy. Yes, it's been ages.

She got her first speaking role, after all, because she could ride. It had been a singing Western. Not anything as big as a Gene Autry or Roy Rogers, but that type. Cowboys and guitars around bonfires, ballads sung against a prairie backdrop, lively hoedowns featuring far too much gingham. When they'd asked the crowd of girls outside the studio who could ride, her hand had shot up. She hadn't ridden since that stay at the Prickly Pear, when she was Anna Louisa, six years old with dark braids, missing teeth, and far too much gumption. She may have lost the braids, but not the gumption. That's why she elbowed her way to the front of the crowd that day on the lot and swore to the casting director that she could ride like Annie Oakley. It worked. After all, in Hollywood, guts count more than talent.

The plain-faced woman doesn't look like she's ever had a bold moment in her life, but she lets her mule drop back until she's alongside Louise's.

"Excuse me," she says, and tugs a button on her brown jacket. "But are you—"

Louise doesn't wait for her to finish her question. "No," she says. She doesn't want to sit and talk to this woman. She doesn't want to acknowledge the faces turning to stare back at her. She wants to enjoy her thoughts and the sky and the warm saddle beneath her legs.

"But you look just like—"

"I'm sorry," Louise says. "I'm not who you think I am."

She feels almost bad as she says it, seeing the woman's pale face flush as she lowers her eyes. The boldest thing this woman has probably ever done before was use cream of chicken soup in her casserole instead of cream of mushroom. And here she's just ridden up to a Hollywood star with nothing more to offer than a plaid shawl and a question.

Louise should've said yes. Maybe signed an autograph on the corner of the shawl. She used to all the time. Time was she fed off the attention. Lit up like a lightbulb. But here, in this eons-old canyon, she feeds off the peace. For someone used to the bustle of the set, she suddenly craves quiet.

The woman returns to her husband, shaking her head. He says, "I told you so," and now Louise is the one flushing. Duane looks back at her, but doesn't say anything.

As she dips farther and farther down the trail, she tries to forget all of that. The braids, the ranch, the casting call ages ago. The fans and autographs. The way her teeth are chattering. She looks out over the canyon, at the clouds stair-stepping from the tree line below into a sky that stretches up forever. No backstory is as big as that sky.

There's nothing but the jingle of mule bells, the creaking of saddles, the clomp of hooves on the sliding rock. No one talks as they wind their way down the trail. The curious look up at the sky or to where the buildings have disappeared along the rim. The bold look over the edge. The nervous look straight ahead at their mules' twitching ears.

Louise, she looks at a bird. A hawk, an eagle, she doesn't know. Something that soars up from the trees below, higher and higher, flexing muscles. Weightless. Effortless. She envies him.

Life hasn't felt so effortless in a long while. Back when she stood tiptoed at the edge of her future, catching each new role as it was offered, glowing under the lights, things had seemed simple. She had her career stretching before her. She had her marriage. Both as easy as breathing. When had things gotten so hard?

They pass a low branch of a scrubby pine, dusted with old snow. She hasn't seen snow in a dozen years or so. There's hardly any around her, just a dusting on the trail that starts to disappear as they wind farther down, but she can smell it. It smells so cold and clean, the way LA never does. She reaches up until her fingers brush needles. They come away icy and tingling.

Duane rides in front of her. He looks even taller on a mule, and uncomfortable, his legs stuck out at awkward angles. He'd pulled himself up on the mule with a John Wayne swagger. He'd wanted to impress her. As she watches him now, bouncing with his bare ankles white above his oxfords, she feels a sudden affection.

She runs fingertips across the mule's stiff mane. Beneath her fingers, the animal quivers. Everything about him – his mane, his neck, his sweaty flanks – is warm. Louise feels it through the backs of her legs. Sweat pools behind her knees.

Duane turns his head and says something to her over his shoulder. The wind cresting down the canyon snatches his words away. Was he asking if she liked the ride? Hated it? Wanted a drink of water? She nods, without knowing what she's nodding to. She's too warm and drowsy to care.

It feels like they've been riding for hours, for days, for weeks, but the sun hasn't moved much beyond the rim of the canyon above. She left her gold Longines back up in the room. Here, time seems to move at its own pace.

The trail narrows, curves close to the edge. Ahead, the woman in the brown jacket gives a quick little cry. Louise almost laughs at her – almost – but then her own mule steps a moment too near to the trail's edge. A stone goes skittering down. She nearly screams. She nearly pulls back on the reins, nearly pushes in her heels, nearly does whatever she can to get the mule to stop.

But she doesn't. She lets go of the reins with one hand and presses it to her chest. She feels her heartbeat beneath her fingertips. *One, two, three, four, five, six, seven, eight, nine, ten.* When she gets to ten, she lets go with the other hand. She stretches both out, like a ballerina. She balances on the back of the mule and she looks out over the edge.

Because, at that moment, of course, she's no longer Louise Wilde. She's little Anna with the braids and the gumption who did the hard things, the brave things, exactly because they terrified her.

It's steep, right alongside the trail. Almost a sheer

drop here. It's green, so green, a snow-speckled carpet unfolding down one side of the canyon and up the other. Trees, she realizes, finally, belatedly. Trees so far away that they look like bushes. Trees that, from up here, are nothing but a smear of color against the bottom of the canyon.

The trail is a jagged line of brown through all that green, winding like a snake's track in the sand, meandering like a snail's silvery path across the windowsill. It zigzags until it disappears into the viridian. She never knew the bottom of anything could be so far away. In a place so vast, her own problems feel so small.

The bird she was watching before soars up again, spiraling on a burst of air. Or maybe it's a different bird. Maybe that's all they do, every last one of them. Spend their days floating in the wide space between the canyon walls. It looks so easy. Arms still outstretched, like an eagle, she leans forward in her saddle.

Duane turns around again, but when he sees her, he stops smiling. "Hey!" he cries, twisting in his saddle. "Hold on, will you?"

Automatically, she takes the reins again. She's not a bird. They have feathers to hold them up. She has nothing but dreams that are quickly losing air.

When the mule train set off, she wondered whether Duane would lead his mule in front of or behind hers. In front, he'd be the one who leads the way, puts down the trail, directs her where to go. Behind, he'd watch to be sure she doesn't fall off the edge. Arnie always went behind, when they were bike riding or climbing up to the

Hollywood Sign. "I'll always be there to catch you," he'd say. "Lou, I won't let you fall."

She doesn't have feathers; she never will. But maybe she still has Arnie.

She's drained when she gets back to the El Tovar. Duane doesn't notice. He wants a flat iron steak and potatoes.

"Not hungry?" he asks, when she stops at the entrance of the dining room and passes him the cowboy hat. "Not even for a hamburger? My treat."

She shakes her head, but she's too tired to even force a smile. More than anything, she wants to be alone.

Duane hesitates for a moment. "Meet for a drink after dinner?" He asks it casually, too casually, and then adds, "Or . . ."

He leaves the word hanging, and she knows exactly what he means by it. She's heard too many "ors" in her life. *Sure, you could go wait in line with the other girls. Or . . . Louise, sweetheart, do you really want to stay in the chorus? Or . . . I can drop you off by your place on my way home. Or . . .*

"I'm heading out in the morning," she says, fumbling for a polite refusal. "I really should turn in."

For a second she thinks he's going to repeat the "or," maybe adding more after the word, embarrassing them both.

But he doesn't. "If I didn't ask, I'd always wonder. You know?" His Adam's apple bobs.

She doesn't answer.

"Anyway, I'm sorry. I shouldn't have. I was thinking . . .

181

Well, who the hell cares what I was thinking. I just shouldn't have."

Maybe he shouldn't have. But he's the first in a long line of "ors" who had apologized. The first who didn't seem to expect her to actually say yes.

"I don't think you would've known what to do with a 'yes' anyway," she says lightly.

This draws out that boyish grin. "I'm a man, so of course I'm supposed to say, 'The hell I wouldn't,' but maybe you're right."

"Your boots," she says, and bends to slip them from her feet, but Duane stops her with a gesture.

"Keep them. Consider them my fan letter to you, Louise."

"I'm going to call Arnie." She touches Duane on the cheek, just once. "You should think about calling Mavis."

He smiles, ruefully and maybe even sadly, then nods. She watches while he walks into the dining room.

"I'd like to place a call to Los Angeles," she says to the desk clerk. "Please have the operator keep ringing back until there's an answer." She scribbles down the number and slides it across the desk.

"Something to drink while you're waiting for the call?" he asks.

She wants to say "Yes, a Manhattan." She almost does. But "Nothing" is what she says, then adds, "Maybe coffee."

The plaid shawl comes off. In the corner is sewn a tag from Montgomery Ward. She begs a piece of paper from the clerk and writes: *Thank you for lending your shawl.*

You are kinder than most. Louise Wilde." She rolls the note up and tucks it beneath the loop of the tag.

She folds the shawl up and slides it across the counter to the desk clerk. "A guest lent this to me earlier."

"Of course. What is her name?"

"I don't know. She looked like Flora Robson." This elicits a nod of understanding. "Would you see that she gets this?"

"Of course."

She doesn't have to wait long for the connection to go through. Amazingly. Before she's walked the length of the lobby, a uniformed boy comes to her with a phone in hand, trailing the cord behind him. She almost drops the cup of coffee. The boy swiftly takes it before passing over the phone.

"Arn?" she asks, cradling the receiver against her ear. "It's really you?"

"Who else do you expect to answer the phone in our house?" He sounds peevish. She doesn't care.

She edges around a massive lighted Christmas tree. She carries the phone over to a chair in the corner and sets it on her lap. "Guess where I am?"

It's a silly question. She realizes it the moment it leaves her mouth. "The operator said the El Tovar."

She should've asked how he was doing. If he'd eaten today. If he'd changed his pajamas. "I'm at the Grand Canyon. I've never been. Have you?"

On the other end of the line, he's quiet.

"I took a mule ride. Can you believe it? Me, on a mule? I wore boots and everything." She knows she's just babbling, but she finally has him on the phone. She doesn't want to let him go. "The canyon goes on for miles. For forever, maybe. To look across onto the rock and the river below and see nothing but what nature's built . . . Well, it's peaceful to see. It's like the ocean, but right here on land. Do you know what I mean?"

The line crackles, but then he finally says, "I think I do."

His voice has lost a bit of its peevishness. She tries to imagine where he is right now. Maybe at his desk. Maybe he's been reading or just sitting with a drink in hand, the way she had so many evenings. Ice clinking. Or maybe he's talking on the kitchen phone, while he's making himself scrambled eggs or a fried bologna sandwich.

"What are you having for supper tonight?"

She swears she hears him sigh. "Saltines."

"You can't live on crackers." She straightens in the chair. "You should make some eggs. Fry up some liver. There should be some in the Coldspot. I might have cheese for a rarebit. You can make toast." There's probably not much in the refrigerator. She closes her eyes and tries to picture what she might've left in the pantry. "Deviled ham. Fruit cocktail. Or just warm up a can of soup. There should be some on the top shelf of the pantry."

But as she's picturing the red Campbell's cans on the shelf, she's suddenly picturing Arnie trying to reach them, from his wheelchair, and she realizes why he's so silent on the other end of the line.

"I'm an idiot," she says softly. "I'm sorry."

"I can reach the crackers," he says.

Even if she'd stocked the lower shelves for him, he can't

reach up to the toaster oven. He can't fill a pot up from the sink. He can't cook on the stove without catching his sleeve on the flame.

There, in the lobby of the El Tovar hotel, her eyes fill with tears. She turns toward the wall and wipes at them with the cuff of her shirt. It comes away streaked with buff powder.

"I was in such a hurry to get out the door, I didn't leave anything for you to eat. I didn't even *think* about that." Tears are soaking through her sleeve and running down her face to her chin. She'd borne the past few days of travel – the empty gas tank, Mr Steve, the suspension, the nights of loneliness – but this right here, and she's crying right onto the lobby phone. "I'll turn around. I'll start driving back tonight. I'll probably get there late tomorrow, but I'll make you meatloaf or hash or spaghetti and meatballs. Piles of them. I'll make whatever you want."

He doesn't say anything and, for a moment, she's worried he's hung up.

But then, quietly, he finally asks, "So why aren't you in Vegas?"

She holds the phone away and sniffs. "Not in Vegas?" Her tears slow. "It's not important now."

"But you were going to go. You were all set to do it. And now you're in Arizona, riding mules?"

Spending the day riding mules and eating a picnic lunch with ten strangers and Duane. While her husband sits at home eating crackers and, probably, drinking days-old coffee.

"It's not important now." Her drive across the country, to

eat Christmas dinner, to ask Dad if he'd divorced Mom – it all sounds so selfish now. "I was going to go visit my dad – for Christmas, you know – but he won't miss me. I'll go to pack up and head back . . ."

"You should go."

His voice is so low, she wonders if she heard him correctly.

"You should go," he says again. "To New Jersey."

"But I . . ."

"You haven't been home in years."

"Home." There's that word again. But this time, she doesn't think of snow and pine trees and carols at Dad's piano. She hears "home" and thinks of last Christmas, when she strung lights around the fan palm in the backyard and Arnie cooked two beautifully rare steaks on the barbecue. Just the two of them, lying barefoot on the hammock, singing Christmas carols up to the stars.

Maybe he's thinking the same thing. Maybe. Because he asks, "You will come back, won't you?"

She smiles through her tears and wipes her eyes again. "I can't stay in New Jersey forever."

Through the crackle of the line, she hears, "Don't."

And suddenly, that's all she needs. "I'll call Pauline. She'll bring hot food over. I don't want you to fade away to nothing."

"All right."

"Remember to do your exercises. You know you're supposed to."

"Lou . . ."

"And if the studio calls, tell them to get bent."

186

She imagines he's smiling. "I will."

"Is that all? Oh, water the African violet in the kitchen."

"Lou." He hesitates. "Just come home?"

Arnie, you're *home,* she wants to say. "I promise."

Francie and Beryl lie on a blanket beneath a sky overflowing with stars.

FRANCIE

(wondering)
There isn't room up there for heaven.

BERYL

You can't say things like that, Fran. Heaven's always there. It has to be.

FRANCIE

Maybe it's beyond the stars. Up to where the universe is black like velvet.

BERYL

Not dark. It's clouds and light and ice cream.

FRANCIE

Whatever it is, it's quiet, I'll bet.

BERYL

(moving an inch closer)
Just like here?

FRANCIE

(moving an inch closer)

Just like here.

—Excerpt from the unproduced screenplay
When She Was King

Chapter Eleven

1926

Saturday

. . . .

F was a perfect grump this morning. Rushed me through breakfast. I burned my hand on the coffeepot.

I'm the one separated from her daughter. I'm the one on the edge of divorce. I'm the one who aches every morning, from ankle to hip, who swills Vigor Tonic like a drunk with her bottle. What does she have to be grumpy about?

Supper: Salmon patties with celery sauce, toast.

Camp	*25¢*
Gasoline	*$1.30*
Postage stamp	*2¢*

April 24, 1926

Woke up to a throbbing tooth. That same old molar that's been giving me trouble. I thought it had gotten better, but now it's shooting pain again. It's awful. I hate the thing.

I gargled with some salt water and took some aspirin, but they only halfway worked. I still had that bottle of hooch I bought in St Louis and used it to wash down another aspirin. All I wanted to do was get to the next campground and go back to sleep.

Of course, today, of all days, Ethel wanted to putter about the campsite, boiling up eggs and making cheese sandwiches for lunch. It's a beautiful morning, isn't it? she chirped. It was disgusting. I didn't want to sit a second longer. And I definitely didn't want a sandwich.

Later

E made me some sort of fancy dinner. Salmon patties topped with celery and white sauce. I've never had celery before. She said she wanted to cheer me up. Of course I felt like a heel. Later, while digging through my duffel for pajamas, I spotted Carl's letters. Now I feel like an even bigger heel. I put myself to bed with aspirin and hooch.

Sunday

It was raining when we woke up, the kind that AL always calls "frog rain," where it's drizzly and puddly, the sort of weather frogs and worms feel quite at home in.

Aches nudged me awake early today. Ankle. Hip. Everything in between. Took a little extra Vigor Tonic. It gave me enough of a push to get out of bed and limp to the bathhouse.

F an absolute bear again this morning.

Supper: Molasses baked beans + cornbread.

Camp	*25¢*
Gasoline	*$1.30*
Eggs	*28¢*
Postage stamp	*2¢*

April 25, 1926

Tooth worse today. I'd been hoping that it was just a little inflammation, but I can feel it all through my cheek. I think the dreadful thing has to come out. I want to cry. I've already lost two others. It's like I'm eight again, losing teeth left and right. At twenty-eight, it's no longer as cute.

Later

Raining an obnoxiously steady drizzle today, which didn't at all help my mood. We ended up not driving as far. E didn't mind one bit. Used the early stop to cook up some beans and cornbread. She pushed a bowl in my direction and said, Your favorite, just as I bit down on a dried bean not quite softened. Pain down through my shoulder. I know I shouldn't have (believe me, I know I shouldn't have), but I snapped, You don't see me in years and you think you know my favorite? As if it was her fault I disappeared from her life for seven years. As if it was her fault I had a toothache.

I tried to apologize, I swear, but the words stuck to the roof of my mouth, and she went off to bed without eating a bite.

I opened my duffel just to look at Carl's letters. I'm the worst sort of friend.

Monday

· ·

F saw a dentist today. Came back one tooth lighter. Made her warm custard for dinner. What else could I do?

Supper: Custard, a whole potful.

Camp	*25¢*
Gasoline	*$1.00*
Dentist	*$2.50*
Cream, pint	*12¢*
Cinnamon	*27¢*
Postage stamp	*2¢*

April 26, 1926

Oh sweet relief! Of course I'm sorer than a dairy cow, but THAT TOOTH is gone. The dentist said it was bad in there, but fixable. He checked over my jaw, but no decay. Thank God. A few days (and a few nips from the flask the dentist slipped me) and I'll be right as rain.

Custard for dinner, so I know E has forgiven me my bad humor. Bless her.

Tuesday
· ·

F says cross her heart her toothache is better, but her right cheek is swollen like a chipmunk's and I saw her slip some aspirin. Maybe she's angling for more pudding?

Supper:—

Gasoline   *44¢*

April 27, 1926

My dratted throat hurts. The dentist I saw yesterday swore up and down that it was just a toothache that was the problem and nothing more, but of course I worry. How can I not? Before I left New Jersey, Dr Hunt told me what to watch out for. Tooth decay that reached my jaw. Joint pain. Anemia. Aching bones. Broken bones. He said I was lucky so far, said the other girls who'd been in to see him, the ones who'd ended up in the hospital (or worse), had never had "just a toothache." He wrote it all down, all those terrifying words like "necrosis" and "cancer" and "probable outcome" for me to give to my new doctor in California. If I made it that long.

While E made breakfast, I sat by the fire flicking my Djer-Kiss compact open and shut, until E took it away and pushed a mug of coffee into my hand instead. Not that I'd know what I was looking for. What does necrosis of the jaw really look like? Would I feel it clear down to my throat?

Later

Stopped for lunch and it's not even eleven. My throat feels like razors and I'm hot all over. Rode the last ten miles with the window flaps tied open.

Wonder if E would make me more custard. It's ambrosia.

Later

Can't drive anymore. Can't hardly

Wednesday—
. . . .

Thursday—
. . . .

Friday
. . . .

Have spent the past few days in a hospital chair. The nuns give me the boot at night and I have to leave her side. I've been sleeping in the car, wrapped in her sweater.

She's peaceful now. Am content to just watch her sleep.

Saturday

· ·

The doctor called it Ludwig's angina, as if I'm supposed to know what that means. An infection in her mouth and throat that made it hard for her to breathe. She was fine one minute, scribbling in her little notebook, and then collapsed the next, flushed and gasping. Someone helped me bring her to the hospital. Angina, the doctor said. Because of that damned tooth.

I've never been so scared in all my life, not even when AL fell into the swimming pool at Olympic Park.

Sunday

· ·

When they first brought her into the hospital, it was queer. All blue around the lips, she dug in her pocket and thrust a piece of paper at the doctor. I didn't know what it was, but the doctor shook his head. "No, none of those," he said, and Florrie let herself fall asleep after that. It was like it was a relief to her.

Later, I looked in her pocket for the paper. It was from a New York City dentist, a Dr Hunt. I didn't understand it. It was some sort of medical record. Symptoms, treatments, possible outcomes. It had her name on top, but it said "diagnosis of radium poisoning," so it couldn't have been hers. It was just a toothache. Wasn't it?

Monday

· ·

So much better today. She asked for clean pajamas. I realized I hadn't changed in days. When I told her, and about sleeping in the car, she said, "Oh, Eth!" and sent me to find a campground.

Don't know if I can do it without her.

Supper: Can of soup, half-warmed.

Camp	*25¢*
Soup	*12¢*
Ride to campground	*$1.00*

May 3, 1926

Finally have this little book back in my hands. E brought my duffel by. I sent her away after then. She's been here every day since it happened. She needed to rest. Maybe I did too.

I've spent the past few days feverish and cold, angry and scared, and also embarrassed. Eth had ridden with me in an ambulance. She'd watched me lying in a hospital bed, bleeding and weeping pus. She's seen me use a bedpan. I smell like boric acid and carbolic solution.

But it's not just that. She was the one I was worried about. Watching her limping and swallowing aspirin. I was thinking of her, and so I let a bad tooth go for too long, I ignored signs of an infection; I collapsed. I did everything

Dr Hunt told me not to. And all because I was more worried about E than myself.

Maybe it would've been better if she'd never come along.

Tuesday

· ·

Slept in late. Bought a bouquet on the way to the hospital.

Supper: Can of soup (tomato), eaten straight from the pot.

Camp	*25¢*
Soup	*12¢*
Dozen roses	*96¢*

May 4, 1926

Why did I write that? That I wished she'd never come along? Must be lingering morphine. I missed her all night.

The ward sister, Sister Benedict, helped me freshen up. A sponge bath, my Chinese pajamas, a pat of Djer-Kiss powder. She combed my hair and braided it, with a coral-colored ribbon on the end. I chewed Sen-Sen to cover up the bitter smell of strychnine on my breath. I hoped E wouldn't notice my sticky bandage, my flushed face, my hospital bed.

When she came in, it was with a little bunch of pink dollar-a-dozen roses. No one had ever brought me flowers before. She came in almost shyly, with the flowers clutched to her chest, and a blue-checked dress on that I hadn't seen her wear before.

She sat and, for a few minutes, we didn't have much to say. The sisters bustled between the beds, straightening sheets, changing dressings, talking in low voices. E and I just sat without a sound, she fidgeting with the flowers that she'd still forgotten to give me, me fidgeting with my blanket.

I finally asked her how the campground was. Fine, she said. Splendid. I have a site under an elm. She didn't say any more for a moment, and I started picturing it and wondering how she ever set it up. How she ever got to the campground in the first place when she didn't know how to drive the T.

She must've seen the question in my face because she said, Drat it, someone drove me there. Okay? A kid, who ran up the curb twice. I paid him a dollar for driving me, which is probably far too much, but I didn't know what else to do. I saw then that her eyes were smudged gray underneath and her hair was only halfway combed. She might not be in a hospital bed, but she wasn't aces. It's too dark and quiet without you, she said. Those tents are too big for one.

Wednesday

• •

Asked F today about that piece of paper from her pocket from that city doctor. I wish I hadn't.

Supper: Soup (pea). A little bit.

Camp	*25¢*
Soup	*12¢*

199

May 5, 1926

Ethel didn't know. She knew she was sick, she knew it was worse than her doctor said, but she didn't know it was radium poisoning. She didn't know she might be dying.

I told her what Dr Hunt had told me, about all of the other girls who came in with infected teeth and rotting jaws, all girls who'd once worked right alongside us for the US Radium Corporation. Mary, Dotty, Helen, Ruth. Others whose names I'd forgotten. Two dead already. More on their way there.

She told me everything she'd been feeling. The dizziness. The sore hip. The broken ankle that never quite healed right. Here I'm the one in the hospital, but I know, I know that she's the one with bones full of radium. And then she shows me the tonic her idiot doctor prescribed and I recognized the name as one Dr Hunt warned me against. Parson's Vigor Tonic is what she's been drinking, every time she's had a bad night. But I know, oh God, it's really just radium water.

She cried. I'm sure I didn't present it the best way. And the hospital setting, all of the nuns and white sheets and bottles of medicine, probably didn't help. I'd known for weeks that I was dying. That all those days I dipped the brush in radium paint and pointed my lips with it were just letters on my tombstone. I'd known for weeks, but Ethel, she'd only learned. And she had more to lose than I did.

Thursday

· ·

Wrote to C today. Just C. Told him everything F said about
the radium. That it was still there, in my bones, all these
years later. That it was the thing making me sick.

If he knows, will he leave Nevada and come home? If he
knows, will he bring AL back to me? Everything's changed.
Even he can see that.

Supper: Another red-and-white can. Vegetable-beef.

Camp	*25¢*
Soup	*12¢*
Postage stamp	*2¢*

May 6, 1926

*E left the hospital yesterday looking dazed, bewildered, halfway
awake. I knew she'd probably be up half the night crying. I
wanted to follow her right out that door. I wanted to hold her
until she stopped.*

*But even if I could, would she want me to? All she wanted
was to reunite with her husband and daughter. And yet I've
spent the past weeks mooning over her, lying to her, keeping
things from her. So many secrets. The hidden disease, the
hidden letters, the hidden . . . love. And when I finally confess
one, it's that I'm dying and maybe she's dying too. It's a small
wonder she left in shock.*

Maybe she cried half the night, but she wasn't the only one. Of course I did too. It was easier when I thought I was going away alone to California. Maybe I had only days left, weeks, months, but in that time, I could do something, I could be a writer. I'd grown up watching the sun rise over one ocean. I'd end things watching it set over the other. But now Ethel was part of it. I cried because she was sick too. I cried because she missed AL. I cried because I'd lose her in the end, one way or the other. I cried because I thought I'd said goodbye to her back on her doorstep with mashed potatoes on my shoes, and now I would have to do it all over again.

Friday

F's fever up again.

Supper:—

Saturday

Still high. Held her nightgown while the nurse sponged her down with alcohol. She's so much thinner than I remember.

Supper:—

Sunday

Still high. The ward sister let me stay the night, just

holding F's hand. Brought me strong tea and toast after the others fell asleep.

Supper: Toast.

Monday
. . . .

Woke up stretched across the foot of F's bed. She was sitting up eating a dish of ice cream.

She's chasing me out again, to eat, wash, change, sleep. Maybe while I'm at the campground I'll empty out her duffel and do laundry.

Supper: Hot dog and potato salad at the next campsite over.

Camp (4 days)	*$1.00*
Ben Hur laundry soap, 10 bars	*24¢*

May 10, 1926

E came back fresh and scrubbed. She was wearing a gray blouse tucked into, of all things, a pair of knickers. Borrowed them from the gals next door, she said. The rest of our things are drying on the line. I asked her which things, and she said All, and I must have looked panicked, because she said, I took all your crumpled things from your duffel. I must've sounded like a scratched record, asking Which things again, but she touched my hand, just once, and said again, All.

She found the letters from Carl, the ones that I'd hidden. She'd read them, all alone by the campfire, without me to offer shallow excuses. As she told me all of this, I closed my eyes, waiting for a slap or a denunciation, but nothing. She sat quietly by my bed until I opened my eyes and burst out with a string of apologies. I was never very good at making apologies, but Eth, she was always the best at listening to them. It was like talking to a priest. In the end, she kissed my forehead, and I glowed with her forgiveness.

She'd brought the letters with her, tucked in a pocket. They were much creased, either from her rereading or mine. I knew they weren't going to be love letters, she confessed. But I thought they'd hurt more than they did.

She told me he wasn't wrong. Things have been peaceful, but maybe peacefulness wasn't what they needed. They didn't argue, she said. They didn't shout and throw dishes. Not once. They didn't even disagree. But without fighting, there was no kissing and making up. I wasn't sure I wanted to hear. He kisses me on the forehead before we go to bed, she said, but that's as romantic as it gets.

Sister Benedict brought me more ice cream right then and Ethel dropped her voice. Nuns probably didn't want to hear about kisses, on the forehead or otherwise. Carl always said that he didn't think there'd ever be a girl wanting to marry him, but then I wrote to him when he was in France and he thought maybe I would. She shrugged and slumped in her chair. Maybe I should've known, when he stepped off that boat and gave me a handshake. Who brings home a handshake from France? We're friends, and maybe I shouldn't have expected any more than that.

She'd never talked at all about their courtship. Never talked about the days leading toward their marriage. I just remember Carl came home from the war and suddenly the two of us weren't alone any longer. It was the three of us again. She seemed happy at the return to routine, but it left a bitter taste on the back of my tongue. I'd grown used to the days with just Ethel and me. I'd have been happy with those for the rest of forever. Why wasn't she? What did she want that I couldn't give her?

Well, AL, for one. Maybe that was it. Maybe she married for a child. She wouldn't be the first woman and won't be the last. But then for Carl to take that child away. He really is the best of fathers, she said. You'd understand if you saw the two of them together. They're thick as thieves, best friends until the end. She sits on his lap at the piano and they play "Alexander's Ragtime Band." She's probably having the time of her little life. I thought back to all the enthusiastic letters AL has been sending, peppered with capital letters and far too many exclamation points. She misses her mom, or she wouldn't be writing so often, but she is happy. For E's sake, I'm grateful for that.

She didn't cry, but she did look pensive. I was content, you know. Married to Carl. Content. But is that the same as happiness? I don't know.

I didn't know either. I'd been content for all of these years alone, but now she was back in my life and my heart fluttered and I wondered the same thing.

You know what, Flor? she asked. Carl never held my hand. Not once. Can you believe it? Maybe that should have told me something.

My ice cream was melting; I'd forgotten about it during this hushed conversation, these confessions about a complicated marriage. I divided the ice cream in half and took up another spoon from my medicine tray. Eth, I said, if I were Carl, I would've held your hand the moment I stepped off the boat. I don't know that I ever would've let it go.

I said it in a rush, because I didn't know what else to say. I'd been listening without anything to offer in return. Maybe I shouldn't have said it. Ethel flushed and I bit my tongue. But she took the bowl from me and spooned up a bite of ice cream.

Remember when Carl mentioned the note I passed him in class, the one with a row of Xs across the bottom? She licked her spoon and didn't meet my eyes. It was the day after we went to Coney Island, the three of us, and you two dragged me onto Shoot the Chutes in Luna Park. Remember how scared I was?

Of course I remembered. Somehow poor Ethel ended up alone on the very front seat with Carl and me behind her. As the car tipped over the top, she reached behind and caught up both of our hands, squeezing them all the way until we hit the water at the bottom.

The note said, "Holding your hand, I suddenly wasn't as scared. Almost didn't let go at the bottom." She finally looked up from her ice cream. Carl opened the note, but, Flor, I wrote it for you.

BERYL

Conversation is so easy with you.

FRANCIE

It's because you already know all of my best punch lines.

BERYL

"Best"?

FRANCIE

(after sticking her tongue out)
It's because we've known each other for so long.

BERYL

I've known Cal just as long and it's not this easy.

FRANCIE

Well, of course not. He's a man.

BERYL

What does that have to do with anything?

FRANCIE

Women are different. We understand the way men never could. We hold on to friendships with our fingernails. We love fiercely and absolutely, but we know just how to wound. When we talk to one another, it's with our hearts.

You're right. You do have the best punch lines.

—Excerpt from the unproduced screenplay
When She Was King

Chapter Twelve

1952

When Louise first met Arnie, it was through a folded note passed across a library table.

"Didn't know a girl could look so pretty reading The Grapes of Wrath.*"*

She'd just started filming *High Noon Hootenanny*. It was her first real role, the singing Western she'd climbed on a horse for. After leaving the studio lot, she wanted nothing more than to sit in the quiet of the Wilshire library. She didn't need winks or ill-placed sentiments.

She took a pencil stub from her little handbag and flipped his note over.

"Didn't know a guy could look so pretty reading Tarzan the Magnificent.*"*

Without looking up, she pushed it across the table and went back to her book.

When the note came back, it said, *"Well, at least you think I'm pretty."*

She'd looked up then. He wasn't, really. Not in a Hollywood sort of way. Too skinny, with thick glasses and a crooked bow tie. But behind the lenses of the glasses, his eyes were blue like oceans. He smiled, showing a single dimple. "Hiya. I'm Arnie," he whispered.

This earned him a stern look from the librarian. He tore another sheet from his notebook.

"I'm Arnie. I'm a writer."

"You could've fooled me."

The next day, he was back. This time, when he pushed the folded note across the table, it was with a purple tulip. She ignored it and kept to her reading.

The next day, it was with a See's chocolate sitting on top of the paper. She ate the chocolate and kept reading.

The next, the note was folded on top of a green-bound screenplay. Finally, then, she looked up. Over the top of his bow tie, Arnie was looking somewhat smug. She opened the note.

"It's not Grapes of Wrath, but it's a movie. If you read it and show up at the studio at ten tomorrow, you have yourself a screen test."

She lifted the note to look at the typewritten title on the front. "MGM presents *Betsey Barnes,* Screenplay by Richard Rachmann, Sidney Weller, and Arnold Bates."

"PS Told you I was a writer."

Writer or not, she had no idea how he'd arranged for a screen test.

But she didn't care. She took that screenplay home, no questions asked, and read it up and down, forward and back. Before ten o'clock, she *knew* Betsey, as silly as she was. And she got the part. Maybe because the studio had already seen the rushes for *High Noon Hootenanny.* Maybe because she'd had a chance to study the script, the story, the character. Maybe because, in this whole city, a stranger had given her a helping hand.

When she found him in the library the next time, he was the one reading *The Grapes of Wrath.* She'd brought her own notepaper this time.

"How did you know I was an actress?"

"Isn't every girl in Hollywood?"

"My roommate is a hatcheck girl . . ."

". . . who wants to be an actress."

She looked up from the notepaper with a glare.

He licked his pencil.

"It was the way you were reading The Grapes of Wrath. *You weren't just enjoying it; you were trying to know it."*

And who wouldn't? The biggest book of the year. Winning awards left and right. The *Pulitzer,* for Pete's sake. That movie would make whoever was cast.

"It's already in production, you know," he wrote. *"They're out filming in the desert. You're too late."*

Her disappointment must've been obvious, because he reached across the table. Not quite touching her, but right there.

"You know," she scribbled furiously, *"I won't go out with you for getting me that screen test. Even if you ask."*

"I know."

"The ladder to the stars isn't runged by men with good intentions."

"I know."

"I climb on my own merits. Good actresses do."

"I know."

"Do you want to go to dinner sometime?"

"Yes."

The day after she leaves the El Tovar, Louise reaches Santa Rosa, New Mexico. She'd been seeing signs for Santa Rosa's Club Cafe for miles, with the face of a smiling fat man and advertisements for sourdough biscuits or chicken-fried steak. But when she approaches the town, that's not what she notices. There's a rail bridge over the Pecos River, and she swears she's seen it before.

She parks and gets out. Walks around the car. Something about it is familiar. Something that doesn't involve a ramshackle divorce ranch down the way. It's when she puts her thumbs and index fingers into the shape of a box, looks through them at the bridge, like a tiny, distant movie screen, that she remembers.

A few minutes later, she's installed in the Club Cafe, awaiting her first taste of chicken-fried steak, and she asks the waitress, "*The Grapes of Wrath* was filmed here, wasn't it?"

The waitress looks bored, even for Santa Rosa, New Mexico. Her name tag reads "Bette," just like the actress. "I never saw it." She straightens a pair of rhinestone glasses. "If it doesn't have Tyrone Power, I'm not interested."

"I recognized the bridge from the movie. They filmed it in '39."

"How old do you think I am?" Her hair is bleached platinum, her eyes behind the glasses caked with makeup. Louise has no idea.

"You would've noticed the crew in town. The cameras? The stars? An old overloaded jalopy?"

"Oh, that one? Yeah, maybe I remember it. They filmed by the gas station and out by the bridge, I think." She opens Louise's bottle of Coca-Cola. "You want a straw?"

"You know, I was almost in that movie," Louise says. "In *The Grapes of Wrath*." The truth is stretched so thin she wonders that the waitress can't see the light shining through the other side. "Or, at least I should've been in it."

"Sure, you should've." Bette pops her gum. "You and Tyrone Power."

The steak is hot and fried crisp, with a peppery coating. It's drenched in a creamy gravy, with a mile-high biscuit perched on the side of the plate. She almost sends the plate back because of the gravy alone. But it smells divinely decadent and she didn't bother to see if they had cottage cheese on the menu.

It *is* divinely decadent. She cuts the steak as fast as she can. She can count on one hand how often she's eaten beef in the past year. And to think she'd grown up the daughter of a butcher.

They'd done pretty well during the Depression, Dad and she. She'd been in charge of cooking during the week. Other girls her age were out playing potsy or hanging around the penny candy shop while she was flubbing her way through Mom's old cookbooks. Cottage pie. Shrimp wiggle. Decidedly odd-shaped croquettes. Rinktum tiddy. She'd learned a few things from Mr Steve and the other dude wranglers. How to make creamed chipped beef on

214

toast, chili con carne, slumgullion stew. How to work up an appetite for just about anything that came off the stove.

Come Sunday, Dad would make one of his mother's German recipes. Sauerbraten or schnitzel or some other cut of meat swimming in sauce. The shop wasn't as busy in those days during the Depression. Some of their regulars moved out of the area. Others were reduced to chopped beef and pork chops. Dad ran a neighborhood soup kitchen out of the back of the shop, using up unsold meat. Even with that, there was still plenty to bring home at the end of the week. The good cuts, the kind families in the neighborhood couldn't afford. Others were eating stone soup and the Wilds were frying up steaks and broiling up crown roasts. The butcher shop's leftovers kept them fed.

As she eats the steak, she thinks of the Joads, of the foreclosures, of the soup kitchens and breadlines. Of Spam sandwiches and hobo stew. And here she is eating a dollar seventy worth of beef and gravy, as though there weren't still foreclosures and families driving to California to follow the fruit. She eats the beef and thinks of Dad. He made the best schnitzel.

After she pays her check – leaving a dime tip on the table – she finds a phone booth and places a call to Newark. She calls the shop, but it's Hank who answers.

"Uncle Hank," she says, fingers tight on the phone cord. "Can I talk to Dad?"

"Ann?" he asks. "What did the operator say, you're calling from Mexico?"

"New Mexico, that's all. Is he there?"

"Honey, he's not in today." Over the line, she can hear the bell on the shop's door ring. "Is everything okay?"

"I don't know. Is it? Is the pneumonia back?"

"He's fine as rain. Just stepped out for a bit." He covers the phone with one hand. "Mrs Keene! I'll have those chops up right away. It's Anna Louisa on the phone."

Louise has no idea who Mrs Keene is – one of the blue-haired fussbudgets who appreciates a shop run by two finicky old men – but the muffled exclamations coming across the line remind her that most everyone knows *her*.

"Uncle Hank," she says when he comes back on the line, "I wish you wouldn't." Alone in the phone booth, her face is unnecessarily warm. "I'm not Anna Louisa."

"Well, miss, you can't tell me who to be proud of. I've known you since you were in pigtails. You argued with me even then."

"Only because I was fond of you." She smiles into the phone.

"Anyway, I'm not supposed to tell you this, but your dad is planning a surprise."

"A surprise?"

Muffled, "Mrs Keene, just take your time picking out the chops. Three today? I'm glad Mr Keene has his appetite back!"

"Uncle Hank?"

"Well, young lady, he's pleased as a Cheshire cat that you're coming home for Christmas. Went out and cut down a tree and everything. So he's off today getting a haircut in your honor."

"Oh, Dad," she says. "He does know I'm coming to see him and not what's left of his hair?"

"Ann," Hank chides, but there's a laugh in his voice.

"Well, when he gets back, will you tell him I called?"

"Honey, of course. Oh, beautiful choice, Mrs Keene! I'll wrap them right up!"

"Will I see you at Christmas, Uncle Hank?"

The line crackles and she wonders if he's busy wrapping up pork chops. Hank always ties the twine with a flourish that makes the customers feel they're at Bergdorf's. "Ann," he says finally. "Wouldn't miss it for the world."

She stays the night in Santa Rosa at a motel with a red roof and baskets of drooping begonias. The sign out front advertised air-conditioning, but her room is as stifling as a sauna. She changes into a pair of shorts and a light blouse and glares at the air conditioner in her window. It remains stubbornly silent. In the front office, they seem unconcerned about the inaction from the air conditioner. And, no, they're awful sorry, but she took the last room. It figures.

She walks down the street to a shop that's just about to close and buys a bottle of orange Nehi. It's icy cold and she walks back to the motel with it pressed against her neck. The motel has a dismal little pool to the side. Though she has no intention of putting on a bathing suit for recreational purposes, she pushes open the gate. Apart from a sleeping cat, it's deserted. The sun is going down and the red glow from the sign lights the water. Louise slips off her Keds and sits on the side of the pool. The water is tepid and speckled with leaves, but she dips her feet in.

She's forgotten, though, that she doesn't have a bottle opener. She briefly wonders about asking in the office, but that would mean slipping her toes from the water and walking back across the parking lot. Behind her, the gate squeaks. A woman comes in, barefoot, in a yellowed bathing cap and swimsuit. It's the waitress, Bette, with the rhinestone glasses. She doesn't look any less bored.

Bette walks over and takes the bottle from Louise without a word. She takes it to the fence, hooks one edge of the bottle cap along the rail, and whaps on the bottle until the cap pops off.

"How did you do that?" Louise asks. It looks like a useful skill, even if just as a party trick.

She shrugs and straddles her glasses over the top of the rail. "I'm a waitress," she says, as if that explains everything.

The Nehi is cold and sweet and perfect. "Thank you."

Bette shrugs again. She drops her bathrobe in a puddle by the fence, walks to the far side of the pool, and dives into that red-lighted water.

When she comes up for air, it's to pick a cypress leaf off her nose.

"It's not much of a pool," Louise says. She takes a swallow of her soda and wipes her mouth with the back of her hand.

Bette swipes water off her face. "Expert on pools?"

"I've been in a few. I'm from California."

"Well, lah-de-dah." She squints in Louise's direction. "Some of us take what we can get."

Louise wonders why she ever started the conversation. "You don't have to be so rude."

"And you don't have to be so talkative." Bette deliberately turns around and begins paddling back to the far edge. "If you worked all day too, you'd want a little quiet at the end of it."

Louise understands. That silent car ride home from the studio at the end of the day. That first Manhattan in her Columbia Green living room, then the second. A vermouth-sweet moment before she had to go argue with Arnie again. She understands.

"I have whiskey in my room," she says. "I'll go get it."

"Oh, hell," Bette says, and climbs out of the pool.

They drink it out of water tumblers with a splash of orange Nehi. Louise is doubtful, but Bette insists. "Almost like a Ward 8," she says.

Louise takes a skeptical sip. Not even close. "Almost."

Bette takes off her bathing cap and tosses it next to the pool. It's torn along one side. Limp strands of platinum blond hair snake out.

"Peroxide is better for your hair than bleach," Louise says.

Bette puts a defensive hand to her head. "Who says I bleach it?"

"I haven't always been a brunette. When I was seventeen, I wanted to be Jean Harlow."

Bette runs fingers through her short curls. "I did it myself. Wanted to look like that Monroe actress, the one who was in *Monkey Business*. I saw her pictures in *Photoplay*."

"Try peroxide next time," Louise advises. "You don't want to be bald before thirty."

Bette pretends to ignore her.

They sit without talking. Louise sips her drink. It's growing on her. The light from the motel sign judders. A lightbulb somewhere near the T is going out. Louise tops off her glass with more whiskey.

She doesn't know why conversation suddenly feels awkward. She knows how to talk to people. It's her job, literally. She knows how to chitchat in the makeup chair, how to impress in an interview, how to defer in production meetings. How to gossip in between costume fittings and debate in between cocktails. How to smile and parrot the publicity-approved answers to fans. Louise is an expert talker.

But what does this scene call for? What would the script say?

She studies Bette, outlined against the lighted sign, her eyes closed, her damp hair drying, her empty cup loose in her hand. She couldn't think of a movie she'd played in with a casual scene like this: two women at ease, feet in a swimming pool. She'd never even been barefoot in a film. Heaven forbid audiences realize that actresses have toes.

Come to think of it, though, she's never played this scene in real life. Sitting with a girlfriend, just idly chatting. She goes for drinks sometimes at Donnie Jensen's house. All the guys there are old friends – Tim and Mack and Ray and Little Eddie Flynn – but she's always the only woman in his crowd. She and Arnie used to play bridge with the Wellers, back when Arnie still went out. Lola Weller was a peach, but it was really Sidney who was Arn's friend; the wives were just part of the package. Pauline is maybe the only female friend she has, and, really, Louise only ever sees her for the occasional slice of pie and commiseration about the war. She realizes that she doesn't really know what it is that women talk about together.

When she looks through the photos of her mother and Florrie Daniels, at their smiles and easy friendship, she wonders how it's done. She wonders what she's missing.

Louise runs a finger around the rim of her glass and ponders what to say. Conversation wasn't this hard with Duane. Even Steve at the Prickly Pear was easier to talk to. "Do you live here at the motel?"

Bette is scornful. "Who lives at a motel?"

Sometimes it feels like half of Hollywood is living in one hotel or another. The Garden of Allah, the Sunset Tower Hotel, the Roosevelt Hotel. William Frawley's lived for decades at the Knickerbocker. "People do."

"Prostitutes do."

Louise lets that slide. She's certainly not going to talk about her months living at the Roosevelt. "Do you always swim in places you don't live?"

Bette blows a flop of bangs up from her forehead. "I work here, okay?"

"I thought you worked at the café."

"I'm not the first girl to have two jobs." She looks down at Louise's pristine Keds, pointedly. "Some of us have to work for a living."

Louise takes an eye-stinging swallow of whiskey. What she wants to say and what her publicist likely wants her to say are two very different things. The last time she'd mouthed off to a pushy fan outside the Brown Derby, it had been a headline the very next day. LOUISE LOSES IT. "Bite your tongue, Lou," Arnie used to remind her. "Play your part." *One . . . two . . . three . . . four . . .* She counts, takes a breath, and puts on a Louise Wilde smile.

"That sounds difficult," she says consolingly, confidingly.

Bette waves away Louise's comment. "Well, what's a girl to do? I followed a guy out West not knowing he was a low-down bum."

"And what does he do?"

"Sponge."

Louise shrugs. "Men." She refills her glass. This time she puts only a splash of Nehi.

Bette sits up. "Who are you to talk to me like you're my sister? Like you understand? You with your white shorts and fancy car over there."

Louise pulls her feet out of the water. "You don't have to be rude. You don't know anything about me."

"I serve broads like you all the time at the café. Make your perfumed beds in the hotel. See you driving through town with your husbands and your pearls and your patent leather purses."

"And you never assume that maybe, just maybe, we buy those pearls and those cars ourselves?" Louise can't help it. "That we work, like you do? That we might be the ones bringing home the bacon?"

Bette snorts. "So you have a deadbeat at home too?"

She stops. "Just because a guy isn't working right now, doesn't mean he's a deadbeat."

Just because it's been months since Arnie's written a thing. Since he's called the office. Since he's put on a fucking pair of pants.

"Oh yeah?" Bette asks. "Then what would you call it, sweetheart?"

Louise hurls her drink at the pool, as though it's the

222

drink's fault that Arnie is sitting back at home, that Bette hit too close. It splashes into the water, orange and brown swirling out. The glass bobs away across the pool.

Bette stands and retrieves her bathing cap and robe. "Sister, they ain't all Tyrone Power."

She leaves Louise alone under the blinking sign.

BERYL

When life becomes a routine, it's easy to miss the tiny beautiful things in it.

FRANCIE

Does life do that? Mine always feels too haphazard for monotony.

BERYL

Parenthood is built on routines. Keeping house demands tidiness and repetition.

FRANCIE

And our trip?

BERYL

The freedom to notice everything around me. To marvel at little things like birdsong, like the delicious warmth of a fire, like the absolute joy of that cup of coffee after a day driving.

FRANCIE

Like the taste of burned toast when your friend is in charge of breakfast.

BERYL
(taking plate of black toast)
Like how lucky I feel when my friend offers to make it.

—Excerpt from the unproduced screenplay
When She Was King

Chapter Thirteen

1926

Tuesday

· ·

F is out of the hospital tomorrow. I have a few surprises up my sleeve. I hope they cheer her up. I hope they make up for the rest of it.

Supper: Rice.

Camp   *25¢*

May 11, 1926

They promise I get to go home tomorrow. As much "home" as our little campsite is.

I feel a million and two times better, but I can't help but be nervous. Last time I was out there I collapsed right on Ethel.

I scared her. I don't want to do that again. I don't want her to see me like that.

My stitches came out, but there's still a mark on my cheek from where the incision was. Sister Theodore Mary said I'm lucky that's all I have, better that vanity suffers than life. Sister Benedict braided my hair and said that the scar would remind me of the time God held me in his hand.

I wonder if E will notice. I wonder if, every time she looks at my face, she'll remember the time I almost left her alone in Kansas.

Wednesday

. . . .

She's mine!

Spending today and tonight at the campsite. Will start driving again tomorrow. The two of us need to have a serious talk.

Supper: Soup, this time for two.

Camp	*25¢*
St Rose Hospital, 16 days	*$64.00*

May 12, 1926

When I stepped outside of the hospital, it was to the Model T pulled right up to the curb. Wearing wool knickers, a dark blouse, unbuttoned cardigan, and plain straw cloche, Ethel stood straight by the Lizzie, holding open the passenger door like a chauffeur. She seemed almost nervous, fiddling with the buttons on her sweater, adjusting one drooping sock, but when she spotted me, she broke into a big grin. She left the door hanging open and ran across the sidewalk to catch me in a bear hug. My back was sore from two weeks in bed, my stomach was shrunk, and I felt more than a little tottery on my feet, but I let her squeeze me until Sister Theodore Mary clucked her tongue and told her to be careful not to knock me down.

She looked shamefaced, but didn't let go of my arms. I didn't complain. The nun still glared at us from under her wimple, whether due to the outpouring of affection or Eth's boyish duds, I wasn't sure. Let's get the hell outta here, I whispered right under Sister Theodore Mary's disapproving nose.

As we walked to the car, E said, I sold a few of my dresses to a secondhand shop and got us these togs instead. Your set is back at the campsite.

I'd worn trousers once before, when I went to a speakeasy in Greenwich Village, one of those spots where the women sometimes wore bow ties and paid more attention to one another than to the men. I'd heard of the club, had even spent one evening outside, watching from across the street, as women and men looked left and right before entering in pairs. One woman walked past me in a splendid man's tuxedo, but tailored, you know, so that it was clear she was definitely not a man. Coming in? she asked me, and here I'd thought no one could see me lurking across the street. You'll be among friends.

I did go back the next day, in a pair of trousers I nicked from the neighbors' line. Maybe it was the trousers, maybe it was the gin rickeys, maybe it was the couples sitting far too close, but I blushed from the moment I arrived until I left. The woman in the tuxedo wasn't there that night, but I did meet one in a powder-pink evening dress. When we left, I walked her home.

Being on the road wasn't the same thing. We passed women all the time in waistcoats and knickers, trousers tucked into high boots. Women who still curled their hair and wore red lipstick, and just wore men's clothes. It didn't mean anything, I told myself, that Ethel was dressed like that now. But, oh, if it didn't make me wish I was in a pink evening gown.

But I just smiled and pretended I wasn't looking at her legs. A girl goes to the hospital for two weeks, and look at all the changes, I said.

Oh, and that's not even all. She waved at the open car door with a flourish. Madame, your car awaits.

The thought of getting behind the wheel, of navigating the streets of Great Bend, of not collapsing again made me queasy. But then I realized that the passenger door was the one open and Eth was grinning. Change number two. I learned to drive!

My head was swirling and all I wanted to do was lay it on the pillow of my cot. I put myself in your hands, I told Eth.

It wasn't only the car (what a weird view from the passenger seat!) and Ethel that looked different. The campsite did too. I suppose it was to be expected. She'd been the one to set it up, all by herself, and had been settled in for the past two weeks. The campsite had a lived-in look. The dirt was well-tramped and the fire pit overfull with charred wood. Clotheslines ran back and forth. One tent looked freshly set up for my return; the other needed a good dusting.

She tucked me in to my old cot and for the first time I missed the comparable luxury of the hospital bed. But this was mine, with its scratchy plaid blanket and inflatable pillow, with the smell of canvas and damp wool, with the sound of Ethel rattling pots and pans around the fire. Forget what I wrote yesterday. This is "home."

Thursday

. . . .

Every time I try to think of Nevada, all I can think of is her hair.

Supper:—

Camp   *25¢*

May 13, 1926

I told E I didn't know if I could face the cold showers. Truthfully I didn't know if I could stand upright long enough for one. So she brought the laundry tub into my tent and set all of our pots and pans and kettles boiling over the fire.

The water was only lukewarm, but she'd shaved a little bit of Fairy soap into the tub. The rest of the bar floated in the middle like a water lily. The water swirled milky white around it and the air smelled warm and fresh. She'd folded the cot up out of the way. I draped all of my clothes over the folded cot and took out my hairpins. My hair reaches my waist when it's unpinned. I'd forgotten a comb.

I was facing the cot, balancing the pile of pins on top of my draped pajama top. I wasn't wearing anything at all and a snake of cool air from outside the tent sent a shiver down my back. I shook back my hair and turned around.

The tent was open, and Ethel stood there.

When I turned, she dropped her gaze. But she was there. She'd been watching me. And she hadn't said a word. I forgot your towel. She held a clean one, clutched up tight to her chest. I forgot to ask if you needed any help.

Blushes splotched my arms and my chest. I could feel them on my face. I yanked up my pajama shirt, and pins scattered everywhere. No, I tried to say, no, I don't need any help, but no words came out because she looked up then, looked up slowly from bottom to top until she met my eyes. She still squeezed that towel, her arms so tight around her, but she said, You've just come from the hospital. You're weak as a kitten. Let me help you.

And so I nodded. What else was I to do? I couldn't say a thing.

You look dizzy, she said, and came straight into the tent. Dizzy? I was now. I felt I was going to wilt. She was right next to me and the tent suddenly wasn't big enough. Don't be silly, she said, and took the pajama shirt from my hands. After all, we're both girls.

We were both girls; that was exactly the problem.

I was shivering, but the water felt burning hot as I sat down in the washtub. My knees were up to my chin. She was behind me, very still and very quiet. I wondered what she was seeing, what she was thinking, what she was planning to do. Then I felt her fingers on the back of my neck, light as fairies. She gathered up my hair, twisting it, looping it over one shoulder. My back was bare and cold.

Oh, Flor, she exclaimed, oh, darling! The word shot through me like electricity. You're so thin. With one of those fingers, she traced the ribs across my back. I can see every bone. One, two, three, four, from one side to the other. I held my breath. The bar of soap slid from my hands.

She reached around me for the soap and the floating sponge. I sat motionless while she soaped my back. A few times I heard an intake of breath, like she was going to say something, but she never did. The only conversation was between the sponge and the water.

She stopped, and I heard the sponge dripping. Other side? she asked softly. Turn around.

I didn't move.

Don't be silly, she said again, but maybe she wasn't saying it to me.

I thought about pulling away, like I had all those times before, like every time she mentioned picnics or tents or whatnot. Maybe it was the lingering fever, maybe the morphine, maybe the fact that she'd looked at me from bottom to top, but I didn't pull away, not this time. Instead I got to my knees and I turned around. This time, it was her breath held.

232

I wondered what she was seeing. I wondered what she was thinking, seeing me with my hair hanging tangled over my bare chest.

Then she leaned forward and pushed my hair back.

There was a second where she was close enough for me to kiss her. Close enough for her to kiss me. Maybe she would. She was looking me straight in the eyes. She bit her lower lip and then she glanced down. Then glanced away. Like she couldn't find a safe place for her eyes.

She was the one who pulled away this time. I'm sorry, she said, I shouldn't have . . . I just . . . Well, you can manage. She was still holding the wet sponge. I only came to bring you a towel.

She left, and I let the water in the washtub grow cold.

Friday

. . . .

Learn to drive.
Wear trousers.
Follow byways.
See sights.
Take photos.
Watch the sun set.
Eat chocolate for breakfast.
And lunch.
And dinner.
~~Keep driving past Nevada.~~

Supper: Buttered corn and tomatoes over rice.

Camp	*15¢*
Gasoline	*60¢*

Rice	18¢
Onions	12¢
Tomatoes, two No. 2 cans	15¢
Corn, two No. 2 cans	24¢
Tomato sauce, can	13¢

May 14, 1926

When I woke, E was sitting out by the fire. It was how I left her last night. I wondered if she'd moved since. She was lost in thought, the way I usually was over a blank notebook page. I almost didn't want to disturb her.

But she spotted me and poured out a cup of coffee. Looking far too serious, she said, We need to talk.

No good has ever followed the uttering of those four words, I can guarantee that. If Carl had waited for her to come home instead of leaving a note behind, he probably would've started with We need to talk.

My palms went sweaty. I wasn't awake enough for this. It was the bath, that silly bath. Why had she come into the tent yesterday? Why had I let her?

Or maybe it had been something else. A hundred little somethings that slipped out over the past month, unplanned. Sitting too close. Watching her walk away. Breathing an I love you in my sleep. What had she noticed?

A We need to talk and I was suddenly sure that this was the end. That she'd leave me. Take the train, hitchhike, walk all the way to Nevada if she had to. Anything to avoid me after what happened yesterday.

So I blurted out, I'm sorry, blurted it out quickly to interrupt whatever it was she was going to say. I wasn't one for getting last words in, but I wanted my apology, for everything, to be it.

She looked up from the pot of coffee. For what?

For . . . And what could I say?

She tucked her hair back under her head scarf. Anyway, I'm the one who should apologize. I've been a miserable traveling companion. Though I didn't agree, I let her recite a litany of worries. The car. The roads. Our dwindling bank. Her anemia. Each and every dark campsite. AL. Carl. Carl. Carl. And now, she said, the radium. She was quiet for a long moment, fiddling with her scarf. I don't want to worry anymore, Flor. I want to live.

I understood. Oh, did I. I set off thinking I was going off to die. Instead I'd spent the past five weeks feeling more alive than I had in years. More than I ever had in my life.

She read me a list she'd made in her budget book, of all the things she wanted to do. Eat chocolate. Wear trousers like explorers. Sightsee and take pictures, like we should've been doing all along.

Stay together.

Later

We only drove a little today. E wanted to show off her skills behind the wheel and I was content to sit in the passenger seat and actually watch the passing landscape.

At the campsite that afternoon, I washed my hair; I never did yesterday. I filled the basin halfway and washed it out by the fire, in my blouse and knickers. E avoided the whole operation. She walked to the grocery store and didn't come back until I was drying my hair by the fire. You should put your hair up, she said as she unpacked her paper bag.

By unspoken agreement, the campfire had always been our sitting room, a place to slip off our shoes and unpin our hair. I liked letting down its weight at the end of the day. Especially now, with this new pink scar on the side of my face. Why? I asked.

She stacked cans in our food box. Because you're sitting there with your hair all around your shoulders like Botticelli's Venus and how can anyone get anything done?

No one had ever compared me to a painting and it made my heart beat faster. Oh, no one's looking anyway.

But she turned from the food box. I've got it, she said. Let's bob our hair.

Right now? I asked.

Yes.

And so we did.

Saturday
• •

With my new haircut, I'm a different person. I drive fast. I roll up my sleeves. I drank my coffee black this morning. I might go all the way to California. I just might.

Supper: Meatballs in tomato sauce.

Camp	50¢
Gasoline	$2.28
Ground beef, on special	10¢/lb

May 15, 1926

Marvelous roads today. Straight and, if you can believe it, even paved in some sections! We followed along the Arkansas River for much of the way. Farms and fields flecked green stretched on the other side of the road. We stopped for a picnic (we're back to frugal peanut butter sandwiches again) and E made a daisy chain for me to wear. She had names for all the flowers – bitterweed and black-eyed Susan and I don't remember what else – but there was one, peachy pink with little leaves, that she couldn't identify. I'll call it a "Florrie," she said, tying a posy together with a piece of braided grass. Long-stemmed and beautiful. I can't tell when she's teasing anymore.

Later

Colorado!

Sunday

. . . .

I didn't realize I'd love driving this much. Maybe it's the countryside stretched through the front windshield. Maybe it's the freedom I feel behind the wheel, like I can go anywhere or do anything. Maybe it's the company right next to me.

Supper: Buttered macaroni.

Mountain View Camp	*25¢*
Gasoline	*$2.50*

May 16, 1926

"And where the cowboy galloped on his wild and untamed broncho, the rubber tires of the ubiquitous automobile glide smoothly by." (quote from our little National Old Trails Road map book)

First glimpse of the Rocky Mountains! They're off in the distance, but better than the flat middle of the country we've been driving through so far. Of course we got out of the car and took pictures of each other with that little sweep of mountains far behind.

Farms are giving way to ranches. Wire fences, long-horned cattle, the occasional browned, watchful cowboy, riding the line around his herd.

Monday

• •

We found the most beautiful spot in the world. Just ours. Every now and again I forget about what's waiting for me in Nevada, and I wish every day could be like this.

Supper: One pocket-warm chocolate bar, broken in two.

Gasoline	*80¢*

May 17, 1926

New Mexico!
   Saw my first mesa.

Later

On the advice of another tourist, we turned off the road just after Raton and headed east to the Capulin Volcano. We were told it was magnificent, a single peak rising green in the middle of a prairie. Adventure? I asked E and she reached over to squeeze my hand in reply. We'll see where this takes us!

Later

My camera rides on my lap. I've made E stop every half-mile or so to capture these bits of countryside on film. Dry lake beds, lava-capped mesas, little green creeks, herds of antelopes bunched on the plain.

Later

Stopped in Folsom to fill up our water cans at the train yard. Mentioned to an old man where we were headed. He asked if the fellows who told us about driving up the side of the volcano were selling moonshine. I wonder what that was all about.

Later

Nearly cheated the radium in our bones! Not once, not twice, but three times we teetered on the edge of nothingness. Magnificent? More like steep, terrifying, nearly impassable. A narrow little track of a road winding its way up MORE THAN A THOUSAND FEET. Really. If we weren't meant to stay on flat ground, God would have given us hooves like mountain goats.

If we'd known, we probably would've stayed on the National Old Trails Road, without bothering about this detour. There was certainly nobody else driving up. We learned later that this road was brand-new, drawn into the side of the volcano by the old caretaker, his mules, and a dragged piece of lumber. And to this we trusted our poor little Lizzie?

But we squared our shoulders and headed up the road. More than once I had to get out and push to keep us from rolling backward. More than once I had to bite off a curse when E turned my way. Because her eyes were shining like she was an explorer on the tip of the world.

The road didn't go all the way up. We had to abandon our poor, wheezing car and go the rest of the way on foot.

But we reached the rim, we caught our breath, and we saw exactly why it was worth it. "Magnificent" was too insignificant. We stood impossibly high above the plain. I couldn't see any antelopes. Couldn't even see our car below. Just sky up to forever, trees angling down to the plain. The top of the volcano wasn't flat, like I'd thought below, but indented,

*like someone had pushed a thumb into the top while it was
still warm. A thumb a thousand feet wide, that is. The crater
was as green and rolling as a valley, with cindery gray rock in
the bottom.*

*The sun was just starting to set, yellow and pink and orange
over the green of the plain spreading below. And we just stood
breathless, watching the trees and the sky and the stars start
to appear. At some point, Ethel's hand slipped into mine. She
didn't let go.*

Tuesday

....

I've gotten used to waking up alone. But today I woke up
warm and safe and thinking I could get just as used to
waking up with her by my side.

Supper: Oatmeal with raisins. Coffee.

Orchards Camp	*50¢*
Gasoline	*$3.00*

May 18, 1926

*We spent the night up there on the rim of the crater, just
stretched out on pine needles, covered over with our jackets.
When we woke up with the first lights of morning, E was curled
up along my side.*

*I wanted to move away. Well, I didn't, but I should have
wanted to move away. Instead I just lay still, listening to her*

241

breathe, trying not to do so myself. Birds sang and a spider crept across my stockinged foot, but I didn't move an inch. Above, a red hawk soared.

I knew when she woke. I could hear the change in her breathing and she flexed her toes where they rested against my leg. She didn't sit straight up, but lay curled a few minutes more. Good morning, I said softly, and she stirred then. She rubbed her eyes and sat up. Her face was flushed from sleep, her blouse unbuttoned at the neck, her hair dark over her eyes. I'm sorry, she said. You were just so comfortable and warm and I didn't want to wake up.

Then don't, I said.

Later

Headed back down the mountain (a dozen more pictures on my camera). E had me drive. She was quiet all morning, maybe still tired. After we made it to the bottom, she closed her eyes and didn't open them again until we made it back to Raton.

Later

Two hundred miles today! I'm exhausted. We had to stop for gasoline twice, no easy feat in this part of the country. Service stations are strung out like stars.

Wednesday

· ·

Am painting a picture for F, because she didn't ask.

Supper: Baked beans, no bacon.

| Camp Grants | 50¢ |
| Gasoline | $2.33 |

May 19, 1926

Today we drove by an Indian pueblo at Isleta. I've never seen anything like it. Adobe buildings crouched low together. Round stone ovens, like beehives, in front. Strings of bright red peppers hanging from the side of each building. Women with bright shawls and bangles, short skirts and white fringed boots. I didn't know something so different could be right here in my very own country. Two thousand miles and a world away from Newark, New Jersey.

We stopped. Others were stopping too, all with guidebooks and cameras. Somehow it just felt wrong. As strange as it all was to my eyes, these were people going about their business. Cooking, hanging laundry, herding children in for late afternoon naps. They weren't a tourist attraction; they were people. So I left my camera on the front seat. Watched from the window of the car.

Later that night, I almost regretted it. As much of an intrusion as it would've been, I wished I'd captured at least one little piece of the pueblo. But then E came around the campfire and handed me a paper. And right there, in smudges of watercolor, she'd captured what I hadn't. Because, she said, I know you wanted to be a part of it.

Thursday

There's too much to see. Even if we had a dozen lifetimes apiece, we couldn't see it all or do it all. With the lifetimes the two of us were given, we don't stand a chance.

How many more nights are left?

Supper: I forgot.

Gasoline   *$1.97*

May 20, 1926

Took a detour to a place called Inscription Rock. Centuries-old graffiti, all in Spanish. On the way there, we passed some place known as the Ice Caves, all carved out of old lava and volcanic ash. Hundreds of photos.

Later

The Continental Divide! E laughed and said she didn't think it really existed outside of our history books. It was fairly anticlimactic, but the smile in her eyes made it all worthwhile.

Later

Arizona!

Later

I fell asleep in the passenger seat. Just listening to E hum and tap out a beat on the steering wheel. When I woke up, we weren't at the campsite. We were parked on the side of the road. E sat outside on a water can, her sketchpad on her lap, painting the sunset falling over the rocks. The Painted Desert, she said when she saw me. I saw it on the map and, oh, I couldn't resist. The rocks glowed in stripes of orange and yellow and red. I told her, I'm glad you didn't.

That night we pulled out our cots and slept there under the stars.

Friday

. . . .

Last night was just the stars, the sky, and us. Can't bear to go back to those two tents.

Supper: Cold sandwiches and chocolate.

Grand Canyon National Park	*free!*
Gasoline	*$2.75*

May 21, 1926

E has been driving more and more. Not even looking left or right, but driving straight and sure. I wonder if she is so intent on getting to Nevada. She hasn't stopped at any post offices in a while. She hasn't stopped for any picnics.

245

This morning she was so quiet. Penny for your thoughts? I asked finally. Though, with our budget, better make it a two-for-one.

She didn't answer straightaway. Nothing. Not much. Her gaze dipped. Just realizing something, she said. But maybe you've known it all along.

Later

After lunch, I drove. But E was so desperate to push on. When I said it was too much for me, she had me pull over and give her the wheel. She drove past Diablo Canyon and the Indian cliff dwellings. We ate supper as we drove, sandwiches that I slapped together from the passenger seat. The map helpfully pointed out side excursions and places to stop for a rest, but Ethel kept going.

When the sun set and the night was rising, she pulled up to the Grand Canyon. All I could see was an impossible hole of darkness. Something seemed to go out of her when she pulled into the campsite, this site right there in the National Park, just moments away from the edge of the canyon.

When I came back from the bathhouse, she had the tent set up. Singular. She cut off any protests with a plaintive I'm beat. I could've offered to set up the second. Maybe I should've. But I saw the two cots inside, chastely separated, and I said, Sure. Okay. Fine. She smiled and yawned and crawled in without changing. The whole tent smelled like cocoanut. Besides, she said, as she drifted off to sleep, you snore so beautifully.

FRANCIE

Road trips are like life, aren't they? Moving forward, but still finding time to stop and admire the scenery. Crossing your fingers that you won't have to make a U-turn.

BERYL

You and your metaphors.

FRANCIE

I'm a writer. I have an excuse.

BERYL

Sometimes there are no U-turns. Some things we can't ever go back to. Once you pass them, you pass them.

FRANCIE

Like New Jersey?

BERYL

Like all of those firsts. The first time you see the ocean. First time you see a movie. First heartbreak. First kiss?

FRANCIE

(quietly)
First kiss.

BERYL

Cal was mine. Did you know that?
(when there's no answer)
Who was yours?

FRANCIE

Ask me again later.

—Excerpt from the unproduced screenplay
When She Was King

Chapter Fourteen

1952

Louise is done with brochures. She's done with touring and sightseeing and leisurely hamburger lunches. This morning when she checks out of the motel, she spots a Lucite calendar between the tinsel on the front desk, one of those that you rotate each morning for the new date. It's shaped like a roulette wheel.

Christmas is only days away and she knows it doesn't much matter, that dates are only numbers on paper. It'll be Christmas when she gets there, whatever the date. Dad will hold the fruitcake for her.

But it *does* matter. Somehow it does. In this messed-up tangle that her life has become, Christmas Eve is still there. Trees are being cut down, mistletoe hung, Santa's list made and twice-checked. Things are almost normal.

She forgoes breakfast and hits the road. She has a map now, bought from a Phillips 66 in Winslow, Arizona. One night, over her hotel tumbler of whiskey, she traced out her route with an eye pencil, at least as far as Oklahoma, where the map cut off. It hadn't been necessary. After thirteen years of memorizing scripts, she had the map in her head, clear as rain.

The skies are gray so she drives with the top of the Champ up. As she passes each town, she mentally kohls out each name. Newkirk, Tucumcari, San Jon. Then across a slice of Texas. Glenrio, Adrian, Vega. Lunch in Amarillo, a "super de-luxe ham sandwich" from the Woolworth's lunch counter. The menu promises "You Will Like It." She doesn't.

By suppertime she's made it across the Oklahoma border. But she keeps driving. Erick, Sayre, Elk City. Up and through country that winds flat and scrubby with brush. In Hinton Junction, she thinks about stopping, but the little town is dusty and quiet, so she drives on to El Reno, to a stuccoed motel stained pink by years of desert dust.

She finds a restaurant near the motel, a peeling place advertising the world's best hamburgers on a cardboard sign in the window. Her stomach is growling after that ham sandwich that was anything but "de-luxe." Of course she wants a hamburger.

It's small inside, but bright. There isn't room for much beyond a counter with a few stools and an ancient cash register at one end. As narrow as the counter is, someone has made room for a potted poinsettia and a crowd of cheerfully waving Gurley snowmen. A domed glass cover curves over a cream pie of some kind, a second over a thick chocolate cake. She slides onto a stool right by the cake and eyes it through the glass.

A waitress dressed in a limp pink dress pushes through the doors in the back. She's older, maybe how old Louise's mother would be, with gray curls and remnants of blue eye shadow in the crease above her eyes. She's humming "Lawdy Miss Clawdy" around a wad of chewing gum. She doesn't notice Louise.

"Catchy tune, isn't it?" Louise says.

The waitress blinks. She blows a bubble and lets it pop as the door swings shut behind her. The place is deserted and she seems faintly disappointed to find someone sitting on a stool. "Sorry, lady, we're closed." She pushes the gum to her other cheek.

Louise rests her feet against the foot rail. "The sign says 'Open.' "

The waitress sets a pile of folded cloth – maybe napkins or aprons or dish towels – on the end of the counter and shuffles over to the door. She flips the sign hanging on the glass door until the "Closed" points out to the street. "Not anymore."

Louise is tired. Tired of motels and diners and surly waitresses. Tired of heat waves shimmering above roads, of legs sweating against vinyl, of smelling nothing but dust and asphalt. She's drunk more cups of overboiled coffee than she can count and hasn't had a semi-decent Manhattan in a thousand miles. She wants her Columbia Green living room, the percolator in her blue-tiled kitchen, the bed in her room, with Arnie breathing, sighing, pretending to sleep, right next to her.

But this waitress, with her faded lipstick and white lace-ups, is probably tired too. Louise looks again at the folded cloth on the counter. It's a jacket and gloves.

"I don't mean to keep you. Honest. I've just been driving all day and could do with a bite to eat." Louise leans her elbows on the counter. "Even a slice of cake. Could I take it in a bit of waxed paper?"

The waitress sighs and removes an apron from a peg by the kitchen door. On the strap is pinned an enameled red poinsettia. "I don't aim to let you go hungry, now." She nudges open the kitchen door with a shoulder and hollers into the back. "Frankie! Come on out here."

As she ties on the apron, a man comes through from the kitchen with a half-empty glass of beer and a copy of *The Old Man and the Sea* tucked under his arm.

"Frankie, we got one more." She jerks her chin at Louise, perched on the counter stool.

Frankie just nods and takes a long swallow of his beer.

"Can I get one of those?" she asks.

It's been years since she's had a beer. Not since the days when she and Arnie got through the week with nothing but a package of hot dogs and a six-pack of Brew 102. They lived in a tiny apartment then, barely big enough for the Murphy bed and for Arnie's typewriter. That single shared beer each evening, passed back and forth as they sat cross-legged on the bed going through scripts, it was practically champagne.

She shrugs out of her jersey jacket and unpins her hat. It's a peach basket hat, covered all over with glossy brown feathers. When she sets it on the counter, it's as if a flock of sparrows has flurried in for a rest. "I'd like a beer and one of those world-famous hamburgers."

Frankie gives a hint of a smile and disappears into the

kitchen. When he returns, it's without his book, but his glass balances on a plate with sandwich fixings. He holds a pink ball of ground beef on a paper.

"You ever have a burger the way we cook them out here in El Reno?" The waitress, whose name tag says "Ruby," asks as she fills up a glass.

"I didn't know you cooked them any different here."

Ruby grins and passes her the drink. "Something has to make them the world's best, lady."

The beer is pale yellow with the barest hint of foam on the top. Louise takes an experimental sip. It's awful, but, come to think of it, she's always thought about beer that way, even back when she split a can with Arn.

"No potato salad left," Ruby says, sliding a plate out from a rack. "Coleslaw?"

"No, no thank you." Louise runs a finger around the damp outside of the glass. "Just the hamburger is fine." She closes her eyes slightly, just enough to block out the chatty waitress. She hears the sizzle from Frankie's griddle and smells onions frying.

Dishes clink and Ruby keeps talking. "People who drive this way, they know our hamburgers. That Steinbeck fellow, he even wrote about them."

At this, Louise opens her eyes all the way. "John Steinbeck? The novelist?" It's like he haunts the whole length of Route 66.

"Yeah, that's the guy. He wrote that book all about the grapes and the fruit." Ruby waves a hand. "I didn't read it, but Frankie over here did. He was pleased as punch to see a hamburger shack like ours right there in the book."

The hamburger in question, of both world and literary fame, slides across the counter on a white plate.

"Well?" Ruby asks. Both she and Frankie are watching expectantly.

The hamburger is flat and crispy, with onions cooked straight into the meat. It's sharp with mustard, tangy with relish, sweet with the caramel-ey brown onions. Louise orders a second before she's even halfway through the first and she watches over the counter as Frankie cooks it. A pink ball of meat is whacked flat with a spatula, then a pile of shaved onions are pressed straight in with the frying meat. A smear of pickle relish and of mustard, a steamed and buttered bun, and her mouth is watering. She finishes her beer while she waits for the second burger, and she takes Ruby up on the coleslaw offer.

A half hour later, she waddles out of the restaurant, three hamburgers heavier but only a dollar lighter. Somehow, in all of that, she feels closer to Steinbeck. She feels more a part of Route 66 than she has this whole trip.

Sometimes Louise thinks about *The Grapes of Wrath* and how things might have been different. She wasn't the only hungry young actress in Hollywood scouring the book, memorizing Rose of Sharon's few lines, wondering how to get a screen test. In the end, Dorris Bowdon was cast. She had no more credits to her name than Louise, but she was dating the screenwriter, and that's how it goes.

And what had Dorris done with it? Gotten married, pregnant, and right out of the business. Louise would've killed for that part. Metaphorically speaking. For the chance to emote, to stagger, to cry on camera, to do just about anything other than sparkle and tap-dance. It could've been the first step on a path to something better. It could've been the role that set her up as a serious actress.

But instead she took the script that Arnie Bates pushed across the library table and went to that screen test. Because it was a job. Because, stranger though he was, he believed in her. And when they asked whether she could sing, whether she could tap-dance, whether she could ride a unicycle, she said, "Yes, sirs!" because, really, what else was a girl to say? For an actress famished in the chorus, parched among the extras, faint with walk-on roles, you say what you need to. You take what's offered. If a producer asks you to jump, you ask if he wants it done with jazz hands.

Betsey Barnes was no Steinbeck, but she couldn't blame Arnie for that. The kid had been in Hollywood for just as long as she had with nothing to show for it apart from a few unofficial rewrite credits. Then his pal Sidney Weller pulled him in for a quick revision. The script was inane, something that Rachmann, studio darling, had put together from a frothy piece in a lady's magazine. Could Arnie give it glitz and glam and a healthy dose of Technicolor? Of course he could. Did Sidney want that with jazz hands?

And so, instead of literature, Louise had tap shoes and a feathered skirt, false eyelashes and a big splashy musical number. She didn't have an Academy Award, but she had packed audiences and a dedicated fellow in the publicity department who signed her pictures and marked them with a rose-pink kiss. A job was a job and, a dozen years later, she's here with fifty dollars in her purse and a bungalow on Rodeo Drive. *Betsey Barnes* hadn't been so bad. So why did she still wonder, sometimes, what if?

Arnie'd never complained. He worked on the scripts the studio passed him. Fluffy musicals, serious costume pictures, the occasional noir thriller. He was good at those. And, in between, the occasional piece for the Hollywood magazines and, less frequently, the newspapers. He always had two or three things going at once. Hollywood adores jugglers.

But no matter how many projects he had going on, no matter how many deadlines loomed, Arnie was always home for dinner. It was an unspoken promise, rarely and reluctantly broken in ten years of marriage. So when he started coming home late, started making excuses, started shutting the door to his office when the phone rang at night, she felt the first prickles of fear down her arms. It wouldn't be the first time a Hollywood marriage was broken up by a lipsticked chorine.

She took to doing the laundry more often, checking his collars for pancake makeup, his undershirts for traces of perfume. Once he caught her at it. He swung around the doorway of the bedroom to see her with her face buried in his white shirt. She felt guilty, as though she were the one at fault. And maybe she was. A few missed cues and she was acting as if he'd rewritten the script.

"What are you doing?" he'd asked.

She'd had the chance right there, the chance to ask if he was stepping out on her. They'd always been honest. Was he still? "Biting off a loose thread" was what she said. She was afraid of what his answer might have been.

That night, Louise was fast asleep when the phone rang. Arnie hadn't come to bed yet and was shut in the office. Though she wanted nothing more than to go back to sleep, she pulled herself out of bed. In her bathrobe, she crept into the dark kitchen. She could hear Arnie in the office next door, the creak of his desk chair and the murmurs of his end of the conversation. She hid a yawn and, breath held, lifted up the other phone.

She expected an airy voice, maybe a giggle or two. Whispers of love and promises of a rendezvous.

Instead, she heard Arnie say, "I don't know, Sid, I think he gives away that he's the murderer with that line," and Sidney Weller's voice saying, "Yeah, it could do with a dab more of subtlety." She hung up quietly.

No wonder Arn was sneaking around. Sid was his mentor and a friend, but he was blacklisted. They couldn't exactly meet for a coffee or talk via the studio switchboard. She poured milk into a pan, added a cinnamon stick and a splash of brandy, and waited for Arnie.

When he came out of the office, she was leaning against the kitchen counter, drinking a mug of warm milk. He paused in the kitchen doorway in his shirtsleeves and bare feet. "Hi."

"I couldn't sleep," she lied, pouring out a second mug.

"Me neither." He ran a hand through his hair. He desperately needed a haircut and a shave. How could she have thought he was having an affair? "Sid was talking through a script with me."

"What are you working on?"

He pushed himself off the doorway. "I know what I'd like to work on." He crossed the kitchen and took the mug of milk from her hands. "I'm sorry I've been so busy lately."

She ran hands down the sleeves of his shirt to his graphite-smudged fingers. "I'll forgive you if you kiss me."

He did, wrapping his arms around her waist and lifting her up on the counter. He kissed her until she was breathless and happy and no longer the least bit sleepy. "You taste like Christmas," he said.

She forgave him.

The next morning, before leaving El Reno, she places a call to Arnie. It rings and rings without answer. She tries to tell herself that it's early, not much after six a.m. there. Arn's probably sleeping. Maybe in the bathroom. Maybe making a pot of coffee.

She waits five minutes, packing her wicker suitcase back up, loading it into the trunk of the Champ, then tries again. He could be out of the bathroom now. Back in the bedroom, changing into fresh shorts and undershirt. Combing his hair.

He doesn't answer.

El Reno is chilly. She wears her navy Dior dress, long-sleeved with a wide collar and a black underskirt peeking out from the scalloped back. She picks a black velvet turban hat that comes down low on her ears. Last night she rinsed out her white gloves, and she wears them now, more because her knuckles are cold than for any attempt at politeness. When she steps out and the wind sneaks into the space between her cuffs and her gloves, she shivers and decides that she doesn't like Oklahoma after all.

She stops in the diner before leaving, for a plate of plain, dry toast to atone for last night's orgy of hamburgers. Of course, this is canceled out by the generous slice of chocolate cake she impulsively orders on her way out. Ruby wraps it in waxed paper and slips her a fork when Frankie isn't looking.

She has a new map. This one she plots on in lip pencil. By her math, done stretched on a motel bed last night, she figures she drove somewhere near to four hundred miles yesterday. Surely she can do just as much today. More if she eats her chocolate cake for lunch while driving.

Oklahoma seems the longest state she's driven through. On the map it's shaped like a saucepan. She imagines tomato soup in the pan, bubbling until it splashes on Kansas. When she reaches Kansas in the afternoon (all eleven miles of it on 66), she apologizes for the soup. There's no denying it. Here on the road, she's cracking up.

She really is. She's lost track of the miles. At one point she swears she sees a buffalo standing on the side of the road, watching her. Of course it's only a bush, but she can't help thinking that they're all buffaloes. One after another, lined up across Oklahoma and Kansas and Missouri. She's only going halfway across Missouri today and already she's tired of it.

The radio holds on to stations for only a little bit. Just when "Tennessee Waltz" fills the car with three-quarter time, it crackles out and suddenly it's "Blue Tango." Once, the radio picks up "Silver Bells," but, before she can conjure up the ring of sleigh bells, the smell of snow and pine trees, the song is lost. When she finds the next station and it starts to play "I Saw Mommy Kissing Santa Claus," she switches it off.

Instead she listens to the rhythm of tires on pavement, like drums, like maracas, until the sound blurs. The window, cracked open a hair, lets in a high whistle of air. It's almost like her own little band. For a while, she sings along with it. All of the Betsey Barnes songs, all of the ones she hears over her kitchen radio in the evening, all of the ones she's seen in movies lately. *Singin' in the Rain* (of course), *Skirts Ahoy!*, *April in Paris*, *Bloodhounds of Broadway*. She's better than Mitzi Gaynor.

She tries singing "Silver Bells," but the song is too new. She doesn't know all of the words yet. It wasn't one that she used to sing around Dad's piano. Not like "We Three Kings" (Dad's favorite) or "The Twelve Days of Christmas" (hers). With the latter, she had a dance and everything. She wonders if she still remembers it.

So many miles with nothing but her own thoughts for company. She thinks about Christmas. She thinks about the ocean. She thinks about Arnie in the Columbia Green living room. She thinks she sees another buffalo. With her fingers, she eats the chocolate cake.

She thinks about Las Vegas, about the script she walked out on. A cabbie's daughter steps in for a showgirl friend, only to become the hit of Las Vegas. *She Trades Her Saddle Shoes for Dance Shoes!* shouts the tagline. In the end, she hangs up her saddle shoes for good and heads out of town, strumming her ukulele in the back of Daddy's cab. Louise is too old for parts like this.

She'd read the script. It was awful, really it was, but somebody wrote that. Someone spent time working on it. And she knew how to play that kind of part. Girl thrust into the spotlight, only to retreat when the going got tough. *Not* because it got tough, mind you. But because there was no place like home. Thank you, Dorothy Gale.

So she thinks about the script. *The Princess of Las Vegas Boulevard* is the working title. Maybe she should go back. Maybe she should tell the studio that she'll do it. But then she thinks about the other scripts, the ones written on an old Underwood Champion and crammed onto the shelves in Florence Daniels' apartment. Stories about women strong enough to stay put when the going got tough. Women who didn't hang up their shoes, saddle or otherwise. Yes, she thinks about those.

That puts a fresh burst of speed on. Bush-buffaloes whip past her window. When she finally gets tired of driving, she's in Rolla, Missouri, and starving.

Instead of a motel, she stops at a tourist court. It looks like something straight out of an earlier century, with neat rows of tiny red-roofed white cottages. The red and the white and she's suddenly thinking of candy canes. Cracked.

She steps from the car and is instantly freezing cold. It's not cold enough for snow, not here in middle-of-nowhere Missouri, but it's not Oklahoma. Or New Mexico. Or

Arizona. Or any of the other scraps of Western states she's driven through. She digs for her coat, her scarlet-lined mink. It's all she has.

The tourist court has a newer hotel building, promising modern rooms and a TV in the lobby, but she takes one of the little cottages. Inside it's just big enough for a bed, a chair, and an ashtray stand. The girl at the front desk said that the original owner had converted old chicken coops into the first few cottages way back in the 1920s. Louise isn't sure if she believes the story, but, then again, she's never actually been inside a chicken coop. Maybe they're roomier than she thinks.

She sets the wicker suitcase on the chair and closes the curtains. Pink and green flowers. The curtains are faded and old-fashioned. Maybe they've been hanging since it was a chicken coop.

Not for the first time, she wonders if her mother stopped here. If she was driving the same roads, sitting in the same diners, walking the same three-house main streets that Mom and Florrie Daniels had all of those years ago. Did they stay in Rolla, Missouri? Did they eat in El Reno, Oklahoma? Did they stand at the edge of the Grand Canyon and want to touch the sky in the middle?

She slips from her mink and drapes it around the back of the chair. There's a telephone in the room, and she puts a call through to New Jersey. She hadn't known she needed to talk to her dad until this very moment, but suddenly she's monstrously lonely. All that precious solitude she'd craved, and now all she wants is someone to share the trip with. Like Mom had.

When her dad answers, she asks, "Why don't you ever talk about Mom's last trip?"

"Al?" She can almost hear the blink in his voice.

"Did she drive on Route 66?" Louise peels off her gloves, one by one. "Did she hate Missouri as much as I do?"

"No 'Hi' or 'Ho' or 'Hanging in there, old man'?"

"Sorry." She blows a noisy kiss through the phone.

"What's going on? You sound tired, Al."

"You can hear that through my kiss?"

"When I pick up the phone and you start peppering me with questions, something's going on."

The phone cord stretches as far as the little bathroom. "Driving alone on the road all day, a person has time to think." She drops the gloves in the sink and turns the faucet on.

"You?" He chuckles. "You can't sit still long enough to think."

She delicately ignores that. "Anyway, it made me realize I've never been in a car for this long. I've never seen this country from side to side." She attacks her gloves with the bar of hand soap. "But Mom did, and I know nothing about that trip. I've been driving along Route 66 this past week and I realized, well, she might have driven the same road."

"Oh, honey, I don't know much about it either. You expect me to remember maps and itineraries from a trip I didn't even go on?"

"You'd remember more than me." The water from the faucet starts running from warm to scalding hot. She shuts it off. "I was only six."

"Al." She can imagine him taking off his reading glasses, rubbing the bridge of his nose.

"All I know is that she drove across the country and never came home. You never told me what road she took, what states she passed through, what sights she saw. Until I saw the pictures, I didn't know that she traveled with Florence Daniels. I didn't know—"

"Pictures?"

She hears the catch in his voice, and balls up the dripping gloves in her palms. "I found them in her apartment."

He coughs. "Florrie's apartment? You know her?"

"Knew. And no, I didn't, not really. Dad, she died a week or so ago."

He's quiet for a good long time. She squeezes down the length of each glove finger. Water spatters back down into the sink.

"We were good friends," he finally says. "The three of us – Flor, Eth, and me. We were inseparable as kids. Then we grew up, graduated, and war hit. I went overseas and, well, it all changed."

"War does that," Louise says quietly.

"Yes, it does."

She drapes the damp gloves over the edge of the sink.

"Eth wrote to me a few times while I was Over There. Flor didn't. I knew they were still as inseparable. Work, dances, Saturday matinees. I wondered if there would be room for me when I came back."

"Oh, Dad. You're worth making room for."

"Eth thought so, but Flor . . . Well, I don't know. I'm not sure if your mom started keeping company with me because

Flor drifted away or if it was the other way around." She hears water on his end of the line. He's maybe washing his hands or filling the kettle for his evening tea. "But you knew Florrie? You never said that."

"I didn't, Dad. Well, not more than in passing. We were at the same studio. She had quite a reputation." She amends, "A *good* reputation."

"I've seen all of her pictures," he says, and she's not surprised.

"But out of the blue, she dies, and I inherit everything. I didn't think she even knew me from set dressing."

"She knew you." A cabinet slams. Evening tea it was. "We kept in touch."

"Really? For all this time? But—"

"Al, this is costing a sultan's fortune," he interrupts. "I'll tell you all about it when you get here." She imagines him unfolding a Red Rose tea bag. "Scout's honor."

"Okay, Dad." She shakes water off her fingers. "I'll be there soon." She hears the murmur of a voice in the background. "Uncle Hank's over? It's not Sunday."

Now her dad is the one to sound tired. "We're doing a jigsaw."

"Circus animals, like we used to do? Bears? Boy and his dog?"

"Trains."

"I love you, Dad . . ."

". . . as big as the prairies."

The line goes dead with a click, and she wipes her hands on the bathroom towel.

In just a moment, she thinks, she'll go find dinner. A

sandwich. Chicken soup. Maybe some of that barbecue the desk clerk told her about. She sits on the bed, eases out of her pumps, leans back to test out the pillows. In just a moment.

In just a moment, she's asleep.

FRANCIE

Do you remember the time we saw that tightrope walker at the circus?

BERYL

Remember? I can't forget.

FRANCIE

I didn't watch her, you know. I watched the people below holding the net.

BERYL

You wanted to see if she would fall?

FRANCIE

I wanted to see who would catch her.

—Excerpt from the unproduced screenplay
When She Was King

Chapter Fifteen

1926

Saturday

· ·

Bought AL a turquoise bracelet, set in silver stamped
with lizards. Traded my tortoiseshell comb to a Hopi
woman for it. AL loves lizards more than she loves
dolls.

Supper: Rice.

Camp   *25¢*
Bracelet   *tortoiseshell comb given to me*
                          by C, our wedding day

May 22, 1926

We stayed at the Grand Canyon one day. One whole day
where we could wake up and watch the sun rise and fill up the

bowl of the canyon and then set, leaving impossible stretches of stars. One single day where we forgot to write, forgot to photograph, forgot to even talk. One wasted day in our rush to Nevada that wasn't wasted at all.

Eth was quiet. We both were. I didn't know if she was thinking about Nevada or Carl or the divorce. I didn't know if she was thinking about the radium in her bones. I knew she was thinking about AL, when I saw her bartering with a Hopi woman. She came back without her hair comb, but with a present in her pocket for AL. Parents can't go away and not bring back a souvenir, she said. Share the adventure.

I didn't remind her that C was the one who went away. That she never would've left New Jersey in all her life if it hadn't been for that empty house and note on the table. That C pushed her into adventure. Do you regret it? I asked. The adventure?

She touched the spot in her hair where she'd always worn the comb. Not now.

Sunday

Set out early today. Two hundred miles to think of what to say.

Supper: Rice.

Camp	*25¢*
Gasoline	*$2.71*

269

May 23, 1926

I woke up and the sun was shining. Right outside the tent door, birds and jackrabbits and one persistent bumblebee. It was almost beautiful. But then E came out of her tent, stretching and yawning and scratching the small of her back. Morning, she said. Out of coffee, I guess. Should we pack up? Tomorrow might be my last morning with her and here she was wasting time with itches and the coffee tin when all I wanted to do was to grab her hand and stay right here in Wherever, Arizona, until forever. She yawned and the sun shone and my heart shattered into a million pieces.

Later

While I was strapping in the tents, she went and begged a jar of coffee off the neighbors. She poured it into our two tin mugs. We might not have too many of these left, she said, almost shyly. But we do today.

Thank goodness Arizona is so god-awful long. Because I'm dreading Nevada.

Monday

· ·

My chest is full of butterflies.

Supper:—

Camp	*25¢*
Gasoline	*$1.80*

May 24, 1926

All day, it was as if E couldn't make up her mind. Fast, slow.
Stop, go. One minute she'd be speeding along, pushing the
Lizzie until it shuddered. The next, she'd be pulling off with
one excuse or another. Pretty flowers. Cramped knees. Too
much coffee. I didn't believe any of them. She'd wander and
fill her hat full of flowers, sit on the running board and plait
dozens of daisy chains, but she was a thousand miles away.
Maybe back in Colorado or endless Missouri. Maybe all the
way back in New Jersey. Maybe farther than that. Not on the
verge of Nevada. Not hours away from seeing her daughter
and husband.

Finally, right about suppertime, she stopped. Stopped
clear on the side of the road and refused to go another mile
farther. We could see the state border from where we were.
She looked calm as can be, but the daisy chain in her hand
trembled. I can't show up on AL in the dark, like a ghoul,
she said. It was still handfuls of moments until sunset. One
night more?

Of course.

Tuesday

I saw her from the end of the driveway. She came bursting
out of the front door like a rainbow. Two crooked braids,
too-big overalls, a sunburned nose. She didn't even notice
me. Rushed straight over to a paddock, blowing kisses at
an enormous horse.

271

I swear she was bigger. Had it only been weeks? Surely she was twice the size.

I called out her name, but she didn't even glance up. "Anna Louisa!" and "AL!" And then, like C always called her, "Al!" She looked up, grinned sudden like sunshine, and ran my way.

F was right, I shouldn't have worried that she'd have forgotten me. But she was missing a tooth – her very first – and I hadn't been there to catch it.

But Carl, he didn't come running across the driveway. As AL wriggled and squeezed me and planted kisses straight on my belly button, he stood on the porch of the bunkhouse. He was brown and thin and wore a plaid shirt unbuttoned at the top. He was growing a mustache. He squinted across at me and he waved.

Words I didn't know I had came up like bile in my mouth. Six weeks of sentences unspoken, six weeks of tears hidden in the dark of my tent. But just when I walked forward, when I opened my mouth, when I was ready to tell him every thought that pressed on my heart, when I was ready to tell him that, yes, fine, let's get divorced after all, he straightened. He said, "Good to see you, Eth," and AL wormed her way under my arm and suddenly, suddenly, all those words went away.

Supper: "Cowboy stew," AL told me.

May 25, 1926

She walked off, the way I expected, the way she was supposed to. The car was warm. I went around it, leaned my head against the hood, and cried.

Wednesday

I can't believe I have my little girl back in my arms. But, oh, she doesn't stay there. She's impatient these days. Happy to see me, but then happy to move on to whatever's next. She tags along after the dude wranglers. The first time I saw her on that huge horse, my heart was in my throat. But she just waved away my worry with a little gesture. "Daddy lets me," she said. "They all let me." And I knew, whatever happened, I wouldn't have to worry about AL. So commanding. So *fearless*. So absolutely sure of herself.

But she ran off and I was left alone with Carl.

That's why I left home. That's why I drove three thousand miles. That's why I slept in tents and cooked over a fire and pushed a stubborn Model T through mud. To find him. To beg him to come home.

I'd only thought about the destination. I hadn't counted on the journey.

All day, shaking and sore and sick to my stomach, I didn't know if it was my bones aching or my heart.

Supper: Omelets, fried tomatoes, raisin dumplings.

May 26, 1926

I've been watching AL riding her horse. Her hair never quite stays in her braids, but her chin is lifted and her eyes shine. She looks so like Ethel, it devastates me.

Thursday

....

It's a good thing I'm here. Carl's aunt Marjorie isn't much of a cook and the kitchen is as tossed as AL's toy box. I spent all morning on the spice cupboard alone. She had THREE jars of celery seed and didn't even know it. Who needs that much?

AL has been keeping me company in the kitchen. She has so much energy she's wearing me out. I don't remember getting tired so easily before. She pushes over a chair for my feet and brings me cold water. I know F said to not take the Vigor Tonic anymore, but I almost think it did help.

Supper: Bean soup, cornbread, shoofly pie.

May 27, 1926

E has been in the kitchen all day. I heard AL's voice inside for a little bit, singing in a toothless lisp, but when I looked in the window, I didn't see Carl. Just AL, dancing around the kitchen with a broom, and E slumped in a chair with a drink and a sleepy smile. The table was covered with jars of spices and tins of flour and lard. It must be heaven after our little camp kitchen.

It isn't a bad idea E has. I spent the morning cleaning out the Lizzie. Everything came out and I spread both tents out to air. I wiped flour from the food box and sand from pretty much everything. I scrubbed six weeks of mud from the floor

*and sewed up a tear in one of the side curtains. It all needs
to be done. I can't stay here forever.*

Friday

· ·

Fainted getting out of the bathtub this morning. I told
myself that the anemia is back, that we've been eating
awfully. But maybe that's not it. The world always feels a
little more solid under my feet when F's nearby. Yesterday,
I didn't see her at all.

I had an excuse ready on my lips. I needed to find
her to borrow the car, of course, to go to the grocery in
Searchlight. Aunt Marjorie's kitchen had next to nothing
in it, I'd tell her, and I needed fresh foods, full of iron.
Liver, tomatoes, spinach. It was a good excuse, one she'd
believe, and I practiced it under my breath.

I didn't find her, but I found the Lizzie emptied like a
tornado hit it. Boxes and duffels, pots and pans, tents,
fire grates, everything, scattered all around in the yard.
Tripped over a bucket of cold soapy water. A cleaning was
overdue (our socks could stand up and walk away), but it
made my stomach icy to think of why she was doing it.
Was she going to leave?

Supper: Fried chicken, potato salad, applesauce cake.

May 28, 1926

*Today I did laundry. Marjorie lent me a bigger washtub
than the one I'd carried strapped to the roof. I washed*

*everything in my duffel (my dusty woolen knickers twice),
plus all of the blankets and towels. I ran out of clothesline
space, so took the last load to hang up over the net on the
tennis court.*

*Despite the dude wranglers and horses and sagebrush, the
ranch has a pool and a perfectly immaculate tennis court,
like something you'd see in a magazine. E told me that dude
ranches are tourist destinations. Easterners flock West for a
rustic (but not too rustic) holiday.*

*I'm not sure I believe her. Apart from Marjorie, the
brassy-haired woman who owns the Prickly Pear, and the
dude wranglers, who sleep above the barn, we're the only
guests. Marjorie gave me a suite of rooms all for my own,
but they echo. I half-considered asking if I could set up my
tent out back. The very night we arrived, E moved into
Carl's rooms.*

*Anyway, this morning, I lugged my basket out back to
the tennis court. It's a quiet sort of place. Warm pavement.
Rectangles and right angles. Unpretentious wooden benches. It
was a good place to be alone. These days, that's all I was. But
this morning, someone was out on the court with a tin pail of
tennis balls.*

*Two someones, I realized; one whose head barely came
above the net. Anna Louisa, deadly serious expression on
her face, stood across the net from one of the dude wranglers.
Steve, I remembered. I'd seen him around the ranch. Restless
and arrogant. Watchful. He quite obviously adored AL and
was fiercely protective of her. All of the guys were, but Steve
called her The Empress and lifted her up onto her horse himself.*

Though he was dressed like a Remington painting, he held the racket like a blue blood, impatiently shouting instructions across the net to AL. She didn't seem the least bit deterred. Her swings were furious and white balls flew wildly. It looked immensely satisfying.

I slipped onto a bench alongside the court and just watched. She was Ethel the way I remembered her. Determined. Spunky. Tireless. That little girl, she lit up that tennis court.

Before too long, she broke off. She was panting. She retrieved a battered metal army canteen and, in that moment, she spotted me. With a dismissive wave at the tall wrangler, she came my way.

You're Mother's friend, aren't you? She plopped down on the bench next to me and a ratty stuffed horse.

I've known her for a long time, since we were a little older than you are now.

She thought about this for a space and took a long drink from her canteen. She was wearing the turquoise bracelet E had bought her, wrapped twice around her wrist. I didn't know she had any friends besides Daddy and me.

We haven't talked in a long while, I said. She waited. Sometimes friends lose touch.

Is that why you look so sad? she asked.

I was sad because, every night, Carl brought Ethel a cup of coffee. She looked at me instead of saying good night. She followed him into their room and didn't come out until morning. I'm sad because I have to say goodbye.

She waved her hand again in that beautifully dismissive gesture. When she grew older, she'd simply devastate people with that wave. I won't do that.

Get sad? I scooted closer. Or say goodbye?

Either. She dribbled water out from the canteen, just to watch it fall. I don't have any friends. I'm like Mom. I don't talk to people. Her canvas shoes were getting wet. We get along fine without anyone else.

I took the canteen from her and capped it. That's a lonely way to move through life, Miss Anna Louisa.

She set her chin. I don't need friends. I'm going to be an actress. Years and years ago, Eth used to lift her chin and declare the same. The only thing I'll need is the camera.

I might have to leave Ethel behind. I might have to say goodbye. But to Anna Louisa, swinging her feet above the edge of the tennis court, I said, When you get to Hollywood, I'll look you up.

Saturday

· ·

Making biscuits today. Pulled the stool up to the shelf where the flour tin was and stepped up onto it all wrong. Pain up and down my whole leg. I fell off the stool and pulled the tin down with me.

I was just about fainting from the pain, but I ran fingers down my leg and it didn't feel right. Wasn't the first time I'd broken a bone. These days, they took twice as long to heal.

Tore a dish towel into strips and wrapped them tight around my leg, hoping they'd hold the bones together. Aunt

Marjorie came in then and saw me tying off my bandage with flour settled all over everything like snow. She didn't say anything, but brought me a cigarette. I didn't even look around to see if C was watching.

Supper: Providence chicken, biscuits, canary pudding.

May 29, 1926

Lifted the floorboards, lifted the hood, and attempted to clean and check all of the Lizzie's Important Bits. I cleaned the spark plugs, the timer, the carburetor, the coils. I tightened the clutch and the brake bands. I changed the oil and (I think, I hope) the burned-out bearings. I tried to straighten out the bend in the front bumper.

I worked right through lunch and through dinner. At one point E brought me out a piece of saucy chicken sandwiched between two halves of a biscuit. I hadn't seen her up close in days. I'd been avoiding mealtimes, eating cold travel rations in my room, and only seeing her from a distance. She was limping again and looked pale, but, from under the brim of my hat, I drank in the sight of her.

She didn't leave right away after she handed over the sandwich. She stepped back into the shade of the porch. She took a breath and asked what I was doing.

I didn't want to answer. I'm not sure she even wanted to ask the question. Getting ready to go, I said.

She thought about it for a good, long while. Opened her mouth a few times as though to say something. I kept on with my mallet and the bumper, trying to pretend I wasn't watching out of the corner of my eye.

I thought to make a joke, something about taking as long as Odysseus if I didn't get moving, but then she asked, Do you have to? and the joke died on my tongue.

Before I could answer, before I could say that yes, I did, of course I did, because if I stayed I'd wither away a little bit every day, Carl came from the mess hall with two cups of coffee, like he did every night. He touched her on the shoulder, like he did every night, and asked, Okay, Eth? And, like she did every single night, she turned and followed him into the bunkhouse.

I knocked the bumper clear off the car.

Sunday

This little deception, I never intended it.

I didn't know where to go that first night. After supper, I didn't want to leave AL's side. She fell asleep on my shoulder and I carried her into the bunkhouse they'd been sleeping in. She had a little trundle bed on the floor, next to the bed. F was in a room farther down. C was in the bathroom brushing his teeth. I laid AL down on the trundle and didn't know where I belonged.

I suddenly missed the smell of damp canvas and wood smoke, the sound of Florrie's snoring, the slant of dark tent above my bed, that cheap wool blanket scratching the bottom of my chin. This room was too quiet. No muffled bonfire conversations, no harmonicas, no wind lifting the tent flaps and rattling poles. I missed it all. I missed Florrie.

But this is where I had to be, here in this room with C and AL. It's what everyone expected. Despite him leaving, it's maybe even what C expected now. But C came out of the bathroom that first night, lifted AL up onto the big bed, and said he'd take the trundle while I was here. *While I was here.*

He'd put out the light and crawled into that bed down on the floor. And that's when I tried to talk to him. Then, and every night since. All the words I wanted to say, all of the words I practiced in my head while driving across the West, I thought maybe they'd be easier in the dark. But when I finally said the first word, each night, he'd already be asleep.

I haven't been able to talk to Carl. I haven't been able to talk to Florrie. Always, I'm too late.

Supper: Ham and macaroni, prune whip, and I forget what else.

May 30, 1926

Today was tires. That Lizzie and her poor wheels. They've been taken on and off more times than I can count.

Worked on the front first. Inner tubes cleaned and patched. Tires wiped down with gasoline. Cracks and cuts filled in with rubber compound. Each inflated to sixty pounds. After three thousand miles on the road, I was a pro.

The last tire, though, was stubborn. Try as I might, I couldn't lever the casing up over the rim. It was a newer tire – we'd had to replace it after a particularly disagreeable stretch of Missouri – and refused to budge. I had an excellent profanity that I'd heard a fellow use in Boonville. Carl walked up on me trying it out. He blinked and said, I'll have to remember that one. Then, Can we talk?

We used to be the best of friends, two points of our little triangle, but the angle had grown wider over the years, the line drawn between us too long. When I came to their front door in Newark to say goodbye six weeks ago, it was the first time I'd seen him in years. We looked at each other over Ethel's head, weighing, measuring, evaluating. He was older, tired. Other than nods and hellos, we hadn't had a conversation in even longer.

I was old and tired too. And I was mad. Mad at my rotting body. Mad that I didn't have much time left for my dreams. Mad at Carl for stupidly leaving. Mad at Eth for going after him.

But I didn't have a front bumper left to bash and I didn't have many friends left. I kicked the tire once, pointlessly, then asked, Give me a hand, Carl?

We talked while he levered off the casing, while I hauled out the inner tube and patched it up. He talked about the war. He talked about coming home not fit for anything but soldiering. About how he opened the butcher shop with his army pal, Hank, just so he wouldn't feel so adrift. But it felt like life had moved on without him. That E and I had moved on. She felt it too, he said. She wanted everything to go back to the way it was before the war. I asked, Is that why you two got married so fast? He said, Maybe.

I talked about the past seven years, about the jobs and my very own apartment. I talked about the issue of Variety folded up in my duffel and the MGM contract at the end of this whole, long journey.

When we ran out of everything else, we talked about her.

How we used to all be friends. How maybe we still could be. How everything was just right when Ethel was there. She walked up that driveway and I suddenly realized how much I'd missed her, he said. That's how she gets us to stay. She forgives us and makes us love her and we never want to be anywhere else.

I didn't ask him why he left in the first place. I already knew. Listening to him talk about the war and returning home, about the butcher shop and Hank, about not knowing where he fit in, I understood. I didn't ask him why he wasn't going to leave again. Through the kitchen window, Ethel limped past, and I knew that too.

So, he asked, what do we do now?

Because we both knew that Ethel wasn't going to decide. She'd stay in there, scrubbing out Marjorie's kitchen for eternity rather than choose which direction to go. California or New Jersey. And she didn't have eternity.

We stumbled through decisions neither of us would make. Possibilities that couldn't really happen. Understandings. We wrestled the inner tube back on the car. We wrestled with the future. The inner tube was more gracious. I have to leave sometime, I told him. He said, So do I.

As the sun hovered low, I packed up my toolbox. Carl, we didn't choose this. None of us did. But going forward, what can we choose?

Florrie, he said, I don't know.

Monday

· ·

I was right there and they didn't even see me. Was bringing them out lemonade, of all things.

They always used to look to me for decisions, but now they're taking them away from me.

May 31, 1926

Woke up this morning to the sound of the Lizzie sputtering to life. I pulled a robe on over my pajamas and went out onto the porch to see the car pulling away from the bunkhouse. C came out of his room at a run, barefoot, his shirt untucked.

I ran with him after the car. It wasn't going fast. I could see E's head above the steering wheel. I called her name and she slowed for a moment, but then she put her foot down on the gas. I kicked off my slippers and sprinted after.

Then a hen ran across the driveway and E swerved. She rolled into the paddock fence and stopped in a crunch of metal. C threw himself at the passenger door and cried, Al!

I didn't even realize AL was in there, not until C yanked open the door. She was in the passenger seat, sleepy and dazed, in her thin white nightgown and turquoise bracelet. A trickle of blood ran from her forehead. He pulled her out and squeezed her so hard I thought she'd break in half. E crawled out after, face streaked with tears, and touched AL's little dangling foot. She's okay?

She's fine, C said. Scared, maybe. Eth, what were you doing?

She looked between C and me. You two were portioning me out like a peach pie. Deciding where to send me, as though I didn't have a say in the matter.

C held AL tight. We weren't. Honest. We were just sorting some things between us.

She wiped her eyes. She didn't look convinced. And what did you decide to do with me?

I took a step closer. I wished I could scoop her up the way C had AL. Eth, we didn't.

That's why I decided, she said.

She'd been leaving. In the backseat of the Lizzie I could see her wicker suitcase. A box of food. The tent. AL's stuffed horse was on the floor. She hadn't even said goodbye.

I could see C's face the moment he realized the same. Where were you going? He let AL slip to the ground, but didn't let go of her.

She bit her lip. She was crying again. I don't know. I thought I did. She wrapped her arms around herself. When had she gotten so thin? But I'm running out of time.

It was then that I saw that brightness in her eyes, the flush in her cheeks, the little waver as she stood next to the Lizzie. I hadn't seen her – really seen her – in days.

I didn't think twice. I crossed the few feet between us and put my arms around her. I smelled cocoanut oil and felt her heart flutter against my chest.

I caught her before she fell.

Beryl scrambles out of stopped Model T.

BERYL

You almost hit her!

FRANCIE

Thank goodness I didn't. I'd be picking feathers out of the radiator for a week.

Both watch an unconcerned hen fleeing across the prairie.

BERYL

Is that all you can say? No apologies? No tears? She might have left a dozen orphaned eggs behind.

FRANCIE

Why are you so sad? Your favorite variety of chicken is the dead variety.

BERYL

You're mean.

FRANCIE

And you're ridiculous. We ate fried chicken last night.

You had three helpings.

Beryl pointedly dabs at her eyes with a handkerchief.

FRANCIE
Why did the chicken cross the road?

BERYL
Why?

FRANCIE
To escape Beryl's frying pan.

—Excerpt from the unproduced screenplay
When She Was King

Chapter Sixteen

1952

After Mom died, Dad was uncomfortable in his new role as widower. He fumbled with how to tell people. "Ethel's gone west," he'd say. Not knowing the soldier's expression, six-year-old Anna Louisa took it literally. After all, Mom had driven across the country, from coast to coast. After a while, Anna Louisa began to doubt that there'd really been a funeral. Maybe her memories were mixed up. Primroses, tears, a patch of shade beneath an acacia tree – those could be from anything. "She's gone west," Dad said, and Anna Louisa imagined her mom driving clear to California and never wanting to come back.

She was only a kid, but it was silly, really. All of the tears and handkerchiefs. The gilt-edged cards covered in lilies and indecipherable script. The black armband on her coat. The smell of primroses. She knew, she *knew,* but still she wondered. At every Saturday matinee, in between bites of Jujubes, she'd scan the faces on the screen. Maybe, just maybe, Mom wasn't dead. She'd only gone west.

Even long after she was old enough to know better, long after Dad had sat her down and explained all about radium moving into Mom's bones and causing a ruckus, she still watched those movies every Saturday afternoon.

It was maybe because of this, because of the lingering hopefulness of a girl refusing to accept disappointment, that Louise half-expected to see her mom when she arrived in LA in 1938. She didn't even realize she was half-expecting it, but she stepped from the bus scanning the crowd.

Of course, Mom wasn't there. Primroses.

As she drives along Route 66, she realizes that that bus ride fourteen years ago probably went along this exact road. It probably passed through Arizona and Oklahoma and the endless middle of Missouri. Looking at the expanse of Illinois and Indiana and Ohio on her map, she begins to wonder if Missouri is the worst the country has to offer.

That was the last time she took a bus. In her days as an extra, she couldn't afford more than her own two feet. Then came studio cars. And then – she pats the tawny dashboard of the Champ – a car of her own.

Mom wasn't waiting in Los Angeles for her when she first stepped off that bus, still Anna Louisa Wild, but, she remembers now, Florence Daniels was.

Of course, she didn't know who Florence Daniels was at the time. Just that, as she stood on the platform, suitcase in hand, a tall woman stepped from the crowd. The woman had reddish-blond hair and wore wide trousers, like Katharine Hepburn.

"Looking for someone?" she asked.

That was when Anna Louisa realized she'd been thinking of Mom, and her face got warm. "She's not here."

"Ah," the woman said with something soft in her expression. She had pale lashes and very blue eyes. "Need a stand-in?"

Though the question made more sense now, it was strange then, coming from this tall stranger. Anna Louisa fumbled with her suitcase. She was eighteen and alone.

The woman noticed, and smiled. "Can I point you in the direction of a cab? You look as bewildered as a newborn kitten."

Nobody had ever compared Anna Louisa to a newborn kitten. A filly, sometimes. Or a mule. Once, a wolf. But a kitten was something she couldn't bear. She straightened her shoulders. She remembered that she'd done her hair like Loretta Young, and the curls were still holding. She was ready for Hollywood.

"I'm fine, but thank you. I'll get my bearings."

There was still that little wisp of a smile on the woman's face. "I believe you will. This town isn't going to eat you up."

Suddenly Anna Louisa felt more tiger than kitten.

"But if you ever need a stand-in for whoever was supposed to come meet you, well, look me up." The woman let go of her handbag and offered her hand, like a man. "Florence Daniels. I'm at MGM. Screenwriting."

If Anna Louisa had known how this business worked,

she would've taken both the hand and the connection. But she was young and green enough to think she could make it in Hollywood through talent and sheer force of will. So, while she took the older woman's hand, she merely said, "I'm . . . Louise. And I really should find a cab."

Florence Daniels didn't wear gloves. Her handshake was firm. The newly christened Louise wasn't even sure she was shaking hands correctly.

"Well, Louise," the other woman said. The name sounded somehow right when she said it. "Good luck to you."

Maybe it was the new name, maybe the unexpected greeting, maybe the assurance that she wouldn't be devoured by the movie machine, but with that wish of luck, Louise didn't feel so alone anymore.

"Thank you."

With a squeeze of her hand, Florence Daniels let go and disappeared into the crowd at the bus station.

As Louise passes out of Missouri, she realizes that she's left that battered copy of *The Grapes of Wrath* back in Rolla. She'd been reading it every night since pinching it from the ranch. Flipping the pages, she could almost smell the ink and paste and paper of the Wilshire library. It was like catching up with old friends.

In St Louis, she stops at a bookstore to buy another copy. She's gotten used to falling asleep with the book in hand. It makes the nights fractionally less lonely. Right on the bookstore's shelf by *The Grapes of Wrath* is Steinbeck's newest, *East of Eden*. Impulsively, she buys both.

She's not quite sure why she does. Maybe it's because she was halfway through *The Grapes of Wrath* and doesn't remember what happens after Tom shoots the deputy. Maybe it's because it's been years since she's bought a new book. The last, she recalls suddenly, was Pearl Buck's *Peony*. Maybe it's because the only thing she's bought impulsively in the last week has been yet another hamburger.

At St Louis, she also turns off Route 66. On the map, it veers north, toward Chicago. Instead she takes Route 40 into Illinois. The lip liner makes a straighter line across to New Jersey.

The man at the Sunoco station filling up her car says it used to be the National Old Trails Road. "That was back before there were any highways, you know." He speaks conversationally, hat pushed back on graying curls. Louise gets the impression that he doesn't find many conversational partners in this brown corner of Illinois. "Wasn't even paved. Back then, it was just man, his Model T, and the open road."

Man, or woman, Louise thinks, pulling back onto the road. Maybe two women with a camera and a pair of makeshift journals.

Though *East of Eden* and *The Grapes of Wrath* ride on the passenger seat, she's no longer in Steinbeck country. Sure, there are still turtles and dust and downtrodden farmers, but who writes about them? There are no great novelists capturing the Midwest, in all its dubious glory. No masterpieces celebrating Ohio or Illinois. At least none that she can think of. But as she winds along Route 40, past neat farms and main streets dotted with redbrick drugstores and overstuffed feed stores, she wonders why not. There's something peaceful about these rural highways and cornfields eager for spring's arrival. She would read those books.

As she crosses into Indiana, it begins to snow.

For a while now, she's been passing white-dusted trees and brown fields marked with snow-lined furrows. Evidence of December, with no active precipitation. But she passes over the invisible border between the states and it's as if the sky suddenly has permission to let loose – with snow, first drifting in front of her headlights, then speckled on the windshield, then ghosting across the road in swirls of white.

She's watching the snowflakes, and so she doesn't see the deer step out onto the road.

At first she doesn't know what it is. A smudge of brown up ahead in the middle of all that white. A smudge of brown resolutely standing directly in her way. When it doesn't move, Louise swears and jerks the wheel to the right. Tires squeal and she slides off onto the shoulder.

It's a deer. Not a big one or a particularly decisive one. It stands in the driving snow, staring at her through the side window and not budging an inch. Far enough into the road to be a nuisance, but not far enough along to finish crossing to the other side.

The deer stands, unconcerned, but Louise's heart is pounding. The Champ has slid to a stop just a foot or two from a tree. Apart from her antlered friend, the road is deserted. If she'd smacked into the tree . . . She finally unpeels her hands from the steering wheel. They're freezing cold. When she reaches across for her purse, which is now on the floor, the silly deer finally decides to go on his way.

The snow isn't deep and the shoulder is relatively flat, but it's icy enough that her wheels do nothing but uselessly spin. She needs a tow truck or a strong pair of shoulders or something to get her out of this mess.

She slips her feet from her shoes and rubs her toes. The car is already getting cold. The wind whistles around the edges of the door. Maybe she should stay put. Tuck up her feet and read until someone like Duane stops to lend a hand. After all, she's not dressed for this. She's in heels and a three-thousand-dollar coat.

But no one's coming, she knows that. No leading man with snow tires and excellent timing. She can't stay forever on the side of this road. The next visitor could be a bear. Are there bears in Indiana? She can't say for sure that there aren't.

She puts her shoes back on, buttons her coat, and pushes open the door.

It's cold out. Wind nips inside the collar of her mink coat. The deer has left footprints across the road, but the tracks from her car are quickly disappearing. Snowflakes catch on her eyelashes. She hasn't seen snow since she left New Jersey. She'd forgotten how soft it is, how quiet, how quickly it melts on cheeks and noses. She's left her little veiled half-hat in the car and her hair is already damp. She tips her head back and catches a snowflake on her tongue. In this snowstorm in the middle of the country, she's six years old again.

She goes around to the front of the car and gives an experimental shove, but the car doesn't budge. She tries to get a shoulder under it. She braces against the tree and pushes with her back. She hauls off and gives it a kick. Nothing.

She stands, ankle deep in snow, staring at the red hood, until she remembers that she'd put the parking brake on.

That impediment solved, she again takes up her position in front of the car. This time, it rocks when she pushes it. It almost moves.

She's spent the past decade and a half dancing. When she first got to Hollywood, tap classes, every day, until she could shuffle-ball-change with the best of them. Later, days spent in the mirror-lined dance studio, rehearsing new numbers until her calves ached. Takes and retakes where she waltzed and tangoed, rode and swam, smiled and sang. She knows "strong."

She sets her feet at the base of the tree and pushes again. Pushes for all of the times she was told to sit back and let someone else do it. Pushes for all of the times she was told to not hurt herself or break a nail or work up a sweat. She's sweated. And she's done it in heels.

Inch by inch, the Champ rolls back out to the road. Her shoes are full of snow and her gloves are soaked, but she doesn't stop. Snowflakes speckle the hood. When the car reaches the road, she shouts and doesn't care if the bears hear her.

She reaches through the passenger door to reengage the parking brake, but doesn't get in just yet. In her three-thousand-dollar coat, she lies down and makes the best snow angel she's ever made.

The snow makes driving slower, but Louise isn't tired. Maybe it's the Snickers bar she bought at her last stop, maybe it's the snow still melting in her shoes, maybe it's the reminder that she's more than just smiles and ukuleles. She briefly contemplates driving all night. Teamsters do it.

She stops once for a turkey sandwich and once more for a cup of coffee. When it starts to snow again, she opens the window and invites a wave of snowflakes into the car.

By the time the yawns catch up with her, she's halfway across Ohio. The snow is coming faster and she finds a cheap motel with a packed parking lot. She's not the only one looking to wait out the storm.

She drapes her mink over the backs of two chairs to dry and pours herself a whiskey. Rather than venture out to the front desk with her ice bucket, she breaks an icicle from right outside and drops the entire thing in her glass. She settles in bed with drink, book, and snow outside her window.

East of Eden is full of grand characters, some dreadful, some heartrending, some unnecessarily righteous. They hate and they love in great measure. She bites her thumb as she reads, waiting for them to fight against fate, to reach for hope and freedom.

One character, Lee, mentions the Hebrew word *timshel,* often translated in the Bible as "thou shalt." God casts Cain out of Eden with the command that he shall prevail over sin. But *timshel,* says Lee, more rightly means "thou mayest" – not a command, but a choice. Cain can prevail over sin, but it's in his own hands. The other characters blindly follow what they think are preordained paths. But if *timshel* means "thou mayest" and they hold the opportunity to decide and choose and transform, well, then that changes the whole story.

She keeps flipping pages until she looks up and sees that it's midnight and the ice in her whiskey has melted. She used to read before bed every night. She and Arnie, tucked close to each other, sharing the light of the single bedside lamp. Even when they could afford a second lamp, they still read shoulder-to-shoulder at night.

Louise used to laugh at that. She used to tease Arnie, "See how we're stuck?" These days she thinks that more and more, only now they're stuck on opposite sides of the bed. Now they're stuck in the dark, stuck in the silence, stuck in the stubbornness of inaction. Once, after he first came home, he called his wheelchair his prison. She didn't know what hers was. The studio? Her marriage?

But as she lies here on a hotel bed, cradling a book and a whiskey with a swirl of melted icicle, she wonders if the prisons ever really existed. She'd never pushed a car, because she'd been told she wasn't strong enough. Never taken a dramatic role, because she wasn't good enough. Never told Arn how much she'd missed him, because she wasn't brave enough. Thou shalt fail.

She sets the whiskey down on the nightstand and lets it grow warm. She licks a finger and draws it across the middle of the page. "Thou mayest," she reads aloud, realizing as she does so that, like the book's characters, following "thou shalt" unwaveringly, she needs a new translation. That few things in her life are etched in absolutes. That she may fail or she may not. That the script is hers to write.

BERYL

What kind of story are you writing there in your little notebook? Something tragic? Funny? Beautifully romantic?

FRANCIE

All three.

BERYL

That's too complicated. Stories can't be all three.

FRANCIE

I don't know. Isn't ours?

—Excerpt from the unproduced screenplay
When She Was King

Chapter Seventeen

1926

June 1, 1926

The doctor came from Searchlight.

He was fifty, sixty years old. Maybe eighty. He rode up on a swaybacked mare, wearing a greasy leather coat and glasses so thick his eyes were magnified like stars. His medical kit was in a saddlebag. Murjorie called him "Doc" as she kissed his cheek and maybe that was all the medical qualification he had. But it was better than nothing.

Despite his coat, his hands were scrupulously clean. He was in the bunkhouse for near to an hour looking her over and asking questions in a soft voice. Out on the porch, he made us wait until he'd rolled himself a Velvet cigarette and smoked it all the way down.

He said she'd recently broken her leg and it was healing crooked. Her leg, broken? I could see that Carl was just as mystified. She hadn't said a word. Was that why she was limping again? Because she'd been walking around with a broken shinbone?

Carl went in to ask. I heard his voice rise through the window.

. . . Bandaged with a dish towel, Eth? he said, and Why won't you take care of yourself?

I knew he was scared and sad and angry all at once. When she fell asleep, he came out and I poured him a whiskey.

The doc said she needed an operation.

June 2, 1926

I sat with her while Doc Robinson got things ready for the operation. He has to reposition the crooked bone. Carl was supposed to stay with AL, keeping her away from the makeshift operating room, but he kept buzzing by the porch, asking questions through the window.

One thing both good and terrifying: The doctor said her fracture was spontaneous. Good, because it meant Eth hadn't done anything to cause it, she hadn't been risky or reckless or anything like that. But terrifying because, well, bones aren't supposed to do that.

E didn't seem surprised. I wondered if there'd been other spontaneous breaks, things she hadn't told a soul.

Later

Something's wrong, but the doctor won't tell Carl or me what it is. He sent Steve into town to get a microscope from his office. Ethel is sleeping. Doc Robinson is just sitting on the porch smoking cigarette after cigarette, waiting.

Later

Carl and I, we hovered outside like ghouls. Marjorie came to take AL to bed with her. Doc Robinson pushed those thick glasses up on his head and spent ages peering into a microscope. It was almost dusk when he came out. Ethel was still asleep. A person deserves to know how she's doing before anyone else does. He straightened his glasses. Now you two go to bed. We'll talk when she's awake.

Without any questions, Carl came with me back to my bunkhouse. The bed was big enough for the both of us. We didn't sleep, but, toward dawn, he took my hand.

June 3, 1926

We sat with Ethel, one on each side holding a hand, while the doctor told her what he'd found. A tumor, right on the bone in her leg. That's what he'd been looking at in the microscope. A tumor.

Carl started quietly crying and I think I did too, but Eth just squeezed our hands until they ached. She didn't say a word.

Later

We took turns sitting with her all afternoon. She slept, mostly. Carl pretended to read a dime novel. I pretended to write. We both pretended not to worry.

Sometime in the late afternoon, when the sun was slanting across the bed, Doc Robinson returned. He'd changed into a clean shirt and smelled like talcum powder. He said he didn't mean to be impolite, but he wanted to give her a more thorough examination. Ethel sent me from the room to make a cup of tea.

When the doc finally left, the tea was cold. Eth was sitting up in bed, buttoning up her nightgown. He found more, she said, her voice steady. More masses. Here – she touched the side of her hip – and here – she touched her torso.

I asked if he could fix it. I was sure he could. A doctor who has his own microscope? I trusted him.

But she shook her head. There are operations he could try, but Flor . . . we both know.

I did, but that didn't mean it wasn't worth hoping.

I don't want to waste this time on hope, she said. I want to spend it with you.

June 4, 1926

Today it's my turn to keep AL away from the sickroom. Carl is in there with Eth and both are talking. I suppose it's good. She's telling him all about the journey. He's telling her about the divorce. I catch words here and there, floating out through the open window. No one sounds angry. Sad, maybe. But we've all gotten too quiet for anger.

Later

After a while he came out and took my place at the checkerboard. Eth was sleeping, he said; she'd worn herself out with talking.

I couldn't ask him, not with AL sitting right there stacking up the red checkers into a tower, but I asked, Better? He nodded. I told her everything, he said. Before I even said a word, she forgave me.

AL tugged on his sleeve, asked, What, Daddy, what? but he looked over her head at me. Now, he said, it's your turn.

June 5, 1926

Today, I thought I was supposed to be playing tennis with AL. So did Carl. When we went looking for her, she was stretched out on top of her mother like a blanket. Her dark head was tucked under Ethel's chin and she didn't even turn around when we walked into the room. Mom was cold, she said. Beneath her cheek, the sheet was wet. Will you help me?

And we crawled in, Carl and I, on either side. We'd been trying to keep this little girl from the sickroom, to keep her from watching her mother die, to keep her from suffering alongside Ethel. If we'd been paying attention, we'd have seen that Anna Louisa had been suffering quietly on her own.

So we climbed in that narrow bed with Ethel. Carl on her right, me on her left, and AL stretched out on top. Between us, Ethel was hot and shaking, but she brought a hand up to rest on her daughter's head. You smell like sunshine, she said, and for the first time, she cried.

June 6, 1926

Help me with a bath, Ethel asked.

I knew it wouldn't be like last time, that warm corner of an afternoon in the tent. We had a real bathtub, for starters. Running water. Thick towels. Marjorie even gave me a bottle of rose water to pour into the steamy water.

When I helped her undress, it was with tenderness. It was love, but love far from that bare moment in the tent. All of the wanting in the world, but this here was needing.

Her leg below the bandage was angry, red, and weeping. She was so thin, I could see hollows under her collarbone.

I laid towels down in the bottom of the bathtub for her to sit on and helped all of her but her right leg into the rose-scented water. I tried not to look. Not at the little hints of curves left on her wasted body. Not at the flushed skin stretched over sharp bones.

Not what you were picturing, is it? she asked.

I almost said no, then stopped. I realized what she'd said. As if she knew. As if she'd known all along. I looked up and met her eyes.

You don't need to tell me, she said.

But those words that had frozen in my mouth a thousand times between here and New Jersey, they thawed. Tell you what? I asked. That I love you?

The words echoed.

She smiled and she touched my cheek and, there in that steamy bathroom smelling of roses, I didn't need her to tell me either.

June 7, 1926

This morning Ethel was having trouble breathing.

I brought my notebook and started reading to her the script I've been writing. It's about two friends driving across the country in a jalopy, I said. There were flat tires, rainy campgrounds, the occasional bottle of cheap gin. Love simmering beneath the surface. Sickness chasing them like a headless horseman. But the friends, they were happy. Whatever came next, they had this time together.

Every now and again, Ethel took the notebook from me to reread a line. Once she took my pencil, and shakily added one of her own. I had to keep stopping to let her catch her breath. I had to stop to keep her from hearing the tears in my voice.

I went to get her a cup of tea. When I came back, she was curled up around my notebook. It's not finished.

Of course not, I said. We still have more story between us, don't we?

She didn't answer.

Doc Robinson gave her a little morphine and her eyes grew dreamy after that. Before she slipped off to sleep, she took my hand and pulled me down close. Her lips brushing against my ear, she whispered, Write me a last scene.

I sat by the bed, holding her hand with one of mine, the pencil with the other. She slept and I wrote the last scene she deserved.

She never got to read it.

June 8, 1926

I gave Ethel a bath again. This time Carl helped. We washed her and dressed her, by mutual consent, in the knickers and blouse she'd worn the past couple of weeks.

We worked slowly. I knew once it was done, once she lay under the acacia tree out back, that I'd have no reason to stay.

Carl knew it too. He'd be for New Jersey, for a quiet house with AL, and I'd be for California. So we worked slowly, needing those last few moments with her, but also with each other. I remembered what AL had said the other day, about refusing to say goodbye. Maybe that's what we were doing.

I'll keep in touch, I said, more with politeness than conviction.

He didn't let me get by with politeness. You said that when I joined the army.

Back then, it had been petty jealousies. I hadn't written because I'd wanted to forget him. I'd wanted Ethel to. Of course she didn't. She missed him and I never even knew.

I hadn't believed that love was infinite. That it doesn't diminish with distance or time. Hearts can bruise and go on beating. I'm sorry, I said.

I spent years without one of my best friends, he said, and will spend a lifetime without the other. Please say you will.

I will.

June 10, 1926

I didn't open up my notebook again until I was standing in front of the Pacific Ocean.

I drove from Nevada with hands shaking, fear gripping me around the middle. I couldn't even say what I was afraid of.

Maybe it was what awaited me in California, the uncertain abyss of work, apartments, friends.

Maybe it was knowing who I was.

Maybe it was the quiet car. The loneliness.

Or maybe, probably, actually . . . it was a future without her.

I drove until I heard the ocean and then I got out and walked onto the beach. From one coast to the other. I left my shoes on the sand and walked until my toes touched the water. Each wave pulled a little of my fear and washed it out to sea.

And I opened my notebook.

Flipping through all the journal entries and their painful yearning, through the pages of my script, I found that Ethel had left something behind.

On the very last page, in faint letters, she'd written an echo of that note passed in class all those years ago. "Holding your hand, I suddenly wasn't as scared."

And, just as suddenly, neither was I.

Chapter Eighteen

1926

Scene: Campground somewhere between the desert and the ocean. Browns and yellows and oranges beneath an impossibly blue sky. Sounds of distant conversation, rattles of pots and pans, a lone dog barking. By the angle of the light, it's late in the afternoon.

A Model T stands in the middle, doors open. On one side of the car, Beryl kneels next to a campfire, peeling boiled potatoes into a pot. On the other, Francie sets up a slanted tent, attached to the roof of the car. Both are in well-worn travel clothes – knickerbockers and brown blouses. Francie has a bandanna tied around her neck. Beryl's is tied around her head.

Beryl hums as she cuts potatoes over the pot. Francie

works silently. She seems deep in thought. She doesn't notice a pole starting to fall until it lands on her toe.

FRANCIE

(swearing)

She is clearly not a woman who swears often. In fact, she looks embarrassed.

BERYL

(laughing, glancing back over her shoulder)
Be careful. You only have ten of those.

FRANCIE

(forcing a smile, even though she's clear on the other side of the car)
Sorry.

Beryl stands and brings her most recently peeled potato around the car.

BERYL

You okay?

FRANCIE

(Her smile becomes genuine at the sight of Beryl.)
Yes.

BERYL

(unconvinced)
Well, *(with a sudden wink)* try not to get any splinters.

I have to get these potatoes finished.

*She moves back to the campfire and her humming.
Francie drops her smile. They face the wings, backs
to the Model T.*

FRANCIE

(finally)
Beryl, *(hesitating)* you sure you aren't going to
regret it?

BERYL

Dinner? No. You know my feelings about mashed
potatoes.

FRANCIE

Be serious.

BERYL

Fine. Regret what?

FRANCIE

Running after the car with your suitcase.

BERYL

(hands stilling, just for a moment)
Of course not. We weren't finished with our
adventure. I still haven't seen the Pacific Ocean.

FRANCIE

I know, but—

BERYL

(almost offhandedly)
Oh, I wouldn't abandon you, Fran.
(pouring milk)
We're in this together.

FRANCIE

I know, Beryl. I know that.
(leans against tent pole and looks across to where Beryl is on the other side of the car)
But that's not what I meant. Not when I left the ranch.

In this draft of this script, they've left the dude ranch, all those wooden cacti and scenery flats and lights with amber gels. The curtain didn't fall, the applause didn't thunder, the orchestra didn't soar into a finale. In a theatrical bit of repetition between acts, Beryl chased the offstage sound of a car engine. And, scene.

FRANCIE

(repeating)
That's not what I meant.

BERYL

Then what did you mean?

FRANCIE

Do you regret running after my car that very first time? At the start of this whole thing?

BERYL

(stills with potato masher in hand)
The start? When did it really start?

FRANCIE

(without thinking)
1908. We were ten.
(without noticing the quiet on the other side)
You'd come to try out for the class play I'd written –
maudlin, preachy thing that it was. None of the boys
wanted anything to do with it, so you marched to
the front of the room and said you'd take the part of
King Henry. Truth be told, I was too scared of you to
say no. Scared, impressed, envious. Infatuated.

Beryl starts at the last word.

FRANCIE

That was the start. Do you remember? After that, we
were inseparable.

*She stares across the space between them, as if she
can see through the car. Beryl's face is anguished.*

FRANCIE

Are you still there?

BERYL

Yes.
(shaking her head and standing)

I remember. That silly play.
(She applies wire masher to the pot of potatoes and milk.)
Ha!
(with unnecessary vigor)
You're right.

FRANCIE

FRANCIE

I am.
(straightening)
You didn't ask.

BERYL

Ask what?

FRANCIE

(quietly)
What it was that started that day.

Beryl does not respond. She busies herself putting mashed potatoes into a ceramic bowl, adding butter, adding salt.

Francie stands straight and squeezes her hands together. She looks like she might pace in front of the tent. She looks like she might duck inside under the canvas and not say another word. If the scene had been real, she might have. If they'd really been here, with nothing more difficult than a Model T between them, Francie might have lost her nerve, the way she had at all of those other campgrounds in all those other scenes.

But this scene is her last chance. It's her only chance. She wrote it to say what she needs to say. To give herself more time. After all, she's the only player left on the stage.

So in this version of this scene that played out in her head hundreds of times, Francie doesn't hide in the tent. She steps around the car. She crosses to where Beryl stands by the bonfire with her ceramic bowl. And she kisses her.

FRANCIE

That's what started the day you stepped in front of me and declared you'd be my king. That.

Beryl drops the bowl of mashed potatoes.

This is the place for a monologue. Something long and suitably romantic. Something that reveals decades of wistfulness, asks for decades of promises. In this script, the future's as long as the script writer's paper. On the page, they have eternity.

But the monologue would be unnecessary. It's become a silent movie, close-ups of emotions on faces and gestures that speak louder than words.

Beryl breaks the eye contact first and bends to wipe off her shoes. Francie waits a moment, then goes back around the Model T to where the second tent sits folded. She begins to unfold. On the other side, Beryl picks up the broken halves of her bowl. She's humming "California, Here I Come." Francie smiles and puts the second tent back in the car.

The curtain, now, can fall.

Chapter Nineteen

1952

It's right there on the front page. *MOULIN ROUGE* Picketed by Legion Men.

The continuation on page nine isn't as leading as that headline. There were only a handful of picketers at the premiere, largely unnoticed by the swanky crowd and the hundreds of fans waiting for autographs. John Huston didn't give them a second thought. The pictures make it look awful, though. Placards with John's name, and Jose Ferrer's. Words like "ban" and "Communist." Louise feels sick to her stomach.

"More coffee?" the diner waitress asks, but Louise waves her away. When her hash and toast arrives, she can't eat it. She reads the rest of the paper, but keeps coming back to those photos.

The waitress looks over Louise's shoulder when she comes to clear the table. "Nasty, ain't it?"

Louise pushes the plate of uneaten hash away. "It is.

To step out of your car on premiere night, already nervous about the critics, and to encounter *this*." She stabs a finger at the newspaper. "Poor John," she says, mostly to herself. "Poor Jose! He looks positively bewildered here."

The waitress is staring over her coffeepot. "I meant those actors. Nasty Reds, parading around like they're real Americans." She picks up Louise's mug, accidentally sloshing coffee onto the newspaper. "It ain't right."

Though she's never done it before, Louise neglects to leave a tip.

It was nine months ago when Arnie first got wind that he'd been named.

Louise had been in the kitchen, frying up a mess of steak and potatoes for Arnie, when the doorbell rang. Maybe it was Pauline with a pie or the paperboy collecting. They weren't expecting anyone, not this close to supper.

It was neither. When she came out of the kitchen, wiping her hands on her apron, it was to Arnie and a Western Union boy on the front porch. Arnie was chuckling over a telegram and ignoring the messenger, who was all but holding his hand out for the anticipated tip. Louise picked up her handbag and fished out a nickel.

"Oh, this one is worth a dime." Arnie handed over the telegram, and retrieved another five cents from her change purse.

It was from Charlie, but addressed to Arnie.

WE SHOULD GET TOGETHER BEFORE YOU HEAD OUT OF TOWN. LUNCH WITH R. KENNY?

"Did he spoil the surprise?" Louise asked. It was two weeks until their anniversary. "Where are we going?"

"This is the kind of surprise that needs spoiling," Arnie said, and she knew it wasn't a weekend in Palm Springs or anything nice like that. "Sorry, kiddo. It's just Charlie being clever. Sending me codes through the telegraph."

Charlie had never sent her a thing in code. "So secret lunches with *my* agent and whoever 'R. Kenny' is. A girl might get jealous."

Arnie stopped his chuckling. On the front walk, the Western Union boy was very slowly pocketing his two nickels. And Louise realized suddenly that the code wasn't as secret as all that.

"R. Kenny. Robert Kenny. One of the lawyers for the Hollywood Ten." She lowered her voice, suddenly sick. "Oh, Arn. What did you do?"

The messenger took his delivery log out of his bag. Next door, Pauline waved over the top of her watering can. Arnie took Louise's hand and pulled her into the house.

"I was going to tell you at some point," he said, shutting the door, "honestly I was, Lou. I mean, I figured I'd be named at some point . . ."

" 'Named' . . . " she whispered. She sank against the cool of the door.

"Listen." He put his hands on her shoulders, held her against the closed front door. "I fronted for Sid. That script about the girl in the peach orchard? He wrote it, passed it to me, and I put my name on it. Charlie was letting me know that I've been found out. HUAC has my name. Charlie's message, about Robert Kenny and being out of town, he was warning me to take it on the lam. A subpoena's coming my way."

If Arnie hadn't been holding her, Louise would've slid down to the floor.

"Lou? Did you hear what I said?" He let go of her shoulder and touched the side of her face. "Talk to me."

She couldn't meet his eyes. "I can't."

"Please."

She smelled onions. "Dinner is burning." She ducked from under his arms.

It was – the potatoes and onions were in a charred heap on the bottom of the pan – but really she just needed to retreat. She needed to lean over the sink and catch her breath, run cold water over her hands, look at something other than Arnie's eyes.

He'd lied to her. All of those weeks when he'd been shut up in his office, "writing" that script. All of those weeks he'd been sneaking phone calls to Sidney Weller, freshly blacklisted, Hollywood poison. All of those weeks he spent pretending that they were still out of the HUAC's reach.

Arnie had followed her into the kitchen. "I didn't mean for this to happen," he said. "Lou, you have to believe me."

She moved the pan off the stove.

"If you won't talk about this now, when will you?"

"I could ask you the same question." She attacked the burned potatoes with the edge of a spatula. "You clearly haven't done much talking." The potatoes stubbornly held on. "When were you going to tell me about Sid? When were you going to tell me that you were risking your career, and mine, to help a friend?"

"Lou, don't be like that."

She spun. "Like what? Angry that my husband kept me in the dark? Scared that he did such a risky, stupid thing?"

He gently took the spatula from her hand. "Lou." She hadn't even realized she'd still been holding it. "The less you knew, the safer you were."

He moved the pan into the sink, turned on the tap, and left. By the time he returned with two large whiskeys, her hands had stopped shaking.

She accepted the drink, grateful to have something to hold on to. Her brief anger had abated, and she was suddenly exhausted. "Can we sit down?" she asked.

"I'll turn off the stove."

She sank onto the living room sofa and listened to him rattle around the kitchen, washing the pan, putting the steak back into the refrigerator, taking out the trash. She found his mahogany pipe hiding under the pile of mail. While she waited, she filled it with Old Holborn. A few minutes later he came out into the living room with two peanut butter sandwiches stacked on top of his glass. He hadn't thought to bring plates.

He set to eating his sandwich right away, but she held hers balanced on her knee. She still wore her apron. There were too many questions, many without discernible answers, so she asked, softly, "Why, Arn?" It's what she wanted to know most of all.

He didn't answer right away. He finished his sandwich and stared into the swirl of whiskey in his glass. He wasn't laughing anymore. Mostly he looked tired. "Sid's having doors slammed in his face left and right. He can't get a job writing a radio commercial, much less a screenplay. When he rang me up and asked if I'd front, he said he didn't think I would, not in a thousand years. No one else would give him the time of day, a helping hand, a red cent. What could I say?" He took a swallow of his whiskey and wiped his mouth with the back of his hand. "He'd give me the boots from his feet if mine were bare. That's what friends do." He patted his front pockets for his pipe.

She passed it over to him. "I love Sid – you know I do – but he shouldn't have asked you. He had to have known what would happen."

"So did I. Lou, don't think I haven't been expecting this." He set his glass down on the coffee table and picked up a matchbook from the ashtray. "Half the people I know are hiding out in Mexico. The other half are working as janitors or short-order cooks. And the other half are doing whatever it takes to keep doing what they love to do, even if it means they're doing it from behind a front."

"That's too many halves," she murmured, and the whiskey had done enough of its job so that they both almost smiled.

He lit his pipe. "I said yes, because I knew it would hit me at some point. I'd be named eventually. And if I can't lift someone up on my way down, well then, what's the point in letting myself fall?" He tossed the spent match into the ashtray. "If it's dangerous to help a friend, what kind of world is this?"

"I don't know. An awful one. A suspicious one." She leaned back against the rust-colored throw pillow. "I read in the paper today that Communists have 'infiltrated' nursery schools. Arn, I'm scared."

"I wouldn't be." He lifted her feet onto his lap. "Dr Seuss is still working on that new edition of *The Communist Manifesto*. I hear there's an aardvark."

She kicked him. "You dope, I'm serious."

He caught her feet. "So am I. Well, halfway."

"We're in a time when nursery teachers are suspect. What chance does a bright, opinionated screenwriter stand? One who maybe almost sort of went to a rally or two in his day."

He put a finger to his lips. "Shh."

"You took a leap fronting for Sid and now they've caught you out." She drank, wishing she had an ice cube. "You've been named. You'll be subpoenaed."

"Yeah, but what are they going to ask me? There's no proof. Sid and I were careful."

"So say teenage girls in backseats everywhere."

"Everyone knows it doesn't happen the first time."

"You plan on doing this again?"

"Well, when the right guy asks . . ."

"Think of your reputation."

The banter died. Because that was exactly what was at stake.

She finished her drink but did not refill it. "Why are we cracking jokes?"

"You heard Gene Kelly. All the world loves a clown."

"This is serious stuff."

"The world is full of serious stuff," he said. "War. Smog. Republicans. We can't write them out of the script, but we can write around them. Laugh at them. Make the dialogue sizzle with disdain."

The telegram sat on the coffee table. Arnie had set his glass right on the center of it.

"So, Lou," he asked, "what should I do?"

As though she had all the answers. As though she had any of them. "Let me freshen up our drinks."

It was a stalling tactic. She even went all the way to the kitchen for ice. She wanted time to think.

Arnie was stubborn. He was Tom Joad. He'd stick to his principles, consequences be damned. She didn't ask what he'd do because she knew. He wouldn't go to see Robert Kenny. He'd dodge the subpoena or stand before the committee and plead the Fifth before he'd offer up a single name. He'd never give in.

So he'd asked her. He already knew how he'd answer.

She took her time arranging the ice cubes just so and mixing up two whiskey and waters. Arnie was leaning back on the sofa with his glasses off and his eyes closed. The mail was spread out on the coffee table. Mostly bills. A letter from Dad. The *Los Angeles Times* folded over a story about CARE for Korea packages delivered to troops in Pusan. On the telegram from Charlie, his glass had left a damp ring around the words "head out of town."

She knew how to keep him safe from rumors, from HUAC, from everything here. He had old editors and old favors he could call up. He wouldn't say no to her.

When she sat back down, he opened his eyes.

"You need to do something wildly patriotic," she said.

"Something that not even the Committee on Un-American Activities can argue with."

"Like what?"

"Like doing your part in the fight against communism." She handed him the glass. "Like going to Korea."

Louise tries calling Arnie every time she stops. And there are a lot of stops. Gas stations. Diners. The five-and-ten at the edge of Pennsylvania, where she desperately buys a pair of earmuffs. Outside of the Midwest, the road is frustratingly hilly and she's cold. By the afternoon she's drunk more cups of coffee than she ever does on set. But still, with all of those stops, with all of those calls to Los Angeles, Arnie doesn't answer.

All of this time in the car, all of this time doing nothing but watching the snow through the windshield and thinking, she misses him. She wants to hear his voice. She wants to say that she's sorry.

It's an apology months unspoken. It's guilt that's been building since the telegram that he'd been injured far away in Korea. It's eating away at her.

That unsaid apology, that unacknowledged guilt, it's why she counts to ten. Why she takes a breath and smiles before opening the front door. Why she doesn't nag and why she just keeps buying the tins of saltines. Arnie's in a wheelchair and he's miserable and she knows it's her fault.

Back when he'd gotten that telegram from Charlie, back when they'd stretched on the sofa with whiskeys and nervous jokes, she was terrified. So terrified of the dangers at home that she disregarded the very real dangers in Korea. "Stay safe," she'd said. "Go to war."

Remembering it now, she flushes. And then is instantly furious at her flushes, at her cradled guilt, at her laziness. She's had months to apologize. She's had months to ask Arnie's forgiveness. She hits the steering wheel. The horn sounds. Though it was an accident, something about the blare fits her mood, and she pushes it again and again. A passing motorist slows and stares out of his window, but her frustration has abated. She waves at him to say that everything is all right. Maybe it is.

At the next town, she stops for another cup of coffee and a slice of shoofly pie. She places her millionth call to Los Angeles, but nobody answers. She finishes her pie and places another call, this time to Western Union. "I'd like to send a telegram to Mr Arnold Bates, Beverly Hills, California. 'Strength is when we're together. I'm sorry we were ever apart. Lou.'"

"Is that a Santagram?" asks the clerk on the phone.

"What?"

"Any holiday greetings?"

" 'Merry Christmas, Arn,' " she says. " 'I love you.' "

Chapter Twenty

Excerpt from "Incidence of Osteogenic Sarcomas in Radium Dial Painters" in *The Journal of Practical Cancer Research* (1931)

Case 10: Left work as dial painter in good health. No anemia. No necrosis of jaw. Married and had a child. Five years later pain and swelling in ankle. Later pain throughout leg and in the area of the tarsal scaphoid. Anemia. Two spontaneous fractures, one of the femur and one of the tibia. No tests for radio-activity during life. Necropsy.

E.W., a white female, twenty-eight years of age, worked as a dial painter from 1917 to 1919. She married, quitting her work as a dial painter, and had a child the next year.

After the birth of her child in 1920, she was found to be anemic. It was attributed to the recent pregnancy and she was given liver extract.

In 1924, she began having pain in her right ankle and began to limp. Roentgenograms were normal.

Over the next two years pain was reported throughout her right leg and intermittently in her left hip. In December 1925, she suffered a spontaneous fracture in her femur, just above her right knee, stepping from a porch step. The patient required twelve weeks in a plaster cast for firm callus formation. Early in 1926 the pain in her ankle and foot intensified and she exhibited swelling above the tarsal scaphoid.

She suffered from fainting spells and weight loss and the earlier diagnosis of anemia was reaffirmed by her family physician, Dr A. G. Glass. She was prescribed Parson's Vigor Tonic, a radium water patent medicine, as a treatment for the anemia.

She suffered another spontaneous fracture of the tibia in May 1926, which was not treated. The fracture was malpositioned and, when seen by Dr Barro Robinson, required open reduction. The operation revealed a tumor on her tibia, near the site of the fracture. Large masses of tumor tissue were removed and examined, proving to be a rapidly growing osteogenic sarcoma.

No roentgenogram apparatus was available, but a manual examination by Dr Robinson indicated a mass on the left side of the patient's pelvis, extending into the abdomen. He reported that she was emaciated and had a mild fever.

Over the next week dyspnea developed and pain worsened. The patient struggled for breath. Regular doses of morphine were administered and an operation to remove the mass on the pelvis was discussed. Death occurred on June 7, 1926, nearly seven years after the patient quit working at the dial factory.

Necropsy, performed by Dr Barro Robinson, circuit doctor in Clark County, Nevada: Necropsy confirmed a large mass on the ilium, about 15 cm in diameter. Another small sarcoma was found on the lower end of the right femur. The femur, the tibia, and the tarsal scaphoid on the right side all showed evidence of radiation osteitis.

HISTOLOGIC EXAMINATION: Sections from the tumor on the hip showed a very cellular, rapidly growing osteogenic sarcoma. Sections of the right femur showed a regenerating marrow of the megaloblastic type, with many primitive cells.

ESTIMATION OF RADIOACTIVITY: This has not been completed in this case. Qualitatively, the bones are radioactive.

COMMENT: Though equipment capable of measuring radioactive output was not available, Dr Barro Robinson previously treated miners working with radium ore on the Colorado Plateau. His histological knowledge of radiation osteitis added to the patient's employment history and the presence of osteogenic sarcomas all suggest that this was an earlier case of radium-induced malignancy.

Belzer & Belzer Associates
Newark, NJ

November 15, 1926

Carl L. Wild
18 Daniel Street
Newark, NJ

Dear Mr Wild,

Per your query, the statute of limitations has passed between the time your late wife stopped work at the dial factory and the time of her diagnoses, however there is some precedent that we can use here. In the recent cases of Marguerite Carlough, Sarah Maillefer, and Hazel Kuser (you may have read about their cases against US Radium in the newspapers), an argument was made that tolling the statute should begin not at the time of unemployment but at the time when the symptoms appear or when the diagnosis is made.

You say that Dr Martland has reviewed her case, which will help our argument, given his reputation as an expert in these cases. Do you have copies of Mrs Wild's employment records and her medical records for visits relating to the radium poisoning? Was there an autopsy?

Sincerely,

Harold Belzer, Jr., Esq.

Another Suit Against Radium Corp.

Newark Attorney Seeks Settlement from Company for Family of Deceased Dial Painter

Death from Radio-active Paint

Widower Says Wife Was Misdiagnosed for Years

Belzer & Belzer, Newark attorneys, announced yesterday that they intended to bring a $15,000 suit against the United States Radium Corporation for the death of Mrs Ethel D. Wild, who died after working in their Orange, NJ, factory, painting watch dials with luminous paint. The lawyers allege that Mrs Wild's death was caused by radium poisoning due to radio-active substances in the luminous paint. The dial painters were taught to wet the paintbrushes to a point with their lips, thus ingesting daily amounts of radium and mesothorium. The attorneys claim that women were not told of the risks, but were told that the luminous paint would give them a healthy glow.

Mr Carl L. Wild of Newark, NJ, the widower of Ethel Wild, is the latest to bring a suit against the corporation. He claims that his wife was seen by several doctors over the past few years, receiving diagnoses of anemia and rheumatism, before a Clark

County, Nevada, physician, Dr Barro Robinson, identified several lesions and masses in the patient and diagnosed radium poisoning. The diagnosis came too late for Mrs Wild.

This follows on the heels of recent suits brought by the families of three former dial painters, Miss Marguerite Carlough, Mrs Sarah Maillefer, and Mrs Hazel Kuser. Dr Harrison S. Martland, Essex County physician and chief pathologist of the Newark City Hospital, is carrying out clinical examinations of affected dial workers.

The three previous cases were recently settled out of court.

January 12, 1927

Carl Wild
18 Daniel Street
Newark, NJ

Dear Carl,
I read about the court case, even all the way out here.
It's ridiculous that there should even be an argument.
Lately I've been reading everything I can get my hands
on about radium. I pinched a pair of glasses from the
prop department and read journals in the medical
school library. They all say (and have been saying) that
radium is awful stuff and that a steady diet of it wreaks
havoc on our bodies. I could single-handedly line up
experts from here to New Jersey with the evidence.

I wish I'd read all of this years ago. I wish I knew
before I knocked on Ethel's door with that ad for
the watch factory and a cheerful "What do you say,
Eth?" The years of suffering I could have saved her
from. The years I could have saved you and AL
from. Carl, among all this, despite everything that
happened, for what it's worth, I'm sorry.
Sincerely,
Florrie

Excerpt from "Wild vs United States Radium Corporation"

The plaintiff, husband of the decedent, as general administrator and as administrator ad prosequendum, commenced an action at law for damages caused by injuries to the decedent and her subsequent death on June 7, 1926.

Ethel D. Wild, the plaintiff's intestate, was employed by the defendant, the United States Radium Corporation, from September 9, 1917, to March 14, 1919, to paint watch dials with a luminous paint, containing insoluble sulphates of radium and mesothorium. The mixture was 1 part radioactive sulphate to each 40,000 of paint. The decedent worked 5 days per week, painting, on average, 250 dials per day, and pointed the brush with her lips after painting each of the fourteen numerals (1–12, with 6 not painted). Licking an average of 1 mg. of paint per numeral, at 250 per day, 5 days per week, the decedent ingested approximately 34,000 micrograms of radium over the 18 months of her employment. As little as 2 mcg of radium fixed in the bones has been shown to be fatal.

While the decedent was in the employ of the defendant, no precautions were taken to warn dial painters or to prevent them from exposure to radium in the paint and radium emanation in the air of the factory workrooms.

Carl Wild
18 Daniel Street
Newark, NJ

Dear Carl,
I couldn't believe it when I read the news this evening. The trial is postponed again? Truly, they are heartless.

As it drags on and on, I can't help but wonder, perhaps, Carl, if you've already won. You've got Ethel's name in the papers. You've got US Radium backed against the ropes. You've got people from one end of the country to the other reading about yet another David standing up to that great Goliath. It's the kind of story that heartens folks. It's the kind that I write about.

Speaking of, have you seen The Poet and the Thief? I was one of the "soundless dozens" working on that. Not a peep in the credits, of course, but I expended many typewriter ribbons on that scenario.

So what does AL think of all this? Does she know what's going on in the courtroom?

Sincerely,
Florrie

October 15, 1927

Carl Wild
18 Daniel Street
Newark, NJ

Dear Carl,
Investments? Who are you, J. D. Rockefeller? I'm strictly a shoe-box-under-the-bed kind of girl (the shoe box is Buster Brown; the contents only amount to a dollar forty). I've never set foot in a bank. Do our kind of people invest?

Really, though, that's an awful lot of money (if the newspapers are to be believed; no need to clarify). But Eth would've been happy, honestly she would've. Knowing that AL was set up for college or traveling or anything she wants. Whatever you choose, know that.

Affectionately,
Florrie

NATIONAL BANK OF NEWARK
NEWARK, NJ
DEPOSITED BY
C. L. Wild

NEWARK, NJ	October 23	1927

PLEASE LIST EACH CHECK SEPARATELY

CURRENCY		
GOLD		
SILVER		
CHECKS		
US Radium Corp.	1000	00
TOTAL $	1000.00	

BILLIONS LOST AS STOCKS CRASH

Stock Values Plummet Amid Panic Selling

—

WALL ST STUNNED

Stocks Hit Lowest Levels in US History

NATIONAL BANK OF NEWARK
NEWARK, NJ
WITHDRAWN BY
C. L. Wild

NEWARK, NJ _____ October 30 _____ 1929 _____

PLEASE LIST EACH CHECK SEPARATELY

CURRENCY	1000	00
GOLD		
SILVER		
TOTAL $	1000.00	

LOCAL BUTCHERS OPEN SHOP

Kitchen in the Back Keeps Neighbors Fed

Local residents and neighborhood butchers Carl Wild and Henry Perry are lending a helping hand. With many in the city hit hard by the Depression, nothing goes to waste in their butcher shop. At the end of the day, unsold cuts of meat are salvaged into soup and offered gratis to any local citizen with a bowl and a need.

Mr Wild and Mr Perry have brought the whole neighbourhood into the act. They supply the meat, while other neighbourhood businesses add surplus produce and canned goods. "Stone soup," Mr Wild calls it, after the story he reads his daughter. "Everyone adds a little, but it matters a whole lot."

The two men, veterans of the last war, opened the business together after being discharged from the army.

September 12, 1930

Carl Wild
18 Daniel Street
Newark, NJ

Dear Carl,
Things are golden here! Well, as golden as they can be when you don't have more than two nickels to rub together. But this is LA. A girl can get by on doughnuts and a smile.

I have a roommate now, a singer named Paulette. She has a voice like silk and owns a top hat. I met her at one of the speakeasies around here. She was up on stage and I thought she was a boy at first, but Hollywood is nothing if not full of surprises!

Have you seen Rose at Sunset? They spelled my name wrong, but it's there in the credits!

Affectionately,
Florrie

Dear Mr Wild,

Thank you for meeting with me this morning. Please find included Anna Louisa's marks so far this term. She has no trouble excelling academically, as this report will show, but her classroom behavior does not meet our school standards. Even today, following our meeting, we had another incident. Anna Louisa took advantage of Miss Flanigan's temporary absence from the classroom to perform a tap dance on the teacher's desk. This is unacceptable and, should it continue, we will be forced to ask you to find another situation.

Sincerely,
Mr Peter Ball, principal
McCall Street Elementary School

August 1, 1932

Carl Wild
18 Daniel Street
Newark, NJ

Dear C,
Wanted to dash off a note with my new address. I've finally moved out of the Hollywood Studio Club! I'm in a shoe box of an apartment with a new roommate, a chorine named Lorelei. She's from Iowa. Until we met, I didn't know that people actually came from Iowa.

I'm trying not to look like a complete dolt and have been attempting to teach myself cooking. Do you have any of Eth's old cookbooks you might send my way? She always used to say that just about anyone could impress with a croquette.

F

From the kitchen of E. W.:

Chicken Croquettes

2 cups chopped, cooked chicken
1 small chopped onion
½ teaspoon celery salt
¼ teaspoon pepper
1 to 2 cups thick white sauce
Cracker crumbs
1 egg, beaten

Stir chicken through finely chopped onion. Season with celery salt and pepper. Mix with enough white sauce to hold seasoned chicken together. Divide mixture into equal portions, allowing at least two tablespoons for each croquette. Form into cylinders. Dip each croquette into dry crumbs, then beaten egg, then again crumbs. Fry in hot, deep fat until light brown in color. Serve on plate with dollop of white sauce.

Newark Arts High School
Newark, NJ

June 15, 1933

Anna Louisa Wild
18 Daniel Street
Newark, NJ

Dear Miss Wild,
We are pleased to welcome you to the Newark Arts
High School for the forthcoming school year. Further
communications regarding tuition, registration, and
required materials will follow by mail.
Sincerely,
Mr A. G. Hathaway

Carl Wild
18 Daniel Street
Newark, NJ

Dear Carl,
Sending you my new address. I've moved again, to an apartment about a square inch bigger than the last. This roommate is named Betty and she's a cigarette girl at the Cocoanut Grove nightclub. She also cooks, so no need for me to continue burning croquettes.

Things are far quieter than when I was at the Hollywood Studio Club and I'm able to get a little of my own writing done nights when Betty is at work. Still haven't convinced anyone at the studio to give my original screenplays more than the cursoriest of looks, but they've put me on to the first draft of an adaptation. It's for Paula Fredricks' Veils of Solitude. Have you read it? I hope not, as the novel is utter drivel. But, for the time being, it's my utter drivel and I mean to make it into something people will be willing to pay a nickel to see. The heroine is wishy-washy, but I'm adding a little starch to her spine. Joan Crawford? Maybe.

Florrie

Harold J. R. Pringle, MD
New York, NY

June 15, 1934

Carl L. Wild
18 Daniel Street
Newark, NJ

Re: Anna Louisa Wild

Dear Mr Wild,

I have received the histology results from the laboratory and reviewed them along with those from the clinical examination of your daughter and I have come to the conclusion that Anna Louisa shows no signs of her mother's illness. No radiation emanations are present. Roentgenograms show normal bone structure. Though she shows slight anemia, the levels are not out of the range for a girl of fourteen. Otherwise, she is in good physical health. She is tall for her age, with sound reflexes, and a strong pulse. I can find no medical source for the aches in her limbs that you mentioned and believe them, based on her age and level of activity, to be caused by growth and by exercise.

Please contact my office if you wish to discuss this further, but you have nothing to worry about at the present with regards to your daughter's health. She is a healthy, growing adolescent.

Sincerely,

Dr H. J. R. Pringle

December 12, 1934

Carl Wild
18 Daniel Street
Newark, NJ

Dear Carl,
If you've been watching the marquee for Veils of Solitude, it was scrapped. I've now been put on adapting, of all things, Miss Ogilvy Finds Herself.

I wonder if they knew who they were giving the story to. It's by Radclyffe Hall. I'd bought it the day it came out and then cried myself to sleep reading it that night. Maybe they did know and thought I could bring those tears, that loneliness, that pent-up frustration into the screenplay.

My current roommate, Evangeline, is actually a writer. I thought that would give us more in common. My last few roommates have been little more than pretty faces. But when I showed Evangeline a page I was working on, she just said, "Life is sad enough without stories like this."

If I didn't have you to write to, I wonder if I'd have anyone to talk to.

Florrie

The Newark Arts High School
freshman class presents a production of

A Midsummer Night's Dream

Starring (in alphabetical order)

Miss Kate Barnes
Mr Chester Floyd
Mr Ulrich Pennbottom
Miss Gladys Woods

With (in alphabetical order)

Mr Augustus Buck
Miss Doris Ann Streeter
Mr Francis Tillis
Miss Elizabeth Yates

And (in alphabetical order)

Miss Vera Jean Blaine
Miss Aldona Finklestein
Miss Penelope Gainor
Miss Hazel Gibbs
Mr Archibald Knute
Miss Ruth Prescott
Mr Trent Valentine
Miss Anna Louisa Wild

May 15, 1935

Carl Wild
18 Daniel Street
Newark, NJ

Dear Carl,
I'm done with temporariness, the string of roommates
and of cheap, cluttered apartments. I feel like I've
been waiting all my life for something permanent. I
haven't found it among the former, but I have with
the latter. I've bought an apartment, Carl! It's not
big, but it's new and sunny and has bougainvillea
bright outside my window. Best of all it's mine.

I have Miss Ogilvy to thank for the apartment, poor
sad "William" Ogilvy. Have you seen the film yet? Of
course it's much neatened up and Code-approved (the
casual viewer would never see her as anything but a
crop-haired tomboy), but I did my best. Of course, I
cried dozens of times as I worked on the screenplay.
Knowing how an "odd girl" feels, just on the edges
of everything. I tried to infuse it with notes of hope.
Because, C, don't we need that, people like you and
me? Permanence, hope, and a sense that we belong.

Affectionately,
Florrie

The Newark Arts High School
sophomore class presents a production of

Much Ado About Nothing

Starring (in alphabetical order)

Mr Chester Floyd
Miss Doris Ann Streeter
Mr Francis Tillis
Miss Gladys Woods

With (in alphabetical order)

Miss Kate Barnes
Mr Augustus Buck
Mr Ulrich Pennbottom
Miss Anna Louisa Wild

And (in alphabetical order)

Miss Vera Jean Blaine
Miss Aldona Finklestein
Miss Penelope Gainor
Miss Hazel Gibbs
Mr Archibald Knute
Miss Ruth Prescott
Mr Trent Valentine
Miss Elizabeth Yates

July 1, 1936

Carl Wild
18 Daniel Street
Newark, NJ

Dear Carl,
Things are swimming along here. I've been moved to a new desk and with a new paycheck. I don't think anyone expected Miss Ogilvy to be as big a success as it was. As I worked on the screenplay, I thought it would be such a quiet film.

Working on an adaptation of Elizabeth Cromwell's Such Is Love. The novel is long on descriptions of cocktail dresses, but the dialogue is smart and there isn't a single, solitary man in the whole thing. Sorry to disappoint you . . .

Affectionately,
Florrie

The Newark Arts High School
junior class presents a production of

The Taming of the Shrew

Starring (in alphabetical order)

Mr Chester Floyd
Miss Doris Ann Streeter
Mr Francis Tillis
Miss Anna Louisa Wild

With (in alphabetical order)

Miss Aldona Finklestein
Mr Ulrich Pennbottom
Mr Trent Valentine
Miss Gladys Woods

And (in alphabetical order)

Miss Kate Barnes
Miss Vera Jean Blaine
Mr Augustus Buck
Miss Penelope Gainor
Miss Hazel Gibbs
Mr Archibald Knute
Miss Ruth Prescott
Miss Elizabeth Yates

Carl Wild
18 Daniel Street
Newark, NJ

Dear Carl,
I hate to see you wrapped so full of doubt. You have every right to feel vulnerable. Look at it all. How can we not? With the way we're always on the outside, with the way we can't be honest to anyone, sometimes not even to ourselves.

But maybe you and I have it better than most. I'm here in Hollywood, surrounded by my friends and my work, and you're there with Hank. We have people who make us happy. And, you know, we have each other. Old friends, gold friends. Three thousand miles isn't a match for the US Postal Service.

Your dear,
F

Newark Arts High School

This Certifies That

Anna Louisa Wild

having satisfactorily completed the Course of Study
precribed by the Board of Education is hereby declared a
graduate of Newark Arts High School and is entitled to a

Diploma

Given by order of the Board of Education of Essex
County in and for Newark Arts High School, Newark,
New Jersey

this Fourth day of June 1938

August 12, 1938

Carl Wild
18 Daniel Street
Newark, NJ

Dear Carl,
I know. I miss her every day. But you can't blame AL.
She said what she did because she hardly knew Eth.
Really, what do you remember from before you were
six? I'm not worried about AL. She's young, she's
probably feeling faintly rebellious, but she'll always
love her mother. And, my dear friend, she'll always
love you.
    Love,
    F

WESTERN
UNION

NEWARK NJ
1938 OCT 1 PM 9 45

FLORENCE DANIELS=
BLAUE ENGEL APARTMENTS HOLLYWOOD
CALIF=

OCT 4 6:49 PM GREYHOUND TERMINAL=
LET ME KNOW WHEN SHE ARRIVES=
I'LL WORRY THE WHOLE WAY=

C.

Chapter Twenty-One

1952

It's dark when she pulls into Newark. Christmas Eve. It's started snowing again, fat, lazy flakes that dot her windshield. By the time she reaches Dad's neighborhood, the houses and street signs are covered with a fresh fall of snow. Though she's never driven in Newark, she makes the turns automatically. This street feels like a creaking leather bike seat, that one tastes like ice cream bars, this one smells like water spraying fresh from the fire hydrant. With each block, she slips another year back in time. When she parks in front of Dad's house, she's Anna Louisa again.

A garland of plastic holly twines up and over the front door with a fat, red bow on top. Through the front picture window, she sees a Christmas tree, splendid with colored lights, tinsel garland, strings of mercury glass beads, and dozens of ornaments. From between the edges of the window, she can hear Dad's piano playing "Silent Night."

Someone had shoveled the front path at some point,

but there's an inch of snow on it now. That was always her job as a kid. Shoveling. She'd always get distracted halfway through by the piles of snow on either side of the walk, just waiting to be jumped into. That always led to snow angels, which led to snowballs, which led to the inevitable snowman.

She's distracted now and misses the patch of ice on the walk. Though her suitcase stays intact, her ego takes a hit. Luckily that's all. Though she hadn't intended to examine the snowy lawn that closely, she finds herself doing that. She pushes herself up to a kneel and shakes snow from her coat.

The front door opens. "Al?"

"Daddy!" She stands and brushes snow from the knees of her black pants.

He stands in the doorway, looking rumpled and bewildered, like he'd just woken from an impromptu nap with his *Reader's Digest*. He looks older than she remembers. More gray in his hair. Reading glasses pushed up on his head. A pine-green cardigan, like something an irritable professor might wear. "What are you doing out there?"

She responds with a snowball that hits the doorframe.

"Hey!" He brushes a spatter of white from the shoulder of his cardigan. "That's not fair!"

"Sorry," she says without conviction.

He bends and quickly scoops up one of his own. "No you're not." He throws it without a hint of accuracy. Louise stands, unconcerned, as the snowball sails into a nearby bush.

The piano music stops. "Is that Ann?" Hank steps up behind and peers out over Dad's head. He's always been as tall and lanky as a stork, with thinning hair. Now he's completely bald.

"Hi, Uncle Hank." She tosses another snowball between her hands. "Dad and I are playing."

"Playing? It was an ambush," Dad says with a grin. From the peg behind the door, he takes down his wool coat. The black furry hat he pulls from the pocket is the same one she remembers him always wearing. "I'm on to you now."

The snowball fight is short and laughter-filled. Hank brings out two pairs of gloves. The ones he gives Louise are too big and smell like the Aqua Velva he's always worn. She slips them on and joins Dad in rolling the base of a snowman.

"So why didn't Arnie come out this time?" Dad asks, pushing the ball. It's about the size of a watermelon. "Haven't seen that mug of his in quite a while."

Louise deflects. "That's because you refuse to come out to LA."

"After those crashes? You're not getting me on an airplane." He stops when the base is half as high as his knee.

"You need to get yourself a car and then you can *drive* out to see me." She nods toward where the Champ is parked in the driveway.

"Much easier to make enough pathetic phone calls that you give in and come to New Jersey."

She knows he's teasing, but she reaches across and puts her hand over his. "Sorry it's been so long this time."

He sniffs loudly and squeezes her hand. "The cold is making my nose run." He slips off his glove and fishes in his pocket for a handkerchief. "You didn't answer my question about Arnie. He couldn't come along? It's Christmas."

Christmas in the little house on Rodeo Drive is Bing Crosby records, strings of lights, Tom and Jerrys, and rare steaks. But she says, "Oh, that doesn't mean much out in Hollywood." She tries to sound flippant. "The tinsel in 'Tinseltown' doesn't apply to the holidays. The only day we get off work is Cecil B. DeMille's birthday."

He prudently doesn't ask why she's had a week to drive across the US. "Then Arnie's busy working." He starts another ball rolling.

Even when he was working, Arnie and she always made a pact. Nothing but books and bedroom slippers and late afternoon naps from Christmas to New Year's. "Terribly busy."

Dad stops rolling. "Al." He puts a gloved hand under her chin and tips her face up. "Stop worrying about your lines. There's no script for life, my girl."

"There has to be," she insists.

"Nope. No choreography. No blocking. No score. You improvise and ad-lib and hope you have the right co-stars."

"I do." She might not have been certain when she set off from LA, but she is now. "Does he?"

"I've seen that boy light up when you walk into a room." He kisses her forehead. "He does."

She smooths down the sides of the base. "He hasn't been well," she finally says. "Not since he got back."

"Nobody really is, at least not right away."

"It's been three months, Dad."

"Kiddo, do you realize how long it took me to get a decent night's sleep after coming back from France?"

She shakes her head.

"Longer than three months." He brushes off his gloves. "Soldiers aren't used to getting much sleep. They're not used to being safe or still or a lot of things. And I wasn't even a soldier."

"He keeps pushing me away."

He raises his eyebrows. "So what did you do?"

She sits back on her heels. "I left."

Dad doesn't say anything, not for a while. "Are you going back?"

"Did you?" she asks suddenly. "You left too. That ranch we went to in Nevada all those years ago, it was a divorce ranch." Snow sneaks past the edges of the gloves and touches her wrists.

"Your mother followed us out to the ranch. She wanted to reconcile. Instead she . . . Well, she died out there." He blinks away snowflakes. "Don't you remember?"

She doesn't, not really. Just the acacia tree, the sweaty handful of primroses, the sound of Dad's tears. The unmarked hole beneath the tree. A woman who smelled like Djer-Kiss holding her until she stopped crying. "A little." Snow falls icy on the back of her neck. "I remember how a funeral feels. I didn't remember it was in Nevada."

"It was the radium that killed her," he says. "A job that she had for half a minute during the war. Turns out all those girls poisoned themselves with each lick of paint." He stacks a second snowball on top of the base. "They both worked in that tomb, but Ethel was the one who suffered."

"Dad, Florrie died too," she reminds him quietly. "It was cancer."

He sighs and runs a hand across the back of his neck. "The radium was just biding its time, then."

Louise slides off her gloves to shake out the snow inside. "You didn't know Mom was dying when you went to Nevada. Please tell me you didn't."

"Of course not, Al. And when I found out, I knew I couldn't go through with it. With the divorce."

She crosses her arms and tucks her icy hands in her armpits. "Dad, why'd you want to divorce Mom to begin with?"

The front door opens. Yellow light spills out onto the trampled lawn. Hank comes out with a carrot and a pipe and a scarf for the snowman. And an extra scarf that he drapes gently around Dad's neck. "I have hot cocoa, you two," he says.

That one little gesture explains thousands of others she'd overlooked over the years. All of those Sunday dinners where Hank came with lemon meringue pie and stayed until after she went to bed. The way the two men cooked together and shared a newspaper. The duets they played on Dad's piano, sitting close. That one time she'd found Hank's reading glasses on the nightstand.

Louise looks at her dad, at the way he turns to the sound of Hank's voice, at the way he smiles up through the falling snow. "Perfect," she says, and means it.

Hank helps them up. "I've made meat pie with peas for dinner. It just went in the oven. It's not much for a Christmas dinner, but your dad didn't know when you'd arrive."

"It sounds wonderful." She pushes herself up on her tiptoes and kisses his cheek. "I'm glad you're here, Uncle Hank."

She swears the old man blushes.

They walk up to the front door, but the squeal of brakes makes Louise stop on the porch. She turns. A taxi is parked at the curb in front of Dad's house. "Does Santa come by cab these days?" she says.

Dad scratches his head under his hat. "Hank, we expecting anybody?" he asks, without thinking.

But it isn't Santa Claus who steps out onto the street. It's her agent, Charlie, wearing a ridiculous hat with earflaps.

"My agent," she tells Dad and Hank. "He hates the cold so much, he sneezes just thinking about it. What on earth are you doing here?" she calls.

He looks at her over the top of the taxi and lights a cigarette. "I was in the neighborhood."

"Liar."

"Well, I was in the state." He tucks his lighter back in his pocket. "I came to bring you a couple of Christmas presents."

"Maybe you are Saint Nick after all."

"What?"

"Never mind."

Charlie walks around the taxi to the sidewalk. "Gift number one, we took the pot."

She blinks. "What pot?"

"Poker?" Dad asks.

Charlie grins. "So to speak. Remember that bluff you wanted me to play, LuLu?"

The studio. The contract. "We . . . won?"

"Still have a few details to iron out, but I got you that new contract." He says it almost casually. "It's not perfect, but it does give you script approval, and a nice little pile of dough to boot."

She claps her hands and spins around. "We won!" She kisses Dad and a startled Hank smack on the lips.

"Gift number two?" He picks his way carefully up the walkway. "I have a script for you to peruse. We'll take it to the studio. It still needs a little work, but . . ."

She feels a little fissure of disappointment. "I've heard that before."

Charlie holds up a finger. "Original story by Florence Daniels." He seems to enjoy watching understanding settle on her face. "I stopped by your house to check in on that no-account husband of yours, and what do you know? He was halfway through a revision of a Daniels' script."

Behind her, Dad murmurs, "She left scripts?" but Louise can't answer him right away.

Instead, to Charlie, she says incredulously, "He . . . read them? Arn did?"

"Had to send over to the neighbor for a new typewriter

ribbon," Charlie announces, resting a foot on the lower step. "After he washed the ink off his fingers, he let me take a look. Something about two friends and a Model T. Like I said, still needs some work, but . . ."

This time it's Charlie she kisses. She almost knocks him down into the snow. "You're better than Santa Claus."

But he says, "Just wait," and walks back to the cab.

The cabbie is unloading the trunk. He sets a suitcase on the sidewalk, and then a folded wheelchair. It glints in the taillights.

She steps off the porch.

The back door of the taxi opens. "Merry Christmas, Lou."

She's down the walk in a handful of seconds and kneeling in the snow by the curb.

"I thought about sending you a note," Arnie says. The light from the front porch touches his face in the backseat of the cab. "I am a writer, after all."

"A note?" She takes his hand without waiting to ask. "It's been done before."

He's wearing an old tweed coat and a trilby. She'd forgotten how good he looks in a hat.

"I hope you don't mind. I should've told you I was coming." On the seat next to him, she can see a bouquet of wilted airport flowers.

"Mind?" She lets go of his hand. Behind her on the sidewalk the wheelchair rattles as Charlie locks it open. "Put your arms around my neck."

"What?"

"You can't eat Uncle Hank's meat pie out here in the cab." She slides an arm behind his back.

He pulls away. "Charlie can help me get into the chair. You don't—"

"Arn."

He looks up and she remembers that first glance across the library table. Eyes blue as oceans.

"That's what love is, isn't it? You take turns lifting each other up."

He takes a deep breath and shrugs off her arm. He pivots so he's facing her on the sidewalk. "Then let me show you how to do it right." His voice is soft. "I don't want you to get hurt."

The pain in the middle of her heart that she's been carrying the past few months suddenly throbs less. "Then, Arn? Don't ever fall asleep with your back to me again."

"Don't ever get rid of the Klimt book," he says.

"Don't ever wear the same pajamas twice," she counters.

"Don't ever repaint the living room."

"Don't ever hide subpoenas from me."

"Don't ever leave."

She swallows and just shakes her head. "What did you decide about the hearing?"

He shrugs, trying to look casual. "It's been a long while since I picked a good fight."

She lets out a breath and nods. "Then that's what we'll do."

"Together?"

"Every inch of the way."

He reaches for her, runs a hand across her cheek, through her hair. "Is this the cinematic fade-out over the sunset?"

"The end?" She raises herself up until they're face-to-face. She kisses him like she should've months ago. "This is only Act Two."

Acknowledgments

Between 1917 and the 1940s, thousands of women worked in US factories painting luminous dials on wristwatches, something in high demand in and above the trenches of both world wars. The paint they used was made with radium and mesothorium, which gave the dial the coveted glow so prized on dark battlefields. These women were taught that, in order to precisely shape the digits, they needed to draw the paintbrushes to a point with their lips. They were told that there was no danger in doing so and, in fact, ingesting the paint would give them a "healthy glow," an attitude supported by the influx of radium-infused medicines and products for the home sold in the early twentieth century.

These working women might have been lost to history if it weren't for the complications that arose from their work. Starting in 1923 former dial painters in New Jersey,

Connecticut, and Illinois began appearing at dentists' and doctors' offices with a host of alarming symptoms. Anemia. Tooth loss. Necrosis of the jaw. Spontaneous fractures. Bone lesions. Cancer. At first medical professionals under the pay of the radium companies dismissed the claims, discrediting the former dial painters with diagnoses of syphilis. But women working in New Jersey's Department of Labor, Department of Health, and Consumers' League didn't shy from the challenge of working to give recognition and legitimacy to the dial painters' complaints. Lawyers took up their cases, bringing suits against the radium paint corporations. Some women took settlements offered by the companies, but five, with nothing left to lose, brought their cases all the way to trial. They were dubbed "the Radium Girls" by a sympathetic press and their actions led to a reshaping of labor laws and establishment of industrial safety standards that are in effect today.

Though my dial painters are fictional, their experiences are based on those of very real Radium Girls. I combed contemporary news articles, medical journals, and court documents for details about their cases. I did this not only to make my characters real and vivid, but also to try to understand these women and their tenacity in the face of despair. I hope I have done their story justice. I dedicate this novel to those women who fought on, despite loss and worsening health, so that their children and grandchildren would have safe places to work and live.

I spent the writing of this book communing more with maps, brochures, and postcards than with actual people, but there are a few (people, not postcards) who deserve my utmost thanks.

To Anne Speyer for helping me to sharpen my writing to bring Louise's story and Ethel and Florrie's story to their emotional best.

To Courtney Miller-Callihan for her unending trust when, with only a hint of what I was writing, I hid away with my vintage maps and guidebooks.

To Rebecca Paul, for being my sounding board on Arnie's recovery and therapy. And, also, for being my sister.

To Danielle Lewerenz and Rebecca Burrell for patiently listening to my frustrations, my brainstorming, and my countless "cool history facts."

To anyone else, friend or stranger, who might have innocently asked, "So what are you researching today?"

Eternal gratitude to Jim, Ellen, and Owen for suffering through my enthusiastic responses to our regular "What did you learn today?" dinner-table question. They are now prepared for any spontaneous water-cooler conversations on early-twentieth-century autocamping. They can thank me later.

A Peek into the Archive

Just the other day I came home from an antiques shop and showed a treasure – slightly dusty – to my husband. It was a pre-printed postcard dated 1948 and sent by a local power company. The text on the back announced that the county had standardized road names and a uniform house-numbering system, and could the resident please use their official address as typed on the front in all communications? Handwritten in pencil was a helpful note to the resident: "For trouble nights & holidays" they should call Consumers Power at the following five-digit number.

Needless to say, my husband wasn't as impressed as I was by this crooked little postcard. "Who saves things like that?" he asked. Implicit in the question, I knew, was, "Who wants things like that?" Well, I always answer, historical novelists do.

Finds like that little postcard hold so much for the novelist. The printed message, of course. The one-cent postage stamp, perhaps. The handwriting and the use of pencil instead of pen. The neat, spare address (no zip code yet). The rubber stamp across the front inviting the recipient to buy US bonds. These tiny details help us writers to bring a time and place to life on the page.

When researching modern history, these ephemeral treasures are easy to find. Those who spend their days in past centuries – whether historians or novelists – seek primary sources and original documents. Twentieth-century historians often have it easier than those who explore earlier eras. Not only do we research a period when mass media and mass communication were both cheap and plentiful, but the distance between then and now is obviously shorter. To reach into the past, we don't have far to go.

The things that people save and tuck away in attic boxes often find their way to archives or local historical societies. Letters. Journals. Photos. High school yearbooks. The stories in these are usually right on the surface, ready for a novelist and her "what ifs." I've had many a fun evening (for serious) with a high school yearbook and a census, seeing how a moment in time played out over the years. Did Floyd find success after four years in the school literary club? Did "Most Likely to Succeed" Helen go to college like she planned? Research + imagination = a story waiting to be written.

But my favorites are the little scraps of paper that people usually throw away. Magazines. Road maps. Bus tickets. Restaurant menus. Programs from commencements, football games, school plays. Coupons. Junk mail. They give unexpected and rich details about the era, about the culture, and about the people who held on to them through the years. From these ephemeral fragments of the past, I can piece together entire books.

Woman Enters Left was built from and ultimately pays homage to ephemera. I love to explore characters through their own words and to let them tell their stories directly to the reader. Much of Florrie and Ethel's story is told through the diaries, grocery lists, and screenplay excerpts that they write. But the other fictional documents in the novel, they all evolved directly from the cards and clippings scattered over my research table.

In bringing *Woman Enters Left* and its world to life, I relied on many different kinds of sources. I plotted out Florrie and Ethel's 1926 road trip with the help of National Old Trails Road maps and guidebooks, Automobile Blue Books, ads and articles from early travel magazines, Model T repair manuals, travel diaries, and photos of intrepid women on the road. They drove on roads little more than muddy tracks in some places and in cars needing near-constant patches and repairs, yet they weren't deterred. In all of the photos, these bob-haired, trouser-wearing women are exuberant.

For Louise's trip in 1952, I used things like gas station road maps, motel postcards, diner menus, and scenic attraction brochures to recreate the now-iconic Route 66. I drew on photo archives of Los Angeles in the 1950s, news articles and interviews about Hollywood's blacklisting, and fashion magazines full of midcentury women's fashions. Oh, the hats!

Much of my research centered on the Radium Girls. I read through articles in medical journals on the symptoms of radium poisoning, through court proceedings on the many suits brought against the radium corporations by former dial painters, and through dramatic and sympathetic newspaper columns. By looking at the Radium Girls' story from different angles, I was able to see them as not only patients and victims, but as fighters. Like the fearless women behind the wheels of their Model Ts, the Radium Girls refused to back down in the face of adversity.

So I decided to bring those documents (fictionally speaking, of course) into my book. Just as Florrie and Ethel had told their story of love and adventure through their own words, I let history tell the story of the Radium Girls through fictionalized medical reports, court documents, news articles, financial statements, and to tie it all together, as I'm wont to do, letters. They bring, I hope, more information, an extra touch of realism, and a stronger historical voice to the book.

Those things – the clippings, the articles, the maps and brochures, the magazines, pamphlets, and newspapers – they all hold pieces of history. They all offer glimpses of lives long ago. Like the postcard from the power company I brought home the other day, with its stamps and postmarks and penciled message, they let us sense, for a moment, people from the past. The people who read them, touched them, wrote on them, talked about them, pasted them in scrapbooks, tucked them in glove compartments, held on to them through the years. We can almost see their ghostly fingerprints.

So to answer my husband's unspoken question, about who wants these yellowed pages, these crumbling squares of cardboard, these things saved from the wastepaper basket, I say: We do. Those of us who delve into history want those old letters in attic boxes and those marked-up road maps lost in desk drawers. To us, they are invaluable. Yes, they're expendable and ephemeral, fleeting and fragile. But they've held together through all of those years to provide us with a time machine of sorts. These little bits of paper, put together, create the pages of an entire book.

JESSICA BROCKMOLE enjoys getting lost in second-hand bookstores and can often be found sifting through odd bits of ephemera and calling it 'research'. She lives in Indiana, USA, with her family and far too many books.

jessicabrockmole.com
@jabrockmole

To discover more great books and to
place an order visit our website at
allisonandbusby.com

Don't forget to sign up to our free newsletter at
allisonandbusby.com/newsletter
for latest releases, events and exclusive offers

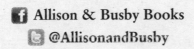 **Allison & Busby Books**
@AllisonandBusby

You can also call us on
020 7580 1080
for orders, queries
and reading recommendations